The Catching
Kind

Bria Quinlan

BREW HA HA SERIES

It's in His Kiss
The Last Single Girl
Worth the Fall
The Catching Kind

BREW AFTER DARK Shorts
Love in Tune
Sweet As Cake

~*~

YA Books by Bria Quinlan

Secret Girlfriend (RVHS #1)
Secret Life (RVHS #2)
Wreckless

J

ONE

I *MAY HAVE* been running late, but at least I was extremely caffeinated. That was the key to dealing with my agent—large doses of caffeine and possibly some type of defensive gear.

If I could wear body armor I would. But I'm pretty sure they wouldn't let me on the downtown train in that.

Catherine Sutter was, to state it simply, a force of nature. And I was a leaf on the wind.

It wasn't that I didn't like Catherine. And I sure as anything respected her. She was exactly what a writer who didn't like confrontation and still wanted to deal with the top publishers needed. Someone to take charge and be the boss of my business life so I could be the boss of my writing life.

I glanced at my phone, which miraculously still had a charge, and rushed on knowing I was going to be late. As usual. But, hopefully by only a minute or two. Not *too* bad.

Well, not bad for me. For Catherine, you'd think the world was ending if someone was thirty seconds late.

I hurried toward the gorgeous Art Deco building, getting my customary shiver just seeing the brass and glass doors. *This is Your Life, Hailey Tate.* A thrill beyond belief. Like tripping over the yellow brick road and landing facedown behind The Great and Powerful's curtain.

There were a few things I loved about being a writer: telling stories, working in yoga pants, and going into my agent's office to discuss my next project.

I'm not gonna lie. It made me feel like a grownup instead of just a girl scribbling stories in math class.

Because, really, when had I used algebra in the last decade? Never, that's when.

Pushing through the front doors, I couldn't help but notice all the security guys hovering around a tall man, head bent over something just on the other side of the lobby.

Advantage, Hailey! I rushed to the front desk to sign myself in so I could sneak upstairs and not be any later than I already was. I got as far as the elevator door when Frank, the very sweet older man who worked the desk, rushed over and stuck his hand into the slowly closing doors.

"Ms. Tate!" He smiled, the welcome I usually got when I came in. "Shame on you, sneaking by like that."

"Don't worry." I gave him a smile, trying to rush this along. "I signed in."

"I know, dear. But, could you bring this envelope up to Ms. Sutter?" Frank handed me a thick FedEx envelope. "I'm a little afraid of her when contracts come in."

He gave me a wink and stepped back, letting the doors start to fall shut again.

"Hold the elevator!"

The voice echoed down the short, tiled hall to where I watched the doors slip inward as I tried to pretend I didn't hear it. I reached for the close-door button. But Frank, sweet man that he was, stuck his hand in again, stopping the elevator. Again.

And all I could think about was how Catherine was going to give me yet another lecture on timeliness.

You'd think she'd save those for if I got too close to a deadline, not just for when I was running a few minutes late for a meeting.

"Thanks." The tall, shaggy-headed blond stepped into view, his gaze crashing into mine for less than a moment.

Connor Ryan. Now middle-aged men hovering in the lobby made sense.

I was probably going to end up in a tabloid just by being on the same block with him, let alone sharing an elevator.

He turned away just as quickly as he'd arrived, standing just outside the elevator, his hand on the bumper, holding it open. I glanced at my watch, wondering why he wasn't stepping in. But his gaze stayed glued to the front of the building, his feet firmly planted on the floor outside the elevator.

"Excuse me," my voice was light and low. It wasn't every day I spoke to a famous person...unless she was a writer. Even though I wasn't a fan—sports or tabloid—it was still a bit intimidating.

Connor Ryan glanced in and down at me with a look that said he was more curious what I was doing interrupting his standing around than he was in what I was going to say.

"I have a meeting I'm trying to get to," is what I came up with.

I'd hoped he'd let the doors shut, but I'd already lost his attention as his gaze turned back toward the lobby. I got a vague, distant *Uh-huh* in response.

"So, if you could just let the doors go," I added. "I'll be all set."

"Uh-huh."

"Pardon me," I pushed, because that wasn't really a yes or no question. "I *really* need to get upstairs."

He glanced back my way, his eyes dropping down to take in my yoga pants and deep purple lululemon wrap.

"I'm sure you can wait another moment." His gaze swept up and away dismissively. "You don't look like you're really needed anywhere."

I couldn't believe he'd just said that. It wasn't every day someone was that unkind to me without even knowing me. Or, to be honest, even when they did.

"That wasn't very nice." The words slipped out, something making me braver than normal...unless you consider the fact that I'd barely whispered them.

"Excuse me?" he shifted his body to glare down at me.

I finally seemed to have his full attention.

"I said that wasn't very nice. You're holding me up for a meeting and…" I faded off, not really sure where I was headed with any of this as he stared me down.

"Sweetheart," he drawled like he had all the time in the world and yet was *still* absolutely right about everything *woman*. "I am an expert on women's appearance. And, trust me. You are not exactly rocking the important vibe." With a shake of his head, he turned back to the lobby.

I fought to keep my jaw from dropping as I registered the clipped sound of heels clicking on the tile floor. Connor

Ryan's expression had changed from one of rude condescension to pleased appreciation.

"Thank you so much for holding the elevator." One of the most beautiful women I'd ever seen outside a magazine stepped into view. Of course, I'd probably seen her in a magazine too. "I'm almost late for an appointment."

"I know the feeling." I'd said it under my breath, but Connor Ryan's hearing must have been worse than his manners.

He angled himself away from me and turned on the charm. "I'd never want to leave a lady in distress."

I may have actually snorted. Or, at least I did in my head. I thought really hard about snorting out loud too.

"Excuse me." I tried again. "Could we maybe…"

I gave them both a smile, hoping they'd just get the idea and step into the elevator. They were so busy scoping one another out, I doubted they noticed. But, to be fair, the model gave me a slight smile…or at least, she tilted her head down toward me and smiled while she ogled the guy holding the doors open. And who could blame her? He *was* stunning to look at.

You don't get named America's Sexiest Athlete by being average.

Finally, they both stepped in and turned their backs to me. She pushed a button and the flirting continued in hushed tones until the doors opened again. She slipped him a card and he leaned out the elevator to watch her long legs strut their way down the hall to the frosted doors of the modeling agency.

I considered pushing him out. Just one big shove and I'd be on my way. My phone read eleven minutes past and I knew I'd never escape an epic timeliness lecture now.

When we got to the seventh floor, I moved to step around him, glad to just get out of his arrogant sphere and instead walked straight into his side as he exited the elevator.

"You're coming here?" All the shock I felt slipped out with the words. Why in the world would a sports guy be coming to our little, boutique literary agency?

He glanced down as if he'd forgotten I was there. He probably had. "And, how is that any of your business?"

"Um…" It really wasn't. I was just surprised.

"Oh, you're one of those people." His arms crossed as his gaze narrowed down to glare at me. All that masculine anger focused on me set my adrenaline pumping. "I'm an athlete, so I must be dumb?"

"No. Actually, almost everyone who comes here writes romance or books for teens." I shrugged. I would have been surprised if any sportsy-god-guy stepped onto our floor. I moved around, finally happy to have the upper hand. Even if it was just for getting to walk away first.

He gave me a look as if he didn't believe me. I gave him back the nicest smile I had.

"Now, if you'll excuse me," I drudged up some bravado out of pure annoyance. "I have a meeting someone made me late for."

I walked by Meg at the front desk, not bothering to have her call back to Catherine since I was late. Also, with how she was drooling over the guy glaring at the back of my head, I figured she wouldn't remember how to use a phone anyway.

Two doors down, Catherine paced in front of her desk, weaving around the piles of book filled boxes. I tapped on the door and watched as she swung in my direction, a look of pure relief washing over her.

This had nothing to do with lunch.

"Thank God you're here. I was afraid you'd heard about the bet and you weren't going to show."

A sick feeling washed through my stomach. I was tempted to turn around and walk right back out.

Instead, I stepped into the room and closed the door. "What bet?"

"The one I lost you in."

TWO

I'M SORRY." I leaned against the door, trying to ignore the fact I'd never seen Catherine nervous before. "I must have heard you wrong. Did you say you lost me in a bet?"

Who would want to win an author? Especially one who wrote books for teen girls. Unless you were desperate to learn suburban high school politics or slang or—since I wrote paranormal—the signs of the zodiac. Otherwise, I was pretty much useless.

"I did. I did say that." She picked up something from her desk and set it back down. I'd never seen her fidget before so this was…disconcerting to say the least. "And I did it too. I know what you're going to say. You're going to tell me it was a stupid move. Of course it was. I thought I had an unbeatable hand. I'd been running hot at the agents' poker game last night when it came down to me and that damn Dex."

She took a deep breath and pointed toward the empty chair across from her desk.

Since I wasn't sure where this was all going, I plopped my rear in the chair. Note to self, memorize my agency contract when I get home. And laws on author trafficking.

"So, are you telling me I have a new agent?" I tried not to panic.

I *liked* Catherine. I liked that she got my writing and she got me. Getting me was sometimes hard. In person I was dry and a bit afraid of publicity and social media…and talking to people I didn't know.

My writing was just off center enough to be a hard sell initially. But, she'd believed in me. Even though I wasn't like her other authors who were bigger sellers. Most of them were huge on social media and liked doing things like giving interviews and being on local newscasts…and talking to people.

"What? No. Of *course* not. I'd never actually *lose* you as a client." Catherine slid behind her desk, rolled her squishy-stress-ball-thingy between her palms, and eyed her ashtray. "Honestly, this is an opportunity. The chance to really bump you into the public's eye."

Her words sent fear rushing down my spine. I tried to think of a response, but since I had zero idea what we were talking about, I just kept looking at her, hoping she'd clarify.

"Hailey, you know I love you, but let's be honest." She tossed the ball on the desk and went back to pacing. "You're not very good at PR. You're a horrible interview, you don't like social media, and you look like you're going to throw up every time someone wants to take your picture. The bet may have been a surprise, but it's going to get you national exposure."

My whole body went cold at the words *national exposure.*

"So, if you think of it that way," she continued. "It's more like we won."

I still had no idea what she was talking about, but when Catherine changed *lose* to *win* that quickly, even I could see the spin.

But, when she said, "Screw it," and lit a cigarette for the first time in three years, I knew I was in trouble.

"Hailey, I lost you to Dex Falco in a poker game and you're going to have to fulfill the bet for me."

Um...

"Catherine, I'm not sure this sounds like something I want to do...I mean, I don't even know what it is, but you're making me really uneasy." Understatement.

"It's not that bad. Like I said, it's a great opportunity. You're going to be the envy of all your girlfriends."

"You know all my girlfriends. If this doesn't involve a Newbury Award, they pretty much aren't going to care."

"I'm betting they'll care about this." She stubbed the cigarette out and came around the desk. Her hand wrapped around my arm and gently urged me to my feet before steering me toward the door. "We'll just head down to the conference room and meet with Dex. Once he explains everything you'll be excited about it."

I figured at this point there was no stopping her. Plus, I was really bad at stopping her...or anyone for that matter. I was Anti-Confrontation Girl. I deserved a cape and some funky bangles to go with a Utility Belt of Anti-

Confrontationalism. Maybe Boots of Avoidance. Compact of Deflection.

She continued babbling as we wove past a still dazed Meg and toward the small office they insisted on calling a conference room.

Her running commentary had gone from *losing* to *winning* to *excited*. My level of anxiety was now on par with waiting for a *Paige & Prejudice* review...and that woman hated me. She said my first book was drivel, but she kept buying them and reading them. Which, honestly, made me feel bad. It seemed like such a waste of money to buy stuff you hate.

But it wasn't that she gave everything I ever wrote a negative review. Not everyone is going to like your stuff. It was the fact that she managed to call me *stupid* or some version of that in every review that hurt.

We reached the conference room door and, after taking a deep breath, Catherine pushed it open with a flourish. There, sitting at the table with his designer shoes propped on the edge was none other than Mr. Dismissive. Connor Ryan.

It wasn't just that he was good-looking. Or famous. Or a known womanizer. It wasn't that he spent more time on the cover of *People* than Mel Gibson after a drinking binge. Or that he'd been rude in the elevator. None of those were what caused me to pause this time. It was the fact that he was one of the best shortstops who ever played the game. I wasn't even a sports fan, but in this town, you couldn't help but be hyper-aware of everything sports-related. And, just like any top tier professional, I expect the best from you. And that's why all other behavior seemed even worse.

He glanced at me, his eyes narrowing, before he dropped his feet to the floor and shot out of his seat.

"No. No way." He pointed at me as if no one knew who he was talking about. "You said she was a stunner."

"I said she was cute." This from the over-suited man seated next to him. He glanced at me and then frowned at Catherine. "You said she was cute."

"She cleans up well."

Thanks for the support, Catherine.

"She's not my type," Connor stated as if I weren't right there.

Not that it wasn't true. His type was high-profile, famous women. Models, reality *stars,* actresses, news anchors, senators' daughters...basically, anyone seven-to-twelve times more famous than me.

"That's the entire point." The man in the very expensive suit, who I could only assume was Dex, crossed his arms, looking at his client in a way I hoped Catherine didn't typically look at me.

"I don't care if that's the point." Connor Ryan raked a gaze over me in disgust. "I won't be seen with someone who doesn't even know how to blow-dry her own hair."

Everyone's gazes drifted up toward my hair and I knew—I *knew*—I was entering nightmare land. I was wrong. This was *worse* than a Paige & Prejudice review. This was a general assault on my person and I didn't even know why.

By this point, I could pretty much guarantee I was not one bit "excited" about this situation.

"She does." Catherine waved in my direction. "I've seen her use a hair dryer on book tour. She's really handy with the mascara too."

I glanced at Catherine like she was nuts—because I was beginning to think she was. The last time she saw me use mascara it was to put a blue streak down my over-long bangs I'd blown out. Of course, it wasn't even my hair dryer. The truest part of her statement was that it did happen while on book tour.

Besides, I did have a hair dryer. It was in the closet with those extremely uncomfortable boots I enjoyed owning and never wore.

Or, more accurately, wore once and almost killed myself getting my heel stuck in a sidewalk drainage grid.

Connor Ryan came around the table as smoothly as he moved on the field and pulled me about to face him. His eyes were darker than they looked in magazines. A blue so deep it was like the ocean at night. Not a surprise so many women slipped into them. It was like skinny-dipping in a room full of people.

Then, he pivoted to face Dex, giving me his back, and placed his hands on the table in front of him.

"Absolutely not." His voice had dropped, low and sure. Not coming off as angry or upset. Just, strong and filled with authority. "We're looking to clean up my rep, not ruin it."

Without a word, he swung to the door and marched out, leaving me alone with the two blushing agents.

I stared at the door as it slammed shut behind him and grinned. Amazing how all the tension had walked out of the room with the pro-baseball player. "So, that went well."

"I guess we're done here." Catherine pulled on the cuffs of her jacket, a sure sign she was packing it in.

I grabbed my bag, ready to escape to my yoga class. We made it as far as the lobby before Dex caught up.

"Hold on a second." He snapped his briefcase shut as he joined us at the door. "We had a deal. He'll agree to it because he doesn't have a choice. Just—"

He glanced my way, taking me in from the tips of my Pumas to my loosened fishtail braid. Shaking his head, he gave Catherine a look that I wouldn't have wanted pointed in my direction. I was glad she just quirked an eyebrow at him and didn't try to convince him I knew what lip-gloss was.

"Just clean her up, alright? I'll call you with the details."

Before I could ask what details, Dex was out the door and pressing the down button like he could conjure the elevator with the power of his finger.

"Do I want to know what this is all about?" Sadly, I already knew the answer to that question: No. I doubted very highly I did.

She led me down the hall and, instead of going to her desk, she dropped into one of the overstuffed chairs in front of her bookshelves and waited for me to join her.

"You know about the APC—the Agent Poker Collective, right?"

Of course. It was myth or legend depending on who you talked to. Agents from every industry worked their butts off for an invite. Lots of liquor. Lots of poker. Lots of across-the-table deals made.

I'd always leaned toward *myth* myself. Maybe it had been true back in the thirties...or even the eighties. But now? This wasn't only a different generation, it was a different century.

"I've heard of it."

"Well, I've been going for a few years. That's how I got Bria that movie deal to work with a certain celebrity last year.

The bets that are thrown around in that place can get a little..."

"Insane?" I filled in. The word matched my morning so far.

Catherine shook her head and laughed. "I take it you know who Connor Ryan is?"

A year ago I might have thought the name sounded vaguely familiar, but lately, it had been all over the news. And the tabloids. Connor Ryan was the latest playboy athlete to hit town. He'd joined the Nighthawks, made some amazing, sportsy moves, and become the Next Big Thing.

But, sports weren't my gig. I didn't even write jock heroes. Not only did I not watch them, I didn't get the appeal. Of course, Connor Ryan was a celebu-jock, so even I was aware. It was all hard to miss.

"He's the model magnet, right?" As demonstrated earlier.

"Honey, he's more than that. The Nighthawks brought him in near the end of last season to replace Johnson when he blew out his elbow. Connor was our top defense with his speed and accuracy. But it's his batting average that's off the charts. He's the reason we *almost* made the playoffs."

But, if she was being honest, she would have led with what he was known for: Leaving his girlfriend behind in Texas to start over here with supermodels, heiresses, political mogul's daughters, and one cover-worthy night with a reality "star." Oh, and that sportscaster who lost her job for sleeping with him...or if you listened to Connor Ryan, stalking him.

Through it all, he refused to comment on his personal life. If asked a question about any of his off-field shenanigans, he turned the answer to baseball. It was almost magical the way he did it.

I remembered seeing an interview that went something like this:

"Con, tell us about the tall, hot blonde seen stumbling out of your hotel room after the game with New York."

"Bobby, the only stumbling I've seen lately was a certain third baseman who missed that grounder and let us bring home two more runs."

I'd been oddly impressed—and not more than a little jealous—of his interviewing skills. I was pretty sure Catherine was embracing this opportunity because every time someone asked to interview me, I all but created a natural disaster. I've spilt drinks on me…on other people. I've gotten so nervous I'd forgotten my character's name and book titles. She wasn't kidding about every picture of me looking like I was about to throw up.

Any time I was the center of attention, all motor skills went right out the window.

So, yes. I found his skills in front of a camera were awe-worthy.

"Okay. I know who he is," I admitted, because it seemed silly not to. "He's enough of a celebrity that even I've heard of him."

"Great." She stubbed out cigarette number two. "Because he's the man who's going to put you on the map."

Annnndddd…Overstatement.

But, we might as well get this over with before the butterflies in my stomach morphed into huge pterodactyls.

"Alright." I pulled the little notebook I brought everywhere, ready to get down to the details. And then recover from whatever she'd gotten me sucked into. "Don't hold me in suspense. What did you sign me up for?"

"Hailey, come on. You need to look at these opportunities as adventures that are allowing you to never, ever, ever have to work in a bank again. Isn't that what you told me when I signed you? Two books a year, no more banks."

It was true. But her bringing it up didn't help the nervousness she was feeding.

"Right." I sighed, hating that she was right. "I'm sure I can do an event or something with him. I mean, people won't even notice me standing there with him being all flashy, high-maintenance guy."

She smirked. When Catherine smirked, even the most powerful senior editors got nervous.

"Oh, people are going to notice you. Trust me. Noticing you is the entire point."

Her words slipped into my gut, turning over my nerves one at a time as I wondered just what she'd done.

"Catherine, spit it out. What was the bet?"

"If you do this right, you'll get hours of exposure and won't have to give a single interview. Maybe ever. Not that every magazine and local news station won't be asking for one." She paused, all dramatic-like. "And all you have to do is date the hottest guy in town."

THREE

"W HAT?" I GASPED, leaping up and sucking in air. Maybe I was having a panic attack. Or a heart attack. Or some type of attack where you can't breathe and you consider throwing heavy objects at someone.

"Hailey, a fresher image isn't going to hurt." She eyed my yoga pants and shook her head. A sad attempt at calming me down.

I wasn't going to fall for it. This was more than just an image update or charity event we were talking about. One night out even I could live through. Probably.

"Catherine, please stop side-stepping into this and just...spill it."

Another sip. Another sigh. Dead silence. And then, "Fine. But, sit down for goodness sake."

I eased into the chair, inspecting the door to make sure I still had a clear path for a quick escape.

"I made a bet at the APC. One I thought I couldn't lose." Catherine glanced around her office as if the answers might be there for her. "A straight flush. I *shouldn't* have lost."

"But?"

She leaned back away from her desk, away from me and for the first time since I'd known her, I watched Catherine unable to meet someone's gaze.

"I lost." She rolled her eyes as if this was obvious. Which, it was, but still not a plot twist I wanted to admit was coming.

"Yeah, I'm getting that." I paused, taking a moment, trying to piece it all together. "But since there's no longer such a thing as indentured servitude, I'm wondering how you think you're handing me off to another agent. Especially a sports agent. He didn't look like he'd *read* a book this year, let alone knew where to sell one."

Catherine snickered and filled her glass again. "Dex is, luckily, smarter than he looks. He's the best in his field."

Which shouldn't have been a surprise considering how many deals I was betting he'd gotten Connor Ryan.

"What exactly does he think he's going to get from me?" Because the dating thing had to be a red herring.

Catherine glanced away as if she was afraid to admit how ridiculous this was. "Your reputation."

"What is this, 1811?" I laughed at my own joke, because the day I was having, someone had to. "What does my reputation have to do with anything?"

"I'll be honest, he suggested Jenna Drake first. But then he heard about her lovely lawyer-boyfriend. You were next and had what he was looking for. The stats, a certain level of success, a new book coming out in a few weeks, and your very strong following of young women between the ages of fourteen and twenty-six. Which would be exactly the group Mr. Ryan's new, ah, adventure has managed to alienate. It also happens to be the group his latest sponsor is trying to reach. You see the problem?"

I had no idea what Connor Ryan had done to tick off girls fourteen to twenty-six, but I didn't see how anyone might think I'd be able to help. I was just…me. They wanted Taylor Swift.

Where was Tay when you needed her?

Of course, I should have known Catherine would have an answer.

"He needs to be seen with someone nice. Someone smart. Someone who shows he's turning over a new leaf, treating women well, and that he's a good guy."

"He's a rude, egocentric womanizer."

Catherine smiled at me, an odd little smile as if she knew something I didn't. "Maybe you'll have fun being pampered in public by a rude, egocentric womanizer."

"No way. I'm not going out with him." It was pretty much my worst nightmare. Being forced to live in public scrutiny, pictures, people, attention. I just wanted to sit in my apartment and write or hang out with my girls. "He wants arm candy who probably doesn't talk in public."

"Honey, I'm pretty sure he doesn't care if they talk in private either."

Of course *she'd* think this was funny.

"But, here's the problem." I crossed my arms, digging my metaphorical heels in. "I won't do it."

I know a lot of girls dream about the popular jock in her school waking up and realizing she's secretly gorgeous and awesome. But I'd never been attracted to that type. I'd grown up with that type—or grown up with that type sending alimony to my mom—and didn't need a repeat of the last generation.

My dad had been a Division I college football quarterback. Mom had been his hometown sweetie. Or, so she'd thought. But, with the fame, popularity, and potential big career came the ego to match.

Dad may not have made it to the pros, but he managed to keep the ego and drop the *sweetie*.

Catherine studied me, a long look that even after knowing her five years I couldn't read.

"Oh, you'll do it." She leaned forward, bracing her hands on the roughed leather of the chair's arm. "You'll do it because if my career goes, yours goes too. It's not a threat. Dex put us both in a bad place. It's a high-stakes world. And so, if you want to keep publishing with a house who prints more than two-thousand copies at a time, you'll do it."

She wasn't kidding. I could even see she was sorry. But she'd do whatever it took to get both of us on the other side of this ridiculousness.

"There's self-publishing," I challenged. "I have enough of a following to make the jump. A lot of my readers would follow me."

"That's true. You do. And, I wouldn't blame you. Your work is universal enough to do well."

It was as close to a blessing as I was going to get in this situation. Not that I felt I needed it at this moment.

"But," she continued. "One book to hit it big is all you need. We've always said a breakout would raise your boat high enough that it would stay there. And this...this mess I walked us both into, it could be the tide that does it. Free publicity, your face out there to go with your name, young women dreaming of living your life not just your characters' lives. This could be the thing that bumps you over the edge. Look at all the celebrity YA books over the last decade."

And isn't that what we all wanted? The magic bullet?

If there was one thing I'd learned from Catherine, it was never sign a contract without three sets of eyes.

"What's the fine print?"

"You date for four weeks and act like a real couple. A *settled* couple. The kind of couple where everyone who sees you goes, *Oh, they're so sweet.* He cleans up his rep and saves his contract with his sponsor, and you get a month of free publicity." She crossed her arms, finishing off the deal. "You'll go on public dates. Hands will be held. Autographs will be signed. From the sounds of it, you'll be getting a makeover."

I rolled my eyes. Yes, I knew she could see me do it.

"Hailey, a makeover wouldn't kill you."

"I'm not paying for a makeover. Or the clothes to play this part. If he's unhappy with my wardrobe, you're all going to have to find a way to make me have clothes everyone's happy with."

Which wasn't a bad deal. I needed some new things for the conference I'd be speaking at next month.

"Fine. I'll have Meg open you an expense account. One-thousand dollars should do it."

Geez, I could buy six of everything in my size at Target for that much money.

"You," Catherine pointed her pen at me like it was a weapon, as if she knew what I was thinking. "You will shop at socially acceptable stores for a Page Sixer. Actually, you will go with the personal shopper I hire for you to whatever stores she brings you to."

"Fine." It was her money.

I closed my eyes, picturing the woman he'd flirted with in the elevator. Then the look he'd given Dex when Catherine had introduced us. I knew the type. Maybe I'd be more excited about this if I hadn't watched my mom deal with my mostly-missing jock of a father for two decades.

I had a rough time equating them with anything less than untrustworthy.

"This isn't going to work. No one is going to buy this."

Catherine took my hand and squeezed it. "It is going to work. And it's going to be good for you to get out there too. Everyone knows how sweet you are under all that sarcasm. He's turning thirty-two. That's like sixty in ballplayer years. He's settling down. With a nice, smart girl. Someone who makes him laugh and doesn't drain his time and energy. And he's exactly what your book sales need. I almost wish I'd thought of this myself."

It could work. That was the problem.

"I have a few demands of my own."

"Of course."

"One, this is not to cost me a penny. Two, he is to understand what my deadlines are and how they are to be treated."

"Okay. Those are reasonable."

"And finally, he's not to humiliate me. If he does, I will take this whole train down. Him. Dex. You. The mythical Agent Game. Everyone. I'm not becoming a laughing stock because you can't count cards."

"Sweetheart, if he humiliates you, I'll take him down myself."

FOUR

WHAT I LEARNED about Connor Ryan while being shopped for and styled could fill an old-school encyclopedia.

Beyond all the tabloid and Nighthawks' stuff I already knew, there was one final piece I'd missed because I'd been on deadline at the end of the baseball season.

It wasn't his typical shenanigans this time. Connor Ryan was caught in an elevator with a very hot Harbor Island Beer girl wrapped around him who just happened to be his new captain, Ackerman's, girlfriend.

He and Ackerman came to blows in the dugout at the end of their last game of the season, which managed to piss off people in sports, advertising, and fans of his personal life in one swoop. Fines normal people would use for a down payment on their house were involved.

Leverage. It's a nice thing.

~*~

Or not.

I'd dressed exactly like Personal Shopper Becca had instructed. A professional skirt that was short enough to show off what she called toned legs with a loosely fitted pink top to "frame me." She claimed I looked pretty, professional, and feminine.

I sashayed—or at least, my version of a sashay—my way into the posh offices downtown a mere four minutes late. Which was a personal record for me this week. Especially considering I had on makeup and something other than a messy bun going on. I felt more confident. More in control of the situation. But, no sooner had the mirrored elevator doors closed behind me than I realized just how out of my league I was.

The office was gorgeous and screamed *successful money-making rich people.* These guys had image down to a science. If I was here to assist in their PR, we were all in trouble. I started toward the high mahogany and glass receptionist desk and waited while the woman with a throaty voice finished redirecting a call.

"Can I help you?" Her tone had shifted, making, *Can I help you?* sound more like *Are you lost, because you sure don't belong here?*

"Yes. I'm Hailey Tate. I have an appointment."

"With who?" This seemed more of a challenge than a question.

But, I was up for the challenge. Or, at least, I actually did have an appointment and so I really did have an answer.

Thank goodness.

"Dex Falco."

She ran her finger down the third column over in her schedule until she reached the eleven a.m. time slot and tapped it with a hot-pink manicured nail. I glanced at my own nails, one of which I'd already managed to chip, and hid them in my pockets.

"I'm sorry. Mr. Falco already has an appointment. I'm sure if you want to call his assistant later in the day she might be able to..."

Receptionist Girl shrugged, as if to say, even if I called the assistant, there wasn't anything anyone could do for me.

I got it. She worked with super famous people. I had to assume the rudeness was a defense system to keep the press and non-clients—as well as all Connor Ryan's ex-girlfriends—from sneaking into the land of hot ball throwers.

"I assume Dex is meeting with Connor?" I gave her my best *I belong here* smile. "Could you let them know I'm here?"

"Sweetheart." Gone was the cultured, throaty accent. "If I let every girl who was looking to get next to an athlete—especially Connor Ryan—by, I would have lost this job thirty minutes in. Now, if you don't mind, I'll have to call security if you keep this up."

"I completely understand." I tried to stay nice. This was her job. "But they're expecting me."

She looked at me as if I'd just claimed I lived on the moon.

I was beginning to doubt my makeover. I ran a hand over my hair hoping it wasn't doing something weird.

Receptionist Girl finally broke and gave me a smile that most likely cost her more than I made last year.

"I'm sure they are. If you'll just have a seat..." She motioned to the waiting area in a windowed alcove. "As soon as they're ready for you, I'll let you know."

"Oh, great. Thanks." Well, that was draining.

I wandered over to the waiting area and slid onto a butter-soft, oversized leather couch made for giants where my feet just brushed the floor. The glass and chrome coffee table was covered with a smattering of sports magazines and business journals.

There was nothing remotely feminine about the waiting area. Except for Throaty Receptionist, Guardian of the Agents. She more than made up for the testosterone-soaked domain.

I pulled out my Kindle and started a read I was doing to give feedback on a friend's manuscript. Luckily, it was fascinating and the next twenty minutes flew by...until I realized it had been twenty minutes.

Maybe they'd changed their minds and I was off the hook and Catherine had forgotten to tell me. Or she was fighting to try to keep the deal alive since she'd convinced herself it was an Epic Win of PR.

Or maybe, I'd forgotten to charge my cell phone.

That happened about three times a month and sometimes took days for me to realize. I'd grasp that no one had called me and BAM. Dead battery.

I dug to the bottom of my new Becca-approved leather tote, looking for the cell. Pens. Post-its. Gum. All the essentials

When I found the phone, it was...yup. Dead. I must have run it down yesterday doing the catch-up thing with my girls after the shopping death march of makeovers.

Before I could work up the courage to approach the receptionist again, a door opened down the long, polished hall, voices mumble-spilled into the lobby before Dex, Catherine, and Connor came around the corner. I stood, dead phone in hand, the Post-its, pens, and gum falling from my lap onto the floor.

They all came to a halt, looking past the reception desk to the waiting area I'd all but converted into an office in the last twenty-seven minutes.

"Hailey, what are you doing out here?" Catherine moved across the lobby in the strong, sleek way she walked that managed to convey power, yet still be completely feminine. It was halfway between a storm and a swagger. "We were waiting for you."

I brushed my hand down the sides of the burgundy skirt Becca assigned for today.

"I..." I didn't know what to say. "I was told Dex was still in a meeting."

I glanced at Receptionist Girl waiting for her to clarify. But, she looked somewhere between annoyed and panicked.

"Ava," Dex's voice was smooth. Nice. But there was an undertone that made me nervous. "Is there a reason you didn't let me know Ms. Tate was here?"

She glanced between us all and sent me a look that was pleading. I'm not sure what she thought I could—or would—do.

"Well, she wasn't in your planner." She sounded so nervous, I almost felt bad for her. "And, your hour is blocked out as Cross-Promo Meeting." Now she sounded defensive. As if she hadn't been given the correct information.

"That's right. And Ms. Tate is a bestselling author who had been invited to the meeting to discuss a charity event opportunity with Mr. Ryan." Dex leaned against the receptionist counter and laid his portfolio on it.

Receptionist Girl—I mean, Ava—glanced at me. Another accusatory look. I must not have appeared Bestselling Author enough for her. It was obviously my fault. "I'm sorry, Mr. Falco."

While she groveled, Connor moved around Dex to come to my side. Ignoring the scattered office supplies, he held out his hand.

"Connor Ryan." His gaze ran over me in a sterile, calculating way, even as he pasted a charming smile on his face. "It's a pleasure to meet you."

I was so far out of my depth. This must be part of the game, although the drama going on about the missed meeting was beyond me.

But, I'd read too many Rom Coms to not play along.

"Hailey Tate."

"I hear there's a chance we might be hosting an event together." He held onto my hand, even as I gave it a gentle tug. "While these two high-powered types sort out details, why don't we hop down to The Purple Lemon and I'll fill you in on everything."

He gave my hand a quick squeeze. I had no idea what it was supposed to say. *Go along with this? Pay attention?* Or, was he annoyed? Was the squeeze echoing his thoughts about the two high-powered types running our lives?

I'd have to agree with him on that, but I was in. I even had a new wardrobe to prove I'd sold my soul to the devil.

"I'd love to." I tried to bat my lashes, but he just looked at me funny. Oh, well. "Let me get my things together."

It took more than the moment I think he expected. In the meantime, Connor wandered back over to the receptionist desk where Ava was batting *her* lashes at him. Why did it look coy when she did it?

I headed back toward the receptionist's desk, afraid I'd have a hard time pulling him away from the woman throwing herself in his direction. But, before I reached them, Connor had already taken a step back and half-shifted his body toward me.

"Great to see you again, Ava." Connor's hand fell to the small of my back, giving me a light shove toward the door.

We waited at the elevator, which seemed to be where we'd spent ninety percent of our time together since we'd met. Both of us quiet until I realized how odd that was.

"You need to chat me up," I said under my breath, hoping he was as quick on his feet off the field as on.

He knew exactly what I was talking about. First, he glanced toward Ava—who was still watching us with an annoyed look—and then toward Dex and Catherine—who appeared to be quietly banging out a plan for world domination—and nodded just a bit. And then, The Smile.

Dear stars, what did these people do to their mouths to make them look so shiny?

"Italian? I know this great trendy little bar around the corner."

Of course he did. It was probably five-figures out of my pay grade.

"How about somewhere we can talk without being watched?"

31

He turned to face me, giving his back to the rest of the room which I realized wasn't typical of him. He seemed to like seeing everything going on...or have everyone see him.

"That makes sense. Somewhere we don't have to worry about being overheard. Somewhere a fan or two might snap a picture and post it, but not where we'd have to deal with any craziness."

My stomached dropped at the idea of someone taking my picture, but I gave him a smile and a nod, knowing this was my life for the next month. If this worked, if it gave me enough exposure to get my books traction to sell wide, then I wouldn't have to worry about pictures that often.

The ding sounded and we stepped into the elevator. As soon as the doors closed, a subtle tension attacked him, tensing his shoulders, drawing him in on himself just enough to notice in that tiny, enclosed, mirrored area.

I almost didn't say anything, but in the end, I was worried it was something I should know. That the meeting had been worse than expected.

Doubting I wanted the answer, I asked, "What?"

He looked at me as if he'd already forgotten I was there. "What, what?"

"What's all that weird tension about?" When he didn't answer, I tried to break through it with a joke. "I'm sure it has nothing to do with finally getting me alone."

A flash of alarm slipped over his eyes as he glanced up at the slow decent of numbers on the elevator panel and shifted a step away from me.

"Seriously?" My own nerves seemed to disappear as my temper kicked in. "You think I'm Crazy Stalker Girl."

It figured. Every guy with any type of ego thought every girl was hitting on him. What was I supposed to expect from a guy who almost every girl actually *was* hitting on him?

"No." He drew his brow down and shook his head, a complete look of forced denial if I'd ever seen one. "No, of course not."

"I should remind you. I don't want to be here. It isn't my career that was torpedoed by the press...or my own stupidity." I felt bad as soon as the words left my mouth.

I started to apologize, to backtrack, but before I did, he sighed and nodded.

"I know." He said the right words, but he stared at the lit up number on the floor panel. It was the *humor the girl* tone that got me. "I get it. This is a job to you and you've already done a lot to move it forward."

He gave me a once-over that demonstrated he was obviously referring to my makeover.

"So, I meet your standards now?" I asked.

He must have missed the sarcasm, because he shrugged and said, "You'll do."

I...Well, I don't know what I thought I was going to say. *You'll do* had to be one of the most passively insulting things anyone had ever said to me. I tried to come up with a witty comeback, but I was maxing out my together time with Connor after less than five minutes.

"I mean," he backtracked into the silence. "You're invested. I appreciate that. I get that you're not here *just* to date me."

Or to date him *at all*.

I sucked in a breath, knowing I had to do this now before we went any further. If there was ever a time to stand up for myself, it was now.

"Oh." I turned to face him, forcing him to meet me head on or be even ruder. I couldn't believe how mad I was…at him, at the situation. I wasn't someone who got *angry*. But, the words just rushed out, fast and uncontrolled. "Let me put you at ease. You don't have to worry. I'm not here to date you at all. I don't like to be the center of attention. I like smart, funny, laid-back guys who are easy to be around. Someone who has similar interests. I don't like other women looking at me like a human-sized road bump. And I don't like to worry that my guy is cheating."

He had faced me, watching me list the reasons why I wouldn't go after him. I hadn't even pulled out the *how-many-owners-has-this-used-car-had* example yet.

His head cocked to the side and a slight smiled pushed up the left side of his mouth. "I actually believe you mean that."

Wow. I'd known about the ego. I mean, it had been apparent since the beginning, but this was getting ridiculous.

"We're almost to the lobby," I pushed. "You better decide now. Once we step out there and head to lunch, this is pretty much a ball in motion."

He looked me over, starting at the top of my head and slowly working his way down. It was the most insulting perusal I'd ever been subjected to.

"You look different."

I couldn't help but laugh. Maybe in his world that was a compliment. "Wow, hold off the sweet talk 'til there's someone around who matters to hear it."

I had a launch coming up this month with tons of things to do to get ready. I also needed to outline my new series. I just wanted to hunker down and get it done. The elevator lurched to a halt and I stepped out, ready to make my way home. I had a bunch of pre-release stuff to do and a new book to get on paper. I really did *not* need this.

"Well, it was nice meeting you." Kind of. I couldn't even look his way again, afraid I'd get too mad to leave it at that. "Good luck with the ad contract."

I pulled my bag up higher on my shoulder and headed toward the door. It wasn't a bluff, although, I'm betting he thought it was. I had no interest in stepping into his sphere of scandal.

I gave a little wave to the nice security guard who had taken my ID on the way in, and hit the sidewalk. The morning wasn't a total loss. I'd have to send Ava flowers for not forcing me to sit through that meeting. I'd even gotten a good jump on my reading.

"Hailey!"

The street was busy enough to allow me to ignore that.

"Hailey, wait."

Connor jogged up next to me and slowed to match my gait.

I kept walking. If he felt there was something that needed to be said, he should get on with it. But as for me? I'd said everything I needed to.

"Listen," he started with a lovely command. "I'm sorry. I meant you look nice."

"No. You didn't. You meant I looked nice for a plain girl. And that's your problem. No one is going to believe you're interested in me."

"Come on." He put on the charming smile. The one I'd seen him aim at the model yesterday. "You're selling yourself short."

That ticked me off. I had reached my limit. I don't think anyone had ever found my limit before. I stopped—right there on the sidewalk—forcing people to go around us.

"No. I'm not. I'm selling you short. You'd never be interested in anyone other than for how she looks on your arm. I'm five-five and girl-next-door cute. I've been in enough situations where I had to sell me instead of my books to know my assets. And I know no matter how nice my wardrobe and no matter how early I get up to do something besides a ponytail, you'd look right over my head. And, because your fabulous life is splashed all over the front page of *US Weekly*, so does the rest of the world."

I moved on, leaving him standing—hopefully gaping at my back—as I walked—no, make that *strode*—away glad I'd said all that. Seriously wondering just how hard self-publishing would be once Catherine found out I'd tossed her bet out the window.

I'd have to return the clothes. That was the real shame here.

And, I was just beginning to break these shoes in.

Come to think of it, Catherine owed me *at least* what I was wearing today. Even the coat.

Also, that pretty computer bag.

Everything else would go back. I'd box it up and she could have someone come get it. Because there was no way I was facing down more than one ego today.

Even my line in the sand was only so thin.

FIVE

BY THE TIME I got back to my building, I'd walked off my mad and thought through the premise for my next story, a love triangle where the nerdy girl picks the cute, smart boy over the popular jock.

I can't imagine where I got the inspiration for that.

I was unlocking the building's door, thinking I'd call Jenna and see if she was around for an update, when someone shouted my name.

I was more than a little surprised to see Connor standing out on the sidewalk.

"Did you *follow* me?"

I'm not sure if I was more worried someone had managed to follow me for that long without me noticing—maybe plotting and walking wasn't so safe—or that he was still there, looking at me, expecting something.

"Yes. I..." He ran a hand through the blond mass of hair that looked carelessly disheveled in a way I'd bet cost him two-hundred dollars a cut. "You were right. I'd like to buy you lunch and talk about it. And, so you don't think I'm trying to back you into a corner, we could have it here so no one sees us. I'll have whatever you like delivered."

Every Stranger Danger alert I'd ever heard sounded in my mind.

"You think I'm just going to say, *Sure, come on up?*" I asked. It seemed like a bad idea. The kind you don't tell your mom about.

"We could go out. But I thought you might want to avoid that."

It was true. The last thing I needed was for our names to be linked and then wind up *not* dating him. It would end up looking like a lame set up since we'd just come from his agent's office.

"The problem is," Connor braced a foot on the curb, looking like he didn't want to come up any more than I wanted him to. "You're both right. You and Dex. He's right that I need to clean up my image and you're right that you're not the type of girl I typically date." He drew himself up, making me want to back into the door behind me. "You're also right about your assets. You're smart, they said you're funny—I'm still waiting to see that one—and you *are* cute. You're the type of girl my mom would want me to bring home. You're exactly what I need."

"But, you don't really want in on the whole deal, right?" Which was my way of trying to say, *No. Now get off my stoop.*

I'd already made up my mind and I was over it. The scraps of compliments weren't exactly winning me over. I was going to stand strong. Not be backed into a corner.

I am woman hear me—

"And," he continued, as if I hadn't just tried to shut him down again. "I'll do my part. I read the contract they wrote up. It's insane, but it would be good for both of us. Catherine does have your best interest at heart. Some of her clauses might make Dex cry. It was worth sitting through the meeting just to see that."

"Connor, I don't mean to be rude." I glanced around, trying to find the words without being too mean. "To be honest, dating you doesn't bring the type of attention I want."

He didn't even bat an eye, which made me think Catherine might have already tried this line of attack.

"I think you're wrong there. My reputation is a bit tarnished, but that fourteen to twenty-six group is, if not always positive, at least very curious. Even when they're not loving me unconditionally, they're hate-stalking me." He took another step up. "And, Catherine said your mind is like a sponge. It sucks in everything it sees, twists it around, and spits out a bestseller. If you wanted to know anything about professional sports or baseball or celebrity...well, all those connections come into play."

"That's not what I write."

"Not right now. But," he took the final step to join me at the door. "Maybe when you know more you will."

We stood there, staring each other down. Neither one of us wanted to do this, but only one of us was willing to walk away.

"One lunch," he pushed. "I'll have someone deliver whatever you want. We'll chat. I'll win you over."

He gave me what I could only assume was his Disarming Smile.

Consider me armed.

~*~

"The menus are in the drawer next to the fridge. Make yourself at home. I'll be right back."

I hurried into my bedroom, dropping my tote and kicking off the incredibly cute, but not yet broken in shoes.

So, Connor Ryan was in my apartment. I wish I could have gotten more excited about that. But I was just annoyed he was in my space and I didn't have any option other than to let him stay while we figured this all out.

Taking a deep breath, I joined him in the kitchen, heading past him to the "office" I'd built out of the double-sized coat closet in the "dining area." Yes, all those quotes were valid in my tiny world. He overwhelmed the space.

It wasn't even that my apartment was small or that he was an oversized guy. It was him. His presence. It was bad enough in the offices or on the street, but here, in my space I felt dwarfed by him.

I took a minute, sorting my notes and checking my calendar. I brought my email up to make sure nothing insane—*more* insane—had happened. A bunch of excited tweets about launch week. A few new reviews I swore I wouldn't look at. And about thirty emails. I set myself up to get to work once I got rid of His Charmingness and took a deep breath.

Okay, so that may also have been a whole bunch of stalling.

"Your place is really cozy." He'd moved to the living room while I'd been working.

I didn't mean to jump, to give away the surprise I felt at finding him still there.

"I used to think *cozy* was just a word girls used to describe something small, but this really is cozy." He leaned his head back against the worn leather of the overstuffed chair in the corner. "Where'd you find this chair?"

I'll admit it didn't go with anything else in the room. My place was more cottage-chic and the chair was more uptown guy.

"An ex moved to California. He lived across the hall and had movers come get all his stuff. Only, that chair was in here because it didn't fit in his living room. He forgot it…and I didn't exactly chase them down the street when I saw the truck drive away."

His loss. I wrote most of my books in that chair. It was the most comfortable thing I'd ever sat on in my life. Some nights I wished I could stretch it out and make it a bed.

"Serves him right." He stood, rubbing his hand along the worn-to-softness leather of the arm. "You should always arrange for your furniture to be moved yourself."

He prowled the edges of the room, picking things up and then putting them back down. He touched everything he walked by. He glanced at movies and music. He checked out my TV and shook his head—I can only assume it didn't meet with Millionaire Guy TV stature.

At the end of his circle, he collapsed back into the leather chair. Guess I wouldn't be sitting there.

I curled up on the far end of my couch, putting enough distance between us for comfort. Not to mention a cushion for all this awkward silence going on.

"I called Teo's." Apparently he needed the silence broken too. "They said you usually get barbeque chicken pizza so I ordered that, a salad, breadsticks, soda—diet and regular—and two slices of chocolate cake."

If he was trying to buy me off, that was an excellent start.

I breathed in a deep, centering moment, taking him in. One of America's Sexiest Athletes was sitting in my living room and all I wanted was him gone. He looked comfortable, sure of himself, and devastatingly handsome just sitting there.

"Have they ever approached you to do *The Bachelor*?" It would make sense.

He grinned. When other people grinned you knew what they were thinking. Not Connor. Whether it was sarcastic or because I'd called him on something, who knows.

"Here's what I'm thinking." He leaned forward, placing his elbows on his knees and clasping his hands together. "We need this to look realistic. Not just a pick-up or an infatuation. We need it to be just public enough for people to believe it and private enough to convince them we're serious."

I was still stuck on the *pick-up or infatuation* part.

"I'm sorry. Back up a bit." Because, I was pretty sure we'd already covered this. "You still think I'm going to become infatuated with you?"

"I'm just saying, one of us has a bit more experience."

"Yeah. At sleeping around." I shook my head. His ego knew no bounds. "And one of us has a bit more experience with relationships."

"And we all see where that landed you. Single with a really comfortable chair."

Oh, he was ticking me off. This *so* wasn't going to work.

"Stop glaring at me." He glared at me.

"You have no idea about my success or failure when it comes to relationships." I tried not to stand and put my hands on my hips. Only one of us lived in the real world here. "Maybe because it's not splashed all over the cover of every magazine decorating the checkout at the grocery store."

"I'm—You know what. Fine." He all but threw his hands in the air. "You have more experience with *relationships*. I could never possibly have had one."

Again I couldn't tell if that was sarcasm or not, so I steamed ahead, unworried about him and his *relationships*. I'd never met anyone who could push all my buttons like he was.

"I'm also really good at narrative." I paused when he looked at me blankly. "That's storytelling."

"I'm an athlete, not an idiot. Dex showed me your website. Saying I'm good at catching a ball is like say you're good at storytelling."

Since he was one of the top ball-catcher-guys in the country, I was at least a little flattered by the comparison.

"What we need to do is write the story of our relationship." If I was going to do this, I was going to do it write…er, right. "Why wait for the media to do it? We plot it out today and then let them fall into our storyline. That seems safer than hoping we can wing it."

"That seems a little…dry."

"You have me for four weeks. How you handle the time during and after is up to you." I leaned forward, matching his body language. "The one thing—this one thing—is the only deal breaker for me. While we're *together*, you are sweet, considerate, and for Pete's sake you are faithful. When this ends, our busy schedules are forcing us apart. I'll be smart and as adorable as possible. That's my deal. Take it or leave it."

"I'm—"

The high, irritating buzz of my door's bell interrupted him, giving me a chance to escape to the kitchen and ring the delivery girl up.

An excuse. A good one, but still an excuse.

I took the food from the teenage girl standing in my doorway and went to my room to find the tote I'd tossed on the bed. Before I could get back, I knew. I just knew.

Okay. It could have been the squealing "OMG!" that gave it away.

"You're Connor Ryan! Oh my God! What are you doing here! Connor Ryan! Oh my God!"

I tried to step between them and pay, but there was no way I'd get anywhere near him with the mini-tornado swirling around, screaming.

It was quite a sight. I felt like I'd just stepped into some type of movie premiere red carpet line her excitement was so high.

"Could you sign..." She glanced around trying to figure out what he could sign and then started to lift her shirt.

"Whoa there." Connor raised a hand as if to shield his eyes. "My days of chest signing are way over. And starting up again in front of Hailey is probably not the best idea."

Plus the whole she-had-to-be-underage thing, which was pretty wise of him to back away from.

I tried to inch backward out of the room as gazes turned my way, but Connor threw an arm around my shoulders and pulled me into the doorway with them. "Say hello, Hailey."

I smiled. It was a less-than-comfortable smile as I tried to ignore the heat of his arm on my neck and the girl scrutinizing me. I worked hard to remember my lines with new people. What do normal people say when strangers were introduced to them?

"Ahhh…Hello?" I stuttered.

The over made-up teen glanced from Connor to me and back again.

"She doesn't look like a model or an actress…or *anyone.*"

And so it begins.

Connor's arm tightened across the back of my shoulder. Well, tough for him. He knew this was coming. Of course, we hadn't even gotten a chance to leave the house yet, but I was an overachiever.

"No. She's a writer. Actually, she writes books for teenagers."

I had to admit, I was impressed he knew that much.

Her little lip-glossed mouth formed a perfect O.

"So, she's famous too?"

"No. I mean, she's…" He glanced at me, his brows gathering together with a look I could only assume meant he was feeling cornered. "She's popular. I think that's how you'd put it. But, unfortunately, not a lot of writers get famous. Like spot-them-on-the-street-famous."

"So, no one *really* knows who she is?"

This was something I'd always been happy about. I so wasn't a crowds person. I never wanted to be famous…never even understood the desire to be famous. And yet, part of me couldn't understand how the creators of some of the most amazing stories were overlooked in favor of their multimillion-dollar earning cousins.

Actors.

Don't get me wrong, I loved Hugh Jackman as much the next girl. But, watching amazing books get turned into award-winning movies that people didn't even realize had been books first—well, it kind of broke my heart.

"Nope." He grinned, looking like that was a good thing. He even had me fooled.

Connor signed the girl's hat, took a picture with her iPhone that was sure to end up on seven bazillion social media sites and—very nicely—shoved her out the door.

I carried the food to the kitchen island, finding twice as much food as he'd listed, and trying to catch my breath again. Trying to get myself back together after all that energy spent. A nice bubble bath and a good book would be great right now.

Forks. Knives. Plates. Glasses. No wine, it was too date'y. Iced tea. Napkins. What else? What else?

"Hailey."

Placemats. That's what was missing. I grabbed some from the bottom drawer in the island and laid them out.

"Hailey."

Should I put the food on serving plates or just leave them in their boxes? That just meant more dishes to do later, so I was voting no to that.

The counter set, I had nothing to occupy my hands and so—

"Hailey." Connor grabbed my hand as I headed back to the refrigerator for ice. "Stop. Sit."

To prove his command, he pulled me toward my chair then sat in the one across from it.

"Do you want to tell me what's going on?"

"This isn't going to work. I'm not good with people. All we did was open a door to one person and look what happened. Imagine what's going to happen in public. I'm going to be the worst-fake-girlfriend ever. Which, honestly, would serve you right. But I need to look smart. Writers need to look smart. If, by some small chance, someone meets a writer, she needs to believe that person is clever enough to create a whole 'nother world in her head. To create characters and conflict and weave a story that makes you stay up hours past your bedtime." I sucked in a breath, fighting off the panic. "So, yeah. This isn't going to work."

I watched Connor think about that while he watched me try to catch my breath. With nothing better to do, I started opening boxes and dishing myself out enough food for a weekend. With guests. What had he ordered?

"Hailey."

My name was beginning to be one of those words that sounded wrong the more you said it.

"Listen," he continued. "I get that not everyone loves the spotlight. Some of my best buddies hate it. They don't even like giving the ten-second sound bite the team's PR person wrote for them. We can work with this."

He leaned back, watching me as I'd moved on to loading his plate up with food.

"Think about it." He dug into the salad and chewed while I—as ordered—thought about it. "This is actually perfect. You just be yourself and I'll be the protective, handle-the-media guy. People will love that."

I fought rolling my eyes.

"You mean people will love you as Mr. Hero."

47

"No. I mean, we make this a win-win. I'm smart enough to know if it isn't working for you, it's going to blow up in our faces. We can do this." He unfolded his napkin and pointed at my plate. "Eat your food."

"And then?"

"And then, you write us that narrative."

I could live with that.

For now.

SIX

THE MAKEUP ARTIST Personal Shopper Becca hired had gone all out. I couldn't even name everything she'd put on my face. In the end, when I told her there was no way I'd be able to do that—let alone want to—she'd handed me powder, lip-gloss, and mascara for everyday coverage.

Even I could handle that.

Becca called that morning to make sure I was wearing the perfect outfit that would say *I'm the woman he's willing to change for.* Even my clothes were lying now.

With only four weeks on our deal—not to mention our schedules—Connor and I had decided to move our *relationship* up a few weeks.

It had been two days since the pizza delivery girl had posted her picture and mentioned "some short girl" Connor was with. Thinking back, he'd been brilliant. He'd given her all the info we'd want out there without making it seem

49

planted and the girl had completely failed to mention more than my height.

Or, lack thereof.

On top of that, Connor had been caught with Ackerman's girlfriend about three weeks before. Figuring he and I met right after that and I caved to his charm immediately, we'd be halfway through our time together. Probably magically making me his longest relationship ever. So, tonight was a big show of Just Comfortable Enough.

Connor was right on time. I'll admit it was a bit of a shock. I figured him for the wander-in-whenever-he-remembered-to-show-up type of guy. The way he'd held us both up for the meeting the first day didn't scream *I value punctuality.* And may the universe help us all if a model crossed his path.

Luckily, I'd made sure to be on time for this. Or Kasey who was obsessed with timeliness came over to help me get ready and made sure I was on time for this.

I grabbed my wrap and headed toward the door before the buzzer finished echoing against the walls. At the top of the stairs, I ran head-on into a solid chest. Patting my nose to make sure it wasn't broken, I glanced up.

"You're ready?" He gave me one of his probably-patented once-overs.

"You said seven."

We stood there, facing off eye-to-eye, with him on a lower step, because we were both punctual. For once.

"Right. I know. But I've never met a woman who was actually on time." He gave me a look that said, *and that includes you.*

I smiled, trying to portray that my occasional tardiness was part of my charm.

I considered the high-maintenance women he dated. With the hair and the clothes and the whole have-to-be-perfect thing, no wonder he was always waiting.

"Well, I don't have as much work to do as the girls you date."

His eyebrow went up and I realized that didn't come out the way I meant it.

"I mean, I don't do as much to myself to go out...you know? I guess my self-standards are lower. I mean, with the makeup and everything. I'm just...yeah." And thank goodness for that. After my makeover, I definitely did not envy the women who had to look perfect all the time for their job.

He was chuckling now. A deep laugh under his breath, and I couldn't figure out which part he was laughing at, the low-maintenance part or the stumbling-around-for-words part.

"No worries. I know what you mean. I guess I'm just used to sitting on uncomfortable, feminine furniture, sipping a Whiskey Neat for half an hour before each date." He shrugged. "My own personal date ritual."

Oh, geez. Whiskey Neat was Scotch, right? I didn't even own any whiskey. Or Scotch. I was already a fake girlfriend failure.

"Don't worry." He must have seen the panic. "I can order a drink at the restaurant if I want one. I guess I was just looking forward to having a comfortable chair to sit in for once."

Connor rolled his shoulder and I noticed the strap of a bag over it. Please, please don't let him be one of those guys who carried a weird *murse* thing. Or who wore indoor scarves. Or got manicures.

Connor didn't seem like a girly-guy, but he was edging toward high maintenance if any of those things were true.

I scanned him for a scarf or overly fashionable socks before asking, "What's that?"

"I brought some things over. I was talking to my brother Gavin and he pointed out that if we'd been dating seriously for a few weeks, I'd have some stuff at your house. And they'd catch us sneaking out to breakfast some morning wearing something different than the night before."

Stuff? And he was going to put it in my place and leave it there?

This was way more involved than I'd anticipated.

Also, the idea that people would be aware enough of us that they'd know he was wearing different clothes—Well, that was a level of celebrity tracking I hoped my visit to would be brief.

"So...I was thinking we could leave the bag here instead of taking it to dinner?"

"Yeah. Yes. Of course." I turned and force-marched myself back to the door, sliding the key home and ignoring the man behind me until I couldn't. "You're not really going to stay here are you?"

He set the bag down on the couch and glanced around. Taking in my tiny furniture and my small, *cozy* space with the non-guy-sized television.

"Of course I am."

I didn't see how there was an "of course" involved in this.

"But that means sleeping here."

Connor stepped over my miniature coffee table and came to hover over me. His gaze slid over my face before coming back to my eyes. He winked, giving me that trademark smile I'd seen on every website hit I'd pulled up last night. "There's not a lot of sleeping involved when I stay over my girlfriend's house."

I could feel the heat rushing up my neck—part embarrassment, part annoyed.

"Oh. I'm so glad to hear that." I forced a grin as he started in surprise. "Because I can't guarantee the couch is very comfortable."

"I am *not* sleeping on the couch."

"Then it's the floor, because you're not sleeping with me." I crossed my arms, so flustered I feared my hands were shaking. "I don't know you. I'm not dating you. If you're sleeping in this apartment, it's on the couch. Or the floor. Although, as you've pointed out, the leather chair is comfortable."

"Hailey, we're both adults." He turned on the charm for this attempt. "There's no reason we can't share a bed."

"I understand you don't know me. So, I'll say this once. I'm not a prude, but my values around sex and relationships obviously aren't as lax as yours. I don't go sharing my bed— for sex or sleep—with random guys I'm trapped in fake relationships with. If you stay, you know your options."

I pushed past him before he could respond. This wasn't an argument. An argument meant he might have a chance of persuading me. This was a non-negotiable and he better get that if this whole thing was going to work.

I threw the door open, annoyed with myself when it banged into the wall behind it.

"So, we can go to dinner and you can decide if you want to stay here—on the couch—later. Or we can call it off. If you forfeit, you make it very clear to Dex that it's on you. I have a proposal going out the door in a few weeks and I don't need their little agent mafia bad-mouthing Catherine when I need every negotiating super power working in my favor."

"Forfeit?" His voice had dropped to a new low and I realized my mistake immediately. "Sweetheart, I don't lose. And I certainly don't *forfeit.* But get one thing straight. I also don't sleep on couches."

"Then I guess you'll be going home tonight."

I stepped into the hall, forcing his hand.

"Fine." He pulled the door shut behind us. "Let's go to dinner."

Worst. Start. To a date. Ever.

I tromped down the stairs, annoyed at Connor. Annoyed to be breaking in more new shoes. Annoyed I could have stayed in and gotten pages written and maybe watched an old episode of Buffy.

When I reached for the front door, a dark sleeve shot past me, pulled it open, and held it as I attempted to sail through as graceful as a swan. I'm sure I looked more like a waddling penguin. But, hey. At least my hair looked good.

On the sidewalk, Connor stepped forward to flag down a cab.

"Where are we going?"

"Il Giardino." He named a restaurant nearby that was busy enough we'd blend in without the paparazzi of his typical set, but we'd still be spotted out together.

"That's only four blocks from here."

Connor nodded, oblivious to my point.

"Why don't we just walk?" Did the man not realize how much cabs were?

"You want to walk?" The way he asked it had me wondering why it was such a confusing idea.

"Sure. Why not?"

"Aren't you afraid you'll get..." He waved a hand in my general direction. "Mussed? I mean, don't you want the moment where you get out of the cab and everyone glances?"

"Not really." And, did people really do that? Make cab entrances? That sounded stressful. "One more reason to just walk."

He kept looking at me and I had no idea if I was supposed to add something to this.

"You really don't care, do you?"

"Should I?" This was way too confusing between the bag and the whiskey and the cabs. I was going to have to make myself pre-date flashcards at this rate.

"I don't know." He looked like he really didn't. Like he was thinking it through and trying to come to some conclusion.

"Do you?" I asked, figuring I'd messed up again.

"I don't think so." He shook his head, a surprised look raising his eyebrows. "No. Nope, I don't care. Let's walk."

We headed east. The sole sound between us the clicking of our shoes. I was focused on not falling or getting the pointy heels stuck in a crack or grate when a heavy arm fell across my shoulder.

"What are you doing?" I tried to step away, but his hand tightened where it cupped my shoulder.

"There's no way I'd walk down the street without having an arm around my girlfriend. If we're not making an entrance showing up in a cab, then we'll have to look the part this way."

He was right.

It kind of grated.

So far, he'd been right often enough that I was beginning to realize I'd underestimated him. Which could be a problem if I was going to make sure I stayed a safe distance from any dating danger zones.

We walked on, both pretending this wasn't the least bit awkward. Okay, I was pretending I didn't feel awkward. Who knows what Connor was thinking? We were a block from the restaurant when he glanced at his watch.

"We're earlier for our reservation than I expected."

I don't think I'd ever gone out with a guy who bothered to make reservations. Or maybe Connor didn't. Someone who made as much money as he did must have lackeys. The whole thing was suspicious. He probably made reservations and then tipped off the papers himself. I'd heard about the Hollywood wars over actresses doing that to get coverage. Like those just-coming-out-of-the-gym photos where the person looks really surprised to be caught. Not to mention, completely not sweaty.

Because *that* happened in the real world.

"Why did you make a reservation?" I tried to keep the suspicion out of my voice, but when he shot me an odd look I knew I'd failed.

"So we wouldn't have to wait. Also, I have a few favorite restaurants where I've gotten to know the owners. Not letting them know I'd be there was just rude if there's a chance we might have an *audience*." The tone of his voice was not all warm and fuzzy on that last word. "I waited till the last minute though so we could stay low key. I was afraid Dex had called the papers." He steered me across the street at the crosswalk. "He seems to know where I am no matter what. I've tried texting, calling, having my brother call. It's like Dex has LoJack on my phone. Would you believe I actually left it at home for a few days to test the theory?"

No. I wouldn't have, but after seeing Dex in action maybe I should rethink that.

"So, you think he calls the papers on you?" I asked. "You think that's how you have so much coverage?"

He shook his head, not even bothering to look down at me.

"Sweetheart, I was born for this coverage. I have it because I'm the best at what I do, I make a lot of money, I'll help get the Nighthawks to the pennant, and I date some of the most beautiful women in the world. If I wasn't me, I'd be buying those dumb rags just to check me out too."

As statements went, that one was an excellent reality check. His social karma moves would only get him so far.

Connor pulled the front door open and allowed me to pass by him into the restaurant. One thing was for sure. He had excellent manners...when he didn't have horrible ones.

Dex had probably sent him to some etiquette school to get him house broken.

"Mr. Ryan!" The girl behind the hostess stand sounded as if she'd just run the four blocks from my house. "We weren't expecting you for half an hour."

"Not a problem, Sheila. Hailey and I can just grab a drink in the lounge." He flashed a smile so smooth, so charming I thought she was going to drop to her knees and thank him for knowing her name.

Which, I'll admit, I was impressed by.

I jumped when Connor's hand landed on my lower back. All this touching was nerve-wracking. But, let's be honest. He was so used to dating five-foot-eleven girls, he was probably aiming for my butt.

In the bar, we found a low table in a dim corner. The booth was a circular, plush-covered deal and as I slid in, Connor moved in behind me. He was better at playing this game out than I was.

"Okay," I said, trying to get *my* game back under control. I leaned against him in what would hopefully look like a comfy cuddle, but was just to discuss our plan without being overheard. "Tonight we're out in public enough to be seen. We've known each other several weeks. This isn't a first date. It's the date where we just stop caring if we get caught since we've both started to take this more seriously."

He dropped his arm behind me, cupping my shoulder again. His smile was somewhere between condescending and humoring. I made a note to self: Look those up to see how different they are.

"I'm sure you can manage to chill and enjoy yourself." His hand ran down my arm and then back up, slow, soothing movements with just the tips of his fingers that had me relaxing against him. "Will it really be so bad having a few nice meals with me?"

Would it be hard? I didn't know enough about him. I knew he was the bachelor of the hour and he was a big shot in the baseball world. I knew stores had started selling Mrs.

Ryan t-shirts and couldn't keep them in stock. I knew he dated a lot and had a very clear image as a playboy.

But I didn't know if he read or voted. I didn't know if he went to college and, if he attended, how he did. Did he have a pet? Where was he from? Was he close to his family beyond that brother he kept sucking into his public adventures?

When it came right down to it, I knew less about him than the average girl on my block. I doubted between his money and his lifestyle that we had many of those things in common.

"Connor, I just—" How to put this nicely? "I just don't think we're the same kind of person. To me this is part of the job."

His lips flattened and at the same time managed to show an almost cruel smirk. "Are you afraid *I'm* going to fall in love with *you?*"

If sarcasm had a face, it would be the one he was looking at me with right now.

"I have no idea how you even got that out of what I just said." Because, really.

"So you don't think I'd be interested in you?"

"You don't have to be mean about it." I couldn't believe he was bringing this up again. "I know your type. The whole world knows your type. I'm five inches too short, two cup sizes too small, and six years too old. Which, honestly, aren't those girls starting to feel a little young to you? So why don't you leave the sarcasm for someone it will work on?"

I pushed his arm off my shoulder and tried to slide farther down the booth.

"Hailey." He wrapped a hand around my wrist. "Stop. Settle down and listen."

I tried to pull away, but his loose hand had tightened on my arm.

"I'm sorry. I didn't mean that sarcastically. I was joking. I thought you'd see the humor in it."

"You don't know me any more than I know you, so I don't know how you think I'd magically understand anything you'd joke about." I was afraid we'd never be speaking the same language at this rate.

"Okay. Listen. This is what I'm thinking. We're going to—"

"Hi, Mr. Ryan!"

"Sorry it took me so long." She rushed on as if we'd been waiting hours. "What can I get you guys to drink?"

"Hi, Rachel. I'll have a Whiskey Neat." He turned toward me, forcing the attention my way. "Hailey, what did you want tonight?"

I wanted to understand what was going on, to get his intentions and be able to play along. But, in lieu of that, I'd take an adult beverage.

So I asked, "What do you have for white wines?"

She ran through a list and thank goodness there were a couple good ones I recognized.

We sat quietly, waiting for Rachel to bring our drinks, his hand doing that soothing up-and-down thing on my arm again.

After we'd been beveragized and Rachel had wandered off, Connor took a sip of his whiskey then paused, waiting for something.

"Here's what I'm thinking." He set the glass down and pulled his arm away so he could shift to face me. "Why don't we just think of this as hanging out? You know, as friends.

You're smart and clean up to be cute in that girl-next-door way. Maybe it will be fun. Being able to go out with someone and not have any pressure. Not to mention, the whole we're-pulling-something-over-on-everyone thing." He gave me a hopeful grin. I think it was dawning on him that he was the one with something to lose here. "It's kind of funny, don't you think?"

I thought about my rapidly approaching book release, focusing on the fact that this misadventure had the power to make or break it. I pushed those worries aside because I could only handle what I could handle.

"Sure. Why not?" I mean, what did I have to lose? It's not like I was escaping this, so I might as well go along for the ride.

"Great." He eased back and took another sip. "I think this will be just fine."

Yeah. So said the man used to getting everything handed to him on a silver platter.

To be fair, it was amazing how quickly he was adjusting to the plan. I guess when a person was as goal-driven as he was, they embraced the route to a win and went full throttle. Or whatever baseball players did.

"But, I was serious." I wanted this as clear as the short glass his whiskey glimmered in. "Do not embarrass me. No *cheating* on me during this or anything."

I glared, adding weight to my words.

"You're adorable." He grinned, ignoring the weighted words. "But, I promise. I know you seem to think I'm this womanizing jock. And, granted, I'm a jock and I like women, but that doesn't always equal the same thing."

"You've been featured on *TMZ* for goodness sake!" Normal people did not end up on gossip rag TV shows.

"And?"

"And, it's not like you've managed to be faithful to a woman. Every week you're on a cover with at least one new girl under your arm. I especially loved the cover of you on four different dates with four different women in one week." It was my turn to casually sip my drink. I forced myself to take a moment to enjoy the forty-dollar glass before adding, "I didn't even know there were that many rich, beautiful, famous women in town. Do you have them imported?"

I had no idea where this Hailey was coming from. I couldn't even stand up to my own agent, but with Connor…well, I guess I was afraid if I let him get a foot in the door, I'd never gain that territory back.

"This is your idea of relaxing and playing nice?" He leaned in, getting so close I could see the silver flecks in his eyes. "I'm going to say this one more time. I do not cheat. I play fair. Every girl I go out with knows the deal and if things get even slightly serious, I treat them that way. So, if you don't mind, I'd like to be judged on my actions instead of by those supposed stories slapped together that don't represent an accurate picture of my life."

Oh. Um. Yeah. Well…He sounded angry enough that it was kind of hard not to believe him. So, maybe I'd been a bit quick to judge.

"Okay."

"Okay?" he demanded.

"Yes. I said okay, alright?"

We stared each other down and then he laughed.

"Hailey, I have to tell you. For a fake girlfriend, you're really high maintenance."

"*I'm* high maintenance?" I tried to lower my voice but outrage was making me squeak. "You date some of the most high maintenance women on the planet."

"Maybe. But, I show up, my whiskey's waiting, they come down, they're happy to go anywhere, they're good at small talk, and they don't badger me about the tabloids."

"You'll have to excuse me if I have zero experience understanding what goes into a tabloid date. I'm happy hanging out with my girlfriends, meeting guys who don't come with a rule book, and writing. It may sound boring to you, but it's a good life."

"That doesn't sound boring. It sounds nice."

Geez. *Nice.* Kiss of death, if this had been a real date.

Maybe Connor was right. Maybe we just needed to write this off and enjoy ourselves.

"If we're going to pull this off," I said, trying to play nice. "Then tell me something about yourself? Like...where are you from?"

"You don't know that from all those tabloids you buy."

"I wouldn't buy that trash. It's horrible. Plus," I went on, getting to what I *really* found offensive about those cheap rags. "I don't think any of them have hired a real copy editor in forever."

"And yet, you just spouted off about some very specific articles and covers."

"Oh." Oh, if only there were a way out of this. "I *might* have done a little research last night."

"On me?" That grin broke into a full out smile. "You researched me?"

63

"Just enough to find out if you're a serial killer or anything weird like that." And, when he'd known about my website, I'd realized I was behind the ball. If information was a commodity, then I was broke.

"And to take a count of how many famous, beautiful women I'd gone out with in the last month. Just so you know, I've also had an enjoyable evening with a lawyer and a woman who runs her own boutique."

Of course he had.

I refocused, trying to remember to toss my tabloid thoughts out and play fair.

"So, again," I pushed us back toward the right conversational track. "Where are you from?"

"I grew up outside Chicago. Nice suburb. A mom, a dad, a brother. Good times."

I tried to read between the lines, figure out what he wasn't saying. It seemed too straightforward.

"Hailey, I can see that brain of yours trying to create something where there's nothing to worry about. I have a great family. I have another condo there so I can spend time year round in my own place. Somewhere to go home to. I did alright in school. Not amazing, but would have gone to college even without the ball scholarship. I was a business major just in case. Nothing exciting. No dark hidden secret you'll stumble upon."

I'll admit I was disappointed.

Of course, that was just his family background. There was still sex, drugs, and rock-n-roll to cover.

"Ever lived with someone before?" I asked.

"No."

"Drugs?"

"No."

"Really?" I found that hard to believe. You heard all these stories about athletes with steroids and models drugging to stay skinny and energetic. And he was at every A-list party on the East Coast. It seemed difficult to believe he hadn't indulged. "Never?"

"Nope. I went to school on scholarship, which meant getting random tests. Then, by the time we got out, I'd already seen what any type of drug could do."

"Okay."

"Keep going. This is kind of fun." He picked up that whiskey he was nursing.

Those must be the smallest sips ever. I was used to people drinking their drinks. But maybe he felt the same way about alcohol that he felt about drugs.

"Or, maybe I should play this game too." He set the glass down and studied me like there might be some answers written right there on my forehead. "Your bio says you're from New England. Here?"

"Vermont."

"*Really?*" As if no one was actually *from* Vermont.

"Yes. I'm saving my lies for something bigger. Things that if I tell you, you'll have to disappear forever with the knowledge."

I was shocked when he laughed a true, deep laughter that had other people looking our way.

"I hadn't realized you were funny. I mean, your books are supposed to be funny and you say some odd stuff. But, purposefully funny I wasn't expecting."

"I'll try not to do it again." I kept my voice dry and made a strong attempt to not roll my eyes as he laughed again.

"Connor." An older man stood at the edge of our table, his smile more welcoming than I'd expected. "I didn't know you were coming in tonight."

"Mr. Antonelli." Connor slid out of the booth and wrapped an arm around the man. "Last minute plans. I thought it was time I showed Hailey where the good food is." He motioned to me and I wondered if I was supposed to slide out too, but Mr. Antonelli waved me down.

"This Hailey, she's the first girl you've bothered to introduce me to. She must be the reason you haven't been coming around with all those salad-eating skinny girls lately."

My college roommate was Italian. That was the only reason I knew I'd just been complimented instead of being called fat.

"She's definitely keeping me on my toes."

I watched them chat, Connor steering the conversation away from any outright lies.

"Where is Sheila seating you? Did you ask to sit outside? It's a nice night, not too breezy. We have those nice heat lamps, keep things snug. You might enjoy it."

I could see Connor struggling, trying to figure out what the right thing was and I realized something. He was smart enough to make the right call. Sure, we were going to argue more than any two humans should over the next few weeks, but we had the same endgame: Survive, get the right PR, and not kill each other—Or, per Connor's suggestion, enjoy each other's friendship.

"I think we'll sit inside this week. We're still...flying under the radar." He glanced my direction with one of those smiles that made you feel like you were in on a secret with him.

But, of course, I was.

It really was absurd.

We were still flying under the radar because we hadn't existed before this week. And, we didn't want insta-fame as a couple because that would be nuts.

Plus, I'd realized there were a few more people I needed to bring into the secret web of conspiracy to make this work.

"I understand." Mr. Antonelli nodded as if this were very sage and he was in complete agreement. "Let me show you to a table then."

I slid to the edge of the booth and looked up to find Connor there, hand outstretched, to help me out.

One thing was for sure, if the fame, money, and good looks stopped getting him women, his charm could.

Mr. Antonelli showed us to a comfortable table in the corner where we'd be away from the hustle of the front door and the kitchen, but not shoved in a small alcove.

"I'll send Margo over to take your order. You know how she loves to see you." He put his hand over his heart as if he were sharing a secret of the love they all had.

"You just want the latest gossip," Connor accused. "And, look at you willing to send your wife to do the dirty work."

It was funny seeing him laid-back and joking with a restaurant owner. It wasn't something I expected. I kept waiting to see the slick side of him the media showed. The I'm-too-sexy-for-my…well, everything. He shook the man's hand once more before sitting down and giving me his full attention.

But, at the same time there was still something guarded about him. It took me a moment to realize that while he seemed to genuinely enjoy the people he was introducing me to, he also was a little standoffish. His wall was just one of overwhelming friendliness.

"So, where were we?" He snapped his fingers, pulling me back from my study. "Oh, yes. I remember. Any pets?"

"Not since Franklin." I regretted the words as soon as I said them. That wasn't somewhere I wanted to go.

"And Franklin was…"

"A rescue beagle I brought home and hid from my landlord for four years."

"I didn't see any doggie stuff around."

I shouldn't have brought him up. It had been off the cuff—there was no *delete* button.

"No. He…" I really wanted that delete button. "He got away from his walker last spring and was hit by a car. They told me it was really fast. The poor kid couldn't have missed him if she'd been psychic. When I got there she couldn't stop crying."

And I hadn't been able to either. Not for days.

"And you went over and told her it was okay. That it wasn't her fault. That you understood even though you wanted to sit on the sidewalk and bawl?"

The cop who showed up had called me a soft hearted idiot when he'd seen me trying to help the girl.

"Well, what was I supposed to do?" I focused on the sconce over his head and blink-blink-blinked the almost tears away. A year isn't that long to be missing your dog. And, when it happened, it wasn't like I was going to scream at the girl. There was a little blanket laid out over Franklin and she couldn't stop staring at it and sobbing. "Anyone would have said that no matter how upset they were."

"Hailey, you have no idea how nice you are. You're just one of those girls. Let me guess, everyone's best friend in high school. You didn't date much, but always had guys around you. If something went wrong, everyone knew to call you because you'd bail them out. Straight As with the occasional B, but you didn't work too hard at it—just hard enough. Your teachers liked you except the ones who were trying too hard to be cool. Them you annoyed because they didn't know what to do with someone who actually liked books and words and learning. Your parents trusted you so much that if there was a video of a bank robbery with you on it, they'd still believe you when you told them you didn't do it. You've been in like twenty weddings—at least a third of them as the maid of honor. You date nice guys who are a little dull, but you never have to worry about them. You'd never blame someone who was at fault for hitting your pet because they already have to live with it."

I wasn't quite sure what to say. He was close—too close—on too much of that. And I was still trying to figure him out.

"How'd I do?"

I wanted to lie, to tell him not even close. But there was too much truth there.

"I didn't have a ton of guy friends, but you're right about the ones I did have. I am still close with a lot of my girlfriends. The weddings might be a slight exaggeration. My parents would still believe me if they were *at* the bank. So, I guess all-in-all...not bad."

He grinned a new grin. I hate to say almost...*boyish*. Obviously he was more than pleased with himself.

He threw his arm around the back of his chair, stretched out, looking just a tad too arrogant... even for him. "You know you want to."

"Want to what?"

"You know you want to try. But you're going to be wrong or find out I'm not the guy you thought I was. Or," he leaned toward me, lowering his voice, "maybe I'm a good liar."

Okay, now he was just pushing my buttons. The guessing was one thing. The reading my mind was a whole other level of intrusion.

"How do I know you'll be honest?"

"I'll make you a deal—if you're up for it." He leaned forward again in what must have looked like an intimate conversation to others.

"What's the deal?" And how worried I should be?

"For the next three weeks we'll be completely honest with each other knowing the other one will never tell anyone. That includes friends, family, tabloids, anonymous blogs..." He paused, giving me a look that would make an angry fan back down. "Putting things in books."

Oh. Ouch.

"I'm not sure I can promise that last one. I put everything in books. I don't even realize I'm doing it sometimes. You just hear stuff and it's so good it gets worked around in your head and some version of it comes out on the page."

"No wonder your parents wouldn't believe the surveillance tapes." He shook his head as if this were something to pity. "You're way too honest for your own good. Even before we decided on our deal."

"I mean, I can *try*. But that's not always how it works."

"Could you promise to not overtly and knowingly use specifics from our deal?"

I could do that. Anything that specific—or overt—would be obvious. I'd pick it up on my read-through if I didn't notice it while writing.

"Okay. Deal. But, you have to know everything is research to me."

"Fine."

It was my turn to lean forward, watching him closely for a tell, for anything that would help read him like he'd read me. "You were raised in a strict but loving home. Your mom stayed home, but she did stuff on the side. Lots of volunteering, maybe some part-time work. Your brother was your best friend after he was done being your biggest enemy. You had plenty of girlfriends through high school, but somewhere around a year before college you settled on one. Together, you guys were voted pretty much everything. Most popular, best looking, homecoming king and queen. You broke it off when you went to college where you immediately fell in with the jocks and cheerleaders. You annoyed the heck out of your professors and tutors because they all realized how smart you were but you stayed focused on baseball. Not that you didn't do well. Bs were good enough for you. The occasional C wouldn't kill you. You've never been in a serious relationship. That isn't just because of the playboy thing. It's mostly because you know you're not in a place in your career and life to settle down so you don't want to get into something and blow it because that would be too much like losing—instead you get into lots of little things and then ease out of them. Politely."

I have no idea how I was suddenly sure about the last bit. Maybe it was because since we'd started tonight, I'd watched him treat everyone—no matter their job—with respect. Everyone who wasn't forcing him into a deal he hadn't made got nothing but consideration and respect. Maybe it was because I wanted to believe he was a nicer guy than the tabloids made him out to be. Whatever it was, I was pretty sure the playboy thing was a side benefit because he wasn't ready to settle down and not the reason he wasn't settling down.

Or, at least I'd come to like him just enough to hope that was true.

Connor took a long drink from his ice water before putting it down.

"Not even close."

"What?" The table closest to us looked my way. I'd been so sure I was on to something with some of my things. "That can't be true. I have to be close on some of it."

"Okay, the family stuff was pretty right on. In high school I was...I grew four inches senior year and was still shorter than the average shortstop. I grew another five from freshman year of college into sophomore."

I did some quick reverse math and came up with the only thing I could: Connor had been a runt.

"College I was red shirted as a freshman—so I sat out the whole year. They were hoping I'd keep growing. Some of the coaches had no clue how I'd ended up on the team at my size. But my batting average...well, that college record still hasn't been broken. And I was great at fielding, quicker than I looked."

Not at all what I expected. But I could see it. He'd talked about the scholarship and the drugs already. I could see him being a kid who went to college to go into business and stumbled into stardom. It seemed to almost make sense he'd accidentally become a baseball god.

"And the rest?" I asked.

He may have been open about his family and his ball playing, but he shut down as soon as I asked about the relationships.

"Not everyone is built for the picket fence, Hailey."

"I don't even know what that means."

"It means people assume that young, successful athletes that date around are trying to fill a void. Being single is somehow the equivalent of filling up the hole in your heart with drugs or booze or some other adrenaline rush. But the thing is," he leaned in, lowering his voice and I realized he was telling me the truth as he saw it. "The thing is that some people are just happy. They're not lonely being single. They're not feeling the loss of a soul mate or that their house isn't a home because they live in it alone. I *like* my life. I have a great life with lots of opportunities to do things I couldn't do if I were married. Travel, sports, not worrying about getting traded. When this is done I'll do things like rock climb and jump out of planes and other things I'd feel nervous about if someone was counting on me."

He took a long drink of his water, studying me over it. Maybe to ensure I was taking in what he was saying.

"Okay," I said, because it seemed like what I *should* say.

"I'm not saying," he rushed on. "That marriage is bad. I just can't imagine that being married to anyone, to be with someone forever, would make me happier than I am now."

I started running through all the reasons that could be. Horrible childhood, tragic love dying in his youth, the—

"Hailey." He interrupted my thought process. "You're doing it again. Let it go. Just, believe me. I know me. I'm not looking for someone to fill a void. There's no void, so…"

He trailed off and shrugged, as if that said it all.

I guess for him, it did.

And that was obviously all I was getting on that.

I still wanted there to be something else. The romance writer in me couldn't believe that some people were just happy with their lives without that One Person.

When I thought about it, that wasn't a lie. Not everyone was built for the picket fence.

But was Connor?

Who knew…and, really, who cared?

When this was over, he could go back to all the non-picket-fencing he wanted to.

He'd promised to be honest and play fair, and that was all a girl could really expect from a pro-player…I mean, pro-baseball player anyway.

SEVEN

OUR MEAL CONTINUED with lots of light chatter and relaxed laughter. Connor was easy to be around and I found myself telling him funny stories about Jenna, Kasey, and Kasey's friend Jayne who we'd all basically adopted. He wanted to hear more about Franklin and wove us around danger zones that would make me sad.

He told me about his brother Gavin moving out here and getting a house a few blocks from him while claiming it was to keep him under control. Connor said it was probably so Gavin could live it up with him.

I suspected it had more to do with them being inseparable for so long that living five states apart didn't work for them...and he just plain missed his brother.

I was trying to convince myself to say no to dessert when a squeaky voice behind me interrupted my chocolate-focused concentration.

"Mr. Ryan, my mom said it wasn't you but my dad said I could come ask if it was. And I *knew* it was you." The boy gave Connor a smile that screamed *hero worship*. "I was wondering if you'd sign my menu. I asked the waitress if that would be okay."

"Sure." Connor borrowed my ever-present pen and turned back to the boy. "What's your name?"

"Jeremy." The little boy breathed his name out like it was a prayer, a crazed hope that this was real.

I'd seen it before. The magic of meeting your hero. My friend Jenna had a huge following and I watched again and again as girls came up to hug her and take pictures. They talked about her character Chloe as if she were a friend they'd grown up with.

"So, Jeremy, do you play baseball?"

"Yes. On my town team. We got to play a team from one town over for the first time last week."

"Wow. You're already playing other towns? What position do you play?" Connor hadn't even picked up the menu he was supposed to be signing yet. It was as though he was having the most important conversation in the world and couldn't have any of his focus split.

"Catcher."

"*Catcher?*" Shock and awe. "They always amaze me. How do you keep your balance down there all the time?"

The boy giggled, but I guess it was a good question because he went on to explain his squat to Connor, the boy talking, the man nodding.

"Well, let me sign this for you. I don't want to keep you from your meal."

He picked up the menu and spent some time over it before handing it off to Jeremy. While he was writing, a man wandered over.

"Jeremy, I said there and back. I'm sure they'd like to get back to their meal."

I laughed at the accidental echo, both used to politely send a child in the right direction. Amazing how some adults didn't realize hero worship always outranked lasagna.

"It's not a problem." Connor stood and offered his hand to Jeremy's dad. "Jeremy was telling us about the difficulties of being a catcher. Lots of balance needed for that."

The father looked grateful as Connor handed over the menu—and a little surprised.

I'd never thought about what that playboy image might do to his relationship with his younger fans. Obviously, it was something Connor took care to work against.

The dad smiled then, with a quick glance over toward his wife, he lowered his voice and asked, "Do you think we could get a picture? I'm sure Jeremy would love it and the guys at work would get a kick out of it. We're all huge fans. We were even rooting for you when that thing went down with Ackerman's girlfriend a few..."

Jeremy's dad glanced my way, suddenly realizing it probably wasn't the best topic of conversation.

"Oh, sorry about that." Connor rose and came around the table as I stood to say hello. "Guys, this is Hailey. We'd just started seeing each other then. You can see the Ackerman thing got blown way out of proportion."

"This is your girlfriend?" Jeremy eyed me like there was a chance I was an Imperial Stormtrooper.

Connor laid a hand on my shoulder. "Yup."

Now Jeremy's dad was eyeing me too.

"Isn't she a little short?" Only a child could say something like that as a fact instead of an attack. "All those pictures have you with really tall, skinny girls."

It took everything in me to not blurt out, *I am not fat*. But I held it in and gave myself mental permission to have dessert as a reward for being polite to a seven-year-old boy.

"Well, a lot of them were. But then I met Hailey. She's smarter, funnier, and more fun than those other girls. Plus, I think she's pretty."

I grinned. Even knowing it wasn't the truth, it was nice to be upgraded to pretty.

"Does she play ball?"

"Nope. She tells stories."

"Like lies?"

I love children. He was on the younger side and I really did envy their ability—and willingness—to ask anything.

"No. Like fairy tales...or horror stories. Depends on how you look at it." Connor winked at me, letting me in on the joke about my own happy, romance'y books.

"Did you want me to take the picture?" I asked, trying to get the attention off me. "That way you can all be in it."

The dad looked so excited he didn't have to figure out how to ask, that I thought he was going to hug me. Connor seemed a pro at this too. He angled everyone so they'd be tight in the picture and wouldn't look awkward with the height difference. Then he asked to take one with just him and *his buddy, Jeremy*.

You would have thought by the time the father and son headed back to their table they'd been doing Connor a favor.

I watched him over the candle flickering on our table, trying to add one more piece to the Connor puzzle.

"You're really good at that."

"At the pictures? My agent made me take a class."

Oooookay, but no.

"I actually meant the whole thing. The kid. The dad. Keeping them on track and comfortable and then sending them on their way. You let Jeremy teach you about how to be a catcher as if you were going to try it out in your next game."

"Well, no matter what they tell you, baseball is about the fans. We make a ridiculous amount of money to get to do something we love. A team keeps you if you're talented or if you're talented enough but their fans love you. You don't see a lot of guys get traded if they're hometown favorites."

That didn't sound like your typical jock reasoning.

"Then why were you traded?"

Oh. Wait. That didn't come out right.

"Sorry. I meant…well, after seeing you in action, I'm surprised you were traded."

"Yeah." He shook out his napkin, his gaze sliding away. "I was."

I felt horrible. I'm not sure where I went wrong. He was supposed to be one of the top players in the league, but… "I thought you were really talented."

"I was young and stupid when I joined my last team. I burned a lot of bridges. When I got hurt last season and the doctors reported I could be 100-percent or I could stay at half-power, management wasn't willing to risk it."

"How'd you get hurt?" I didn't want him to tell me he was doing something else reputation-damaging. But, any way you looked at it, hurt was hurt. And hurt was a career killer for him.

"I went to cover second during a play that pulled our guy into a weird spot. When the runner slid into the base, I moved to jump out of the way, but got caught on his cleats. The tangle wasn't bad, but I landed wrong. The momentum with the runner dragged me just enough to do some tearing."

"But you got back to one-hundred percent?"

"Yup. And I learned a lot of lessons. One of the captains, a guy I completely disrespected when I'd first gotten there, pulled me aside before I left. Gave me this lecture. Told me he'd seen me smarten up, but not enough. Hoped I'd learned a lesson getting hurt. No one knows everything. Listen to the coaches and the vets. Go with the flow of whatever team I ended up on. Work harder than anyone else. Stay out of trouble, keep my mouth shut, respect the fans."

"That's a lot of advice." Where were the author advice guys? I could use some of them.

Of course, Becca was so good at clothing advice. I bet she'd be willing to do that too.

"I needed it. He said a lot of guys start out young and stupid, the measure is if they get less stupid as they get less young. Then he looked me in the eye and said, 'Dude, you're thirty. This is a young man's game.'"

I'd been told the same thing about writing Young Adult books, but the longer I was in *my game*, the more I saw it wasn't true. Tamora Pierce had been writing when I was a kid and still kicked butt. It wasn't about being young. It was about understanding what was important to your readers.

And thank goodness for that, or I'd be worried about my career ending soon too.

I watched Connor pay for the meal and wondered what that was like. What would it be like to know your career had a shelf life shorter than what it took most people to become competent in their fields? And how strong was the fear? Was it constant?

Did it mean that you did everything a guy would want to do knowing it was all going to come to a sudden halt one fall, maybe sooner if you got hurt?

Talk about pressure.

He rose and held out my coat for me to slip on.

I managed not to jump this time as he placed his hand on my lower back and steered me toward the front door. The air outside had started to change, to catch the damp crispness of late fall.

It was my favorite time of the year. When I'd typically be out and about trying to squeeze in all those last minute enjoyments before the snow came. It was my reset time. I think it was part of the internal clock of my YA brain. When others considered New Years their time to hit the mental, emotional, and spiritual reset buttons and others looked at spring as a rebirth, for me it was always fall.

I'd been known to go back to school shopping...even though I didn't go back to school.

How was I expected to deny myself the pleasure of new pens and notebooks? And those colored binder clips I'd gotten this year? Please, those were a no-brainer.

"Do you want me to flag down a cab?" Connor asked, glancing down the street toward the busier intersection.

"It might be easier to catch one here than in front of my house."

All heads turned when Connor laughed. It wasn't just that it was Connor Ryan. It was the infectiousness of the sound, like it wasn't being held back and was inviting everyone to come join it.

He leaned in, his arm draped around my shoulders again as his nose brushed one of my curls. "I think you forgot where I'm sleeping tonight."

Oh. Yeah. I had.

"Well, I hope you didn't forget what that couch looks like. I think it's a good three inches shorter than you are. Hope you don't mind waking up with a crick in your neck."

"We'll see."

I don't think the crick was what he was talking about.

EIGHT

I T WAS EARLY when we headed to my place. Too early to toss some sheets his way when we got back and head to my room. I considered using work as an excuse, but I didn't want him wandering around my place— no matter how *cozy* it was—without me. I ran through the options of what we could do once we got back. And, with only four blocks to go, I was running out of time to make a plan.

"Board games or movie?" I mean, what else was I going to do with him?

Yeah. *Right.*

He caught my eye, glancing down at me, and I realized how incredibly stupid almost every woman in America—and probably a good number outside—would consider that thought.

"When you say movie, I hear *The Notebook.*"

"Oh good! I was hoping you'd pick *The Notebook.*" I watched his eyes widen in horror. It was kind of cute.

"So, one of your favorites, huh?" He stared straight ahead, just up and over my head, a very neutral look on his face. The creases around his eyes tightened and I wondered just how far those good manners would carry him.

"Yep," I lied. "I'm really excited to see it now. We should stop and get ice cream to enjoy with it. Or are you a popcorn-movie-combo person?"

"Nope. I'm good with ice cream. But it better be chocolate or we're not sharing."

A man after my own heart. We ran into a store and then headed back to my place, my hand wrapped in his free, larger one.

I was starting to get used to the touching. After watching him at the restaurant I realized it wasn't just part of the act—it was Connor. He reached out to people around him, not only with his words, but physically as well. With women, it was almost "instinctual." There was a female standing next to him so he should touch her.

All the way back to the apartment I babbled about the movie. How romantic it was. How sweet it was. How hot Ryan Gosling was.

Okay, so that last one was right on, but other than that I was kind of *eh* about the whole thing. Connor just nodded along, tuning me out.

I realized, as I worked to carry on my false movie love, that Connor was *fun*. He was more laid-back than I'd expected, dinner had been interesting and low stress once we'd decided to be friends, and he was easy to be around. I wasn't even worried about hanging out watching a movie. It would just be chill.

At the front door, we ran into Mike from 12B. You'd think he'd never seen a pro-athlete before. The stuttering was almost cute.

Especially since at a block party that summer he'd gotten drunk and told me he wouldn't date me because I just didn't hit his level, but if I'd get my act together and get a real job, maybe I'd find a boyfriend.

This would have been odd—not to mention embarrassing enough—but I hadn't asked him out. Or even been interested in asking him out. I'd been sitting on a lawn chair chatting with a group of people when he just blurted it out.

For the next week I kept expecting him to sober up and come apologize.

That didn't happen. Whenever I ran into him, *he* gave *me* the evil eye. When I'd had enough, I went to his roommate to ask if I'd said something to offend him or remembered the situation wrong. Or maybe the guy just didn't like writers.

Answer: Nope.

So, when he saw Connor Ryan holding my hand and his jaw almost dislocated itself, I had a tinge of ha-ha-ha. Okay, more than a tinge.

"Hey, Hailey. Hi."

"Hey, Mike." I was kind of surprised to have to stop since this was the first time he'd talked to me since then. "How's it going?"

I'd like to say I hid my smug smile well, but the dislocated-jaw-staring-at-Connor thing was still going on.

Connor went to drop my hand so he could offer it to 12B Mike to shake, but I held tight.

"Connor, this is 12B Mike. That guy I was telling you about the other night."

It was finally my turn to get something out of this. I'd just become an evil genius and there was no slowing me down. This might be even better than the new wardrobe. Not by much, but it was a close call.

"You remember?" I went on, hoping Connor would pick up the thread. "The one who announced out of the blue at a party that he'd never date me and that maybe I should get myself a real job that would pay me instead of letting the state pay my rent."

Connor had been trying to pull free of my grip, but as soon as the words registered, he stopped and gave my hand a squeeze.

"Oh, yeah." He gave Mike a look like he was trying to figure out what was so great about him and then kind of shook his head. "His loss is my gain, right? Well, nice meeting you, man."

He gave me a little tug and pulled me through the door 12B Mike still held open and hurried us toward the stairs.

As soon as I heard the front door fall shut, I almost hugged him.

"That was the best thing ever. Ever-ever."

"What a—well, words I'm too polite to say in front of you."

"No, go ahead. You can say them." I bounced on my toes, too pumped up from finally getting something fun out of this. "But only in regards to 12B Mike."

"I think you underestimate the crass level of a dugout."

This was probably true. But, it was nice to know that 12B Mike rated Dugout Level Bad Words.

Once we got to my place, I stowed the ice cream and then turned, trying to figure out how we were going to occasionally co-exist in my small space. It wasn't just that it was Connor—which, don't get me wrong, was a huge part of it—but my space wasn't that big. I mean, my office was in a closet.

He'd joked about cozy, but even with my last boyfriend it had felt a bit crowded. And I'd wanted *him* there.

"I'm going to put on something more comfortable. And when I say that, I mean those yoga pants you love so much."

Connor just shook his head at me and grinned as I headed to my room.

I changed as quickly as possible, trying to get back to the living room before he started doing things like going through my DVDs and books or checking out pictures of my friends.

But, when I opened the door Connor was nowhere to be found.

"Connor?"

Behind me, the bathroom door opened and he came out, his little bag in hand, in a pair of long mesh shorts and a Just Do It t-shirt on. I guess I wasn't the only one getting more comfortable.

It was a little sad how *not* trying to impress each other we both were. My gaze skittered across the t-shirt stretched tight across his shoulders and the shorts caught on his hipbones. If this was his "not impressive" no wonder women threw themselves at him.

"I thought I'd change now too." He purposefully walked to my bedroom and dropped the bag on the floor just inside the door.

I watched him come out, a little smirk playing around his lips. No matter how great it was to use him as a weapon for good against 12B Mike, he still wasn't sleeping with me in my bed.

"You know, there's nothing in the world that says you need to sleep in the same room with that bag. It's more than welcome to stay where it is."

"Hailey, seriously." His sigh was B-movie star worthy. "We're adults. There's absolutely nothing wrong with us sharing your bed."

"I'm sorry you're so confused about this, but I don't casually sleep with men. I know that makes one of us, but—"

"Two. That definitely makes two of us."

I rolled my eyes.

"Fine, I don't *casually* share my bed with anyone indiscriminately—even just to sleep. There are some lines I don't want to cross. You wanted to stay here so it helps the story and makes you look like Mr. Good Relationship Guy. That's fine. But you stay on the couch."

I couldn't tell if he was annoyed or trying to come up with another argument to wear me down. I was getting a real glimpse of him. One meal and I was ready to cave. Not being able to read a simple facial expression was a huge red flag.

WARNING: Back the heck up.

"Okay. I get it." He crossed his arms as if he were the one being put out. "I'll sleep on the couch."

Note #1: He agreed.

Note #2: He did not go get his bag.

I stood there waiting, watching him. He settled onto the couch, moving pillows around so he could make himself as at home as possible. He flicked the light next to the couch off and then turned back to look at me.

"Well?"

"Well, what?"

"Are we going to watch that movie or not?"

I swear he did things just to keep me off balance. He was good at that too. And the whole charm thing. And the impressive manners. Not to mention his ability to lead conversations with fans seamlessly.

It's almost a shame he didn't have to fall back on that business degree. It would have been interesting to see how he might have earned his first million.

He was kind of fascinating as a character. Diverse and a surprise at every turn.

I should have been taking notes. It dawned on me a guy like this—maybe not the Connor he was in high school, but the Connor he was now—would make an excellent match for one of my heroines. She was feisty, smart, and independent. She hated to be told what to do and I had a feeling even just being handled would drive her nuts.

She'd see through his *handling* skills right away for what they were. She wouldn't be fooled that she was getting her own way or that—

Wait a second.

"You really are sleeping on the couch."

"I know."

"I'm not kidding."

"Yeah." He looked at me like I might have lost my mind. Of course, I might have. "I got that."

I crossed my arms. He was looking way too comfy in my apartment. He looked way too comfortable everywhere, but when the space he was claiming was mine, I wasn't quite as happy about it.

As a character trait, that smooth charm would fit perfectly against my new heroine, Marley. That was the key to my high school, high drama—No one ever fits *with*. They always fit against. *Against* shared a wall, had a starting point, but didn't match up. It left lots of room for working things out while falling in love.

Marley was a bit of a control freak. She didn't like the idea of anyone else telling her what to do, when to do it, or how it should be done. The idea that a guy could swoop in and make her shift her plans around with a smile and some charm would just about kill her.

And, I could use this as research without breaking our agreement. He'd even said I could ask him about his world. "Connor, if a woman didn't give you your way and you absolutely had to have it, what would you do?"

"Is this still about the bed?" He glared at me from where he reclined, graceful yet alert.

That expression I recognized. It was pure suspicion.

"No." I couldn't help it if he didn't believe me.

"Is it something important?" he asked.

"Let's say, no. It's not something important. Just something you want." *Like the bed.*

"Then, I'd try cajoling a bit. Bring my flirt out. If I got the idea it was important to her, I'd let her win."

Let her win. I made a note of that. *It was important in Tucker's viewpoint. He was letting her win. He wasn't letting it go or any other expression. It was about winning. Tucker likes to win. Even when he lets Marley win, he's winning because he chooses to let her win so he didn't really lose.*

"What are you writing down?"

"Nothing." I made a final note and then asked. "What if it was something important?"

"What is this nothing you're doing?"

Connor started to get up and I waved him down again. I didn't like people looking over my shoulder when I was working.

"So, let's say it's something important and the girl—I mean, the woman—you're dealing with is the one who's stopping you from getting what you want, then what do you do?"

"I guess I'd just ask. Explain to her what I want and expect once she saw my side, she'd understand and give it to me."

Hmmmm...Interesting. *Tucker doesn't comprehend that sometimes getting his way isn't possible. To him, Marley must not understand the situation if she won't let him win.*

This was going to be good. These two were going to chew each other up pretty good before they started falling for each other. Maybe this setup wasn't such a bad deal on my end. Research is your friend. It wasn't like Tucker was Connor. They were really different except in a few personality ways. Connor was just a resource, not an inspiration.

Maybe I needed more guys in my life just to get the details of the inner-workings from them.

"Hailey." Connor was off the couch, stretching his arms over his heads, his t-shirt riding up to show a ridiculously flat stomach that had me thinking of Ryan Gosling again. Thank goodness that boy made more movies than just *The Notebook* or my TV would be living with the mute button on.

I slammed the new binder shut before he could get a look.

"I'm good. Ready for ice cream?" I shelved the binder with the bazillion others. Target had been having a sale on the left over school supplies. Binders were down to twenty-seven cents and I couldn't help myself. Although I was working hard at avoiding the one with the dancing bears on it.

They kind of freaked me out.

Connor stayed where he was, half-stretched out on my sofa eyeing me.

"What were you doing?" His glance strayed toward the robot binder leaving me with no doubt what he was asking.

"Oh. Brain flash. I get them sometimes for a story."

"And that had to do with how I'd get my way...how?"

This was going to be sticky. People didn't always like being the inspiration for a character. Even if the character was the hero. People never saw what you expected them to.

And the truth was I'd never stolen a person—maybe a character trait, but not a whole person. But by the time I wrote the story, the person had disappeared and left a new, true-to-himself character behind.

Instead of trying to explain, I just answered the short, honest answer. "It's always good to have a guy's perspective."

Speaking of which...

"Do you always approach the most attractive woman in the room first?"

"*What?*"

I was a little surprised at his disbelief.

"When you're somewhere and you're picking up a woman, do you always zero in on the most attractive woman first?"

"Why would I hit on a woman I didn't find attractive?"

"That's not what I'm asking. There's a difference between who you're attracted to and who you know is the most attractive person in the room." I knew I was going to have to explain. "You see, I *know* Brad Pitt is attractive. Millions of women—and men—can't be wrong. I've even seen those studies on facial balance and blah, blah, blah. But, personally, I don't find him attractive."

"No?" Less disbelief, more confusion.

I shook my head.

"So, if Brad Pitt walked in here and *he* wanted to sleep in your bed, you'd say no?"

"Beyond the fact that I'm pretty sure Angelina Jolie could kick my butt while wearing six-inch heels and holding an orphan? Yes, I'd say no."

"Really?"

"Yes. Also, he may be Brad Pitt, but, like I said, I don't find him hot." I didn't think this was such a hard thing to grasp. "It's like art."

"This I've gotta hear." Connor stretched back out, crossing his hands behind his head.

"Well, I know Picasso made amazing art. It's technically provable. It's also anecdotally provable. I look at it and appreciate it for what it is. I even understand it's beautifully done. But, me? None of his works really move me. No matter what I know about them. Some people like modern art, some like pre-Raphaelite. Etcetera."

"And this ties back to me hitting on women how?"

"I'm curious if how you hit on women is personal or if it's more about social leveling."

"I thought we were just going to eat ice cream and watch a movie."

If he was begging to watch *The Notebook*, I had to have been hitting a nerve.

"I have this theory—"

"Oh geez."

"It's a pretty good theory." I sat back down at my desk chair and swiveled around to face him. "See, everyone who looks at you—even guys—are going to realize you're good-looking. It's not that guys are attracted to you. Well, you know, straight guys. But any guy can look at you and say, *Yeah. That Connor Ryan, he's a good-looking guy.*"

"You think I'm good-looking?" He was getting all smirky-smirk and missing the point.

"Yes. Just about everyone in the western hemisphere would think you're good-looking. The point is, not everyone would be attracted to you."

"So, wait. You're not attracted to me?" He sat up a bit straighter, obviously trying to figure out how this could possibly true.

I found it amazing that this seemed to bother him.

"Do you need everyone to be attracted to you?"

"No." He shifted, looking more uncomfortable than when he'd suggested we just watch the movie. "Just the women."

I should have seen that coming. What was surprising was that he flourished in an all-male profession.

"But that's not how it works. It never is. Tastes aren't universal. Even as people look at you—er, Brad Pitt—and know he's good-looking, that doesn't mean they find him attractive. We all have types. If we didn't then only absurdly good-looking people would find someone and the rest of us would live sad, lonely lives."

He gave me *a look*.

The look said he doubted that we—the mere mortals of the world—didn't actually live sad, lonely lives.

"I have to bring my A-game every time we go out for this to be acceptable to you. The girls you're used to can bring their I-Didn't-Bother-To-Brush-My-Hair game and still look amazing. And yet, this may surprise you, but I'm not exactly dateless."

"I didn't say you were dateless. I—"

I waved a hand between us. "I get it. I'm not dateless. You just wouldn't personally date me." Connor was too nice about everything *except* who he was going to date.

And, hey, I wouldn't date someone I didn't want to either.

Well, this fauxmance was the exception.

Anyway, moving on.

"But," I continued. "That's the point. I get asked out enough. I get asked out by guys I think are attractive who aren't anywhere near as good-looking as you. So, I think it's the hardwiring."

"It's not that you're ugly—"

"Seriously, Connor. Stop while you're almost-kinda-not-really ahead."

"No. I mean…that wasn't what I meant when you came in that day."

I stood and headed toward the kitchen. "Honestly, I'm not doing this backtracking with you. Let's just leave it at I'm-not-in-your-hard-wiring and let it go."

I didn't need to deal with him trying to convince me of something he couldn't convince himself of.

And the dating thing was true. I was picky about who I dated. Writing was more than a full-time job. When a writer's on deadline, she has zero time. A lot of guys didn't get that. A

BRIA QUINLAN

lot of girlfriends didn't get that. So, I kept my circle of friends to people who did. I went on dates after I'd turned in a book. By the time another deadline rolled around, I either knew if I wanted to keep the guy around or not. And vice versa.

I scooped out ice cream, filling his bowl with twice as much. After watching how he ate, I was pretty sure he wasn't one of those people to count calories. Unless he was counting to make sure he was getting enough of them.

Putting two smaller scoops in my bowl, I grabbed some spoons and headed back to the living room—all of seven feet away.

He was already digging into his ice cream by the time I settled on the other side of the couch and hit *Play*.

The previews rolled and then the menu popped up and he turned toward me.

"*Terminator*?"

"Yeah. I kind of love action movies. My best friend and I live on them a little."

"Nice." He reached across me and turned off the other light as the movie started. "But, you're a cruel tease of a woman, Hailey Tate."

It was 108 minutes of perfection. Ice cream, action flick, and a night to just stay in and veg. It almost made up for dealing with the guy taking up half the pillows and the majority of the couch.

When *Terminator* ended, it was still early, so I slipped *T2* in and watched as Connor grinned to himself.

The familiar scenes flashed by, lulling me into a chance to consider my day and figure out how I was going to get through the next month.

It was bad enough I was going to have to deal with book release stuff, but knowing there'd be the added *bonus* of dealing with the attention the bet would bring wasn't gearing me up for excitement.

I must have dozed off, because suddenly the static menu of *T2* was on the screen with the theme rolling on repeat. My feet were cozy-warm tucked under Connor's thighs as he sprawled at the far end, both arms wrapped around a pillow, his head thrown back against the sofa.

I eased my feet out from under him and padded to the hall closet while trying to figure out if I should wake him up. The angle of his head was going to leave a horrible crick in his neck, but it also meant no more arguing about who slept where.

I guess I was a nicer person than I thought, because I opted to wake him up.

"Connor." I gave him a little shake. "Connor."

One of those overly built arms let go of the pillow and pulled me down, tucking me against his solid frame.

Yeah. No.

I slapped his shoulder. "Connor, wake up."

He did that little snuffle thing people do when they don't want to wake up. But, when he glanced down at me, he looked confused. Like he had no idea where he was or who I was.

Who knows how many times he'd been through that.

The arm crossing my waist loosened, letting me pull away.

"What, Hailey?"

Or he did know.

"We fell asleep. I brought you some sheets and a blanket for the couch."

I dropped them next to him and started toward my room. "You can have one of my pillows tonight. But if this is going to be a regular thing, you're going to need to bring one over."

I grabbed my second pillow, the one *I* usually slept cuddled up against, and brought it back to the living room...where there was a half-naked pro-athlete leaning over my couch tucking a sheet into the cushions.

And, while I knew he wasn't the kind of guy I'd ever date, the sight of his black boxer brief clad rear end was a little swoon inducing.

"What are you doing?"

He straightened and glanced over his shoulder. "Making my *bed*."

Yeah, still not happy about that.

"No. I mean, where are your clothes?"

"I can't sleep in my clothes. What will I work out in tomorrow? I have three hours of swinging a bat in the afternoon. I'm not wearing slept in clothes to do that."

"You can't walk around my apartment naked."

"Sweetheart, this ain't naked." He crossed his arms across an overtly impressive chest. "This is me politely not sleeping naked. Which is how I usually sleep."

"It's how you usually sleep at home or with your girlfriend."

"Who is currently you. But, here I am, sleeping on a couch, in my boxers and not doing any of the other things I could be doing with my *girlfriend*."

I threw the pillow at his head and growled when he caught it.

I would have if he hadn't too—I mean, he's *paid* to catch things. With that, I headed back to my room where there was a perfectly good bed, and fell into it.

And I didn't feel the least bit guilty.

NINE

I WOKE TO banging. Not building-something banging or someone's-at-the-door banging. I woke to cabinet banging.

That's when the morning joy of my guest hit me.

I'd hoped that comfortable truce we'd established the night before would carry over.

I pulled my hair into a ponytail, wrapped my little robe over the pajama shorts set I was wearing, and headed out to the kitchen to see if he'd destroyed it already.

"You don't have any coffee." He had thankfully pulled the shorts back on, but between the naked shoulders and the mussed bed head, he looked like an ad for sex...I mean, something sexy.

Yeah. Whatever.

I glanced away because...yeah.

"Good morning to you too."

"How can you not have coffee? I thought writers lived in weird, dark places and subsisted on coffee and cigarettes."

"And you thought wrong. I subsist on tea and chocolate when I'm not eating like a normal person."

"So, there's really no coffee?" He looked at me like I might be lying. Like there was coffee in some secret compartment he just hadn't found yet.

"Nope."

"How do you live like this?" His voice rose with the accusation as if I was living without heat instead of a specific beverage.

I guess we'd found his Achilles heel.

"Pretty easily actually."

"We're going to have to go out. We need to get coffee. This is an emergency."

I almost thought he was joking, but he brushed past me and grabbed the bag he'd left in my room.

"You need to get ready. Do your girl stuff so we can go." He was already keying into his phone. "What's the closest coffee shop?"

The weird, almost British female voice answered, "The. Closest. Coffee. Shop. Is. The Brew. Ha. Ha."

"Thank you."

"Did you just thank your phone?"

I stood back in awe, watching him spiral into a crazed, under-caffeinated lunacy.

"I need coffee, alright? What part of emergency did you not understand?"

Oooookay. Coffee. Emergency. Got it.

But I had needs too. "I need to shower."

He looked at me like I'd threatened to shoot him.

"And to get dressed in Connor–acceptable clothing."

Now he was glancing toward the door.

"Don't even think about it. You woke me up on my sleep-in day. You're buying me tea and a muffin and maybe even a cookie for later."

"Fine." He pushed all the sheets and pillows down to the end of the sofa and reached for the remote. "But hurry up."

I shook my head, but he didn't notice. He already had his feet up and SportsCenter on. Which was funny because I was pretty sure I hadn't even gotten SportsCenter in my package.

The shower was easy. Even blow-drying my hair was simple since it was pretty much stick-straight. Getting dressed wasn't as straightforward.

Luckily, almost as soon as I closed my door I heard the shower come back on. That gave me at least ten minutes to figure out what to wear.

I grabbed the binder Becca created, pretty sure there wouldn't be a fake-morning-after outfit but was shocked to find a whole set of possibilities under "Casual Encounters."

Once my new clothes were on—and retail-gods willing I'd ripped off all the tags—I threw on light coats of mascara and lip-gloss and headed toward the living room, surprised to hear the shower just turning off.

Connor took another ten minutes to get dressed, brush his teeth, and use my hair dryer. He'd probably end up using it more than me if he planned on staying over a few times a week.

I'd actually just bought a new one. When Becca had come over to arrange my wardrobe in some type of order—not to mention kidnap some of my clothes she deemed *unwearable*—she'd insisted there was so much dust in my rarely used hair dryer that it was a fire hazard.

When Connor came out of the bathroom, he tucked that darn bag back in my room before coming out to join me. I guess it was going to be living there for a while.

He glanced my way and stopped, studying me. I was *not* going to change. This outfit was on the Casual Encounters/Daytime list. He'd have to have it out with Becca if he didn't like my outfits.

"You look nice."

"You sound surprised." I tried not to show how surprised I was at his surprise.

"No. Just...Well, I've seen your morning thrown together look." He shrugged. "There's no yoga pants involved today."

Nope. Today I was wearing a little pair of white Capris and a blue t-shirt that cost more than any three t-shirts I owned before. I'll admit, it fit perfectly and it was super soft, but still. Who paid this much for a t-shirt? I'd even thrown on a little ball cap—not one with his team's logo—that was listed in the accepted binder and paired it with strappy flats and new sunglasses, then topped it off with a flowy scarf.

I'd never felt so put together in my life.

Getting ready was typically exhausting, but this hadn't been so bad. It didn't hurt that Becca had emailed more pictures of how to combine outfits that I was supposed to print out and update my binder with.

I grabbed my bag and a light coat before following him to the door.

"Have you been to this Brew Ha Ha place?"

I'd kind of hoped he'd forgotten about The Brew. It was the coffee shop where my girlfriends and I wrote and hung out.

"Yup. I go there all the time." I turned around to put my coat on, afraid to look him in the eye. "Are you sure you don't want to head over to a Starbucks? There's one just a little further down the street."

"I don't think I'd make it." He glanced around as if he might swoon at any moment and needed a soft place to land. "You'd have to get a bag of coffee and bring it back in the form of an IV."

"But, then you know what you're getting. You know? There's no disappointment."

"I like trying new things."

"I'm kind of craving..." I scrambled for a Starbucksy something as I faced him. "A mocha-mocha-soy-espresso-chai." Um, yeah.

"Is there a reason you don't want to go to The Brew Ha Ha?"

Yes. "No. It's just..."

He stopped, his hands going to his hips as he glanced away. "You don't want to introduce me to your friends if they're there."

Kind of.

"No," is what I said out loud. "I just—I'm not ready to deal with it all yet. It was weird enough when it was just the two of us. Now you want to throw my friends into the mix right away."

"You haven't told them yet about the deal?"

"Oh, I told them alrighty." Because that's what girls do when they're venting, they tell the most horrible parts that really upset them. Only, you can't take those things back later.

There must have been something about the tone of my voice, because that smirk came out again.

"And you may not have told them the most flattering things about me, is that it?"

"Well, you weren't exactly kind when we met."

Which was a good reminder for me as well. This was just another game to him.

It would take a while to figure out which Connor was real. The first one, who dismissed me so easily, or the one he was showing me now who was a little insane about caffeine but seemed like a good guy.

"Hailey, you have to understand. A ball player has only two things going for him: his skill on the field and his reputation. I need to be able to get ads and maybe a hosting gig when my knee or my shoulder or my wrist or my ankle or whatever it is that's going to go goes."

I froze, crossing my arms and watching him explain this.

"Then, they tell me my reputation is shot and we need to repair it. They follow that up with, '*Don't worry. We have the perfect girl. Cute, funny, smart. She's one of the darlings of publishing for your target audience.*'"

"And?"

And, I knew where this was going, but I wanted to see if he'd say it. If he'd really go that far.

"Well, Hailey, you have to admit you were a mess that morning."

"I was *not* a mess. You live in a dream world where it's a woman's job to look good. If she didn't look good, then she'd be a sucky model or whatever wouldn't she?"

"It's not just that. I mean..."

I waited him out this time. He hadn't been able to finish a sentence since he realized he was digging a hole so deep he'd tossed out the shovel and brought in a backhoe halfway through.

"Yes?"

"You told your friends I was a jerk." He sounded genuinely upset about this.

"Here's a clue. If you don't want people to tell other people you're a jerk, don't act like a jerk."

We glared at each other eye to eye because of the stairs. I could feel the heat rising up my neck. I was mad. *So mad.* Yes, I'd told the girls what he was like. And it was true. It was also true that yesterday he'd been nothing but nice.

The disparity of it bothered me. How much of yesterday was an act and how much of before was just him being caught off guard?

"I'm not a jerk." He glanced away, his gaze going out the window to the treetops lining the street. "Listen, I know. I know I came off for you far worse than you came off for me that morning. I *was* rude. It's just…"

He took a deep breath, his eyes narrowing as he still stared past me. Then he laughed. Not a typical Connor laugh, but one that was a little sad and self-deprecating.

"Gavin's told me I've lost track of myself." He turned and looked at me with that full attention gaze he seemed to be able to give to anyone. "Hailey, I'm sorry that I was rude and selfish and self-focused in the elevator and that I demeaned you in front of a woman because she was beautiful and dressed for her job. I was angry and worried and I defaulted to the person I put out for the papers, not the guy I like to be when I'm with my family or the few friends I trust. You are not ugly or beneath me. You're…I like you. I'm glad we're deciding to be friends. It's…good, you know? *Friends* is good. I could use more. Especially an honest one."

I stared at him, afraid to move as everything, *everything* about this whole mess shattered under my feet.

I took a deep breath, and, with that…I let it go.

"Fine." Then, I added because it felt correct, "Thank you."

"Okay." He crossed his arms and uncrossed them. "Thank you back."

We headed out the door, both of us caught in our own worlds as we tried to figure out what this meant. I didn't argue with people. Jenna and Kasey, yes. Dane, always.

Either it was because Connor had hurt my feelings and I'd had a hard time letting it go. Or it was just Connor and the way he made you feel like the center of everything, that had me feeling like I *could* argue with him. Like he was a safe zone.

"Listen." I went down the two steps to join him on the landing. "Let's just…let's go back to the friends thing. Especially at The Brew."

"I'll be nice to your friends."

"I know." I knew he would. I was trying to adjust to this new Connor. The one I'd met was so solid-rooted in our short relationship, that doing this one-eighty was making me dizzy.

We reached the lobby and I headed toward the door.

"Hailey." He caught up with me and snagged my hand. "We'll start now."

I had no idea what he meant. Start what?

Connor stared through the glass of the door to the sidewalk, a suspicious look on his face.

"Start what?"

"As of the second we walked out of your apartment, we were *in public*. If we're going to do this, we need to help each other remember. Conversations like that need to happen behind closed doors and when we're out, we need to look like we're together."

I hated this. *A lot.*

"Fine."

He took my hand, rolling it over in his so he stared down at it as if he were reading my palm. His thumb traced a small circle over it, running over the ridges.

"You have tiny hands."

"That's because I'm not six-feet tall. Those hands would look like big Hamburger Helper gloves on me."

Connor laughed as he threw an arm over my shoulder and pulled me into his side.

"It would be worse if it were your feet. You'd be tripping over those things all the time."

I rolled my eyes and tried not to smile. I knew what he was doing. And, because it was easier, I let it work. Plus, to be fair, I believed him when he said he wanted to be friends. It wasn't his fault I wasn't a model—it was only his fault he was a jerk about me not being a model.

We walked down the street, people barely glancing our way. Connor kept up a light conversation, telling me a story about his brother's date a few weeks before and how the girl had thought he was a millionaire because she'd met him coming out of Connor's building.

Of course, hilarity ensued and Gavin ended up telling her where to go.

I suggested maybe she was a better match for Connor and we could double date. He was a bit appalled when I asked if he had a picture of Gavin on him.

Obviously that wasn't going to happen any time soon.

He'd just finished telling me what he thought of me wanting to meet his brother when The Brew came into sight. The cute little sun umbrellas were open giving an extra dash of color to the cottage-looking building with its quaint shutters and gaslights.

"Wow. If the coffee is anywhere as good as the shop looks, this may be my new go-to spot."

I froze. Just stopped walking right there in the middle of the sidewalk, forcing the woman behind us to curse and dodge around us.

"What?" Connor loosened his grip on my shoulders so he could turn to face me.

"I think we need to create some ground rules."

"You mean, about the coffee shop."

"I mean about a lot of things." I glanced down the street, looking to see if anyone was coming. "But, maybe this is one of those apartment conversations you were discussing this morning."

Connor nodded, drawing me back around under his arm. "In the meantime, I won't get attached."

Perfect. That would be my mantra too.

Ten

THE INSIDE OF The Brew was warm and welcoming—just like always. Today it was the guy standing next to me that gave me a bit of a chill. It was like a cool, calm summer evening before a storm, lulling you into going out in shorts without an umbrella.

I was not going to be lulled.

I was lull'less.

I headed toward the counter, Connor following behind me, his hand slipping to the curve of my back again. We were early for the Sunday morning crowd and only had to wait a minute or two before Abby the Barista deigned to greet us in her usual warm and sunny manner.

Yes. That was sarcasm.

"You're early." She pointed toward our empty corner. "Your friends aren't here yet."

"Right. I saw that."

"Maybe you want to come back later and not lounge around taking up space."

"We'd rather lounge." I smiled, trying to rush past this part and get to the tea and muffin goodness.

Abby fixed me with her patent-ready stare. At eighteen she was more hard-nailed than Catherine was. If Catherine ever quit agenting, Abby might be a good person to step in. She'd probably have publishers crying.

"Abby." John's voice came from the backroom. "We've talked about threatening our regulars, right?"

"It wasn't a threat." Abby glanced my way and it felt like a threat. "It was just a suggestion."

John pushed through the swinging door, his arms filled with to-go cups and gave me a warm smile. "Morning, Hailey."

"Hey, John."

I waited. I'd been through too many of these learning situations with Abby. Oddly, the girl didn't seem to mind being corrected in front of an audience and I knew John liked to do it right away. Like you might with a puppy.

I knew a few customers who would pay good money to watch him rap her on the nose with a rolled up paper.

"Abby, you know Hailey and her friends are here more than any of our other customers. They spend more money here than anyone else. They do it because they buy the time to lounge. I've also seen all of them occasionally slip a twenty in the tip jar to thank you, so not only is it rude to suggest she leave and come back when her friends are here, it's bad business."

I'd watched him do this over and over again. Explain not just the soft reasons, but the business reasons for doing something.

Jenna had told me once Abby was in some type of manager-training program for at-risk teens. She was here during the day too, so high school obviously wasn't working out. She'd recently started carrying one of those big GED books around, so I was hoping that she was making the most of what John offered her.

"Fine." She sighed as if he was pointing out a detrimental truth that she was going to have to accept in order to allow world order to continue. "You're right. They spend money."

"And you secretly like me." I grinned. I couldn't help it. She might be eighteen, but there was something about pushing her a little.

"If I liked you, why would I keep it a secret?" This question seemed to confuse her.

I just kept smiling at her, waiting for her next snappy comeback. Abby upset Jenna the Soft-Hearted and confused Kasey the Kind. But me? I got a kick out of her. I knew that girl could do anything she put her mind to, based on pure stubbornness.

"You." Abby had spotted Connor. I'd hoped for a little star struck'ness. "You're the guy who shows up on all those trashy magazines covers."

Oh. Oh, that was even better.

"Um. Yeah?" Connor looked at me not quite sure what to say.

But it was nice someone else was calling him on his public dating habits.

Abby shook her head and looked at me like I'd gone nuts. "What are you doing with him?"

I almost jumped the counter and hugged her. All the looks, all the worry about what he'd be doing with me, and it took a grumpy, eighteen-year-old to ask the opposite.

"Well, you can tell he's a little lost when it comes to women." I grinned at her because she was making me so happy right now. "I'm mostly humoring him. He asked me out and he's kept me amused, so we'll see where it goes."

She nodded like this was the most logical reason for me to be standing there with one of the country's top bachelors.

"Abby." John came back and hovered. "Have you asked them what they're having yet?"

Back to business.

"What are you having?"

"I'll have a green tea and a chocolate muffin."

"Heated?"

"Of course." As if this all needed to be done. Abby could have had the order finished before I reached the counter.

"And him?" She glanced toward Connor and then back at me as if she wasn't sure he could put a whole sentence together.

After a short silence, I answered for him. "Coffee."

"Plain coffee?" She sounded even more horrified by the idea of plain coffee. "He can get plain coffee anywhere. John just bought a new bean from Venezuela. He should try that."

"Okay." I nodded. Let's just move this along. I wanted my muffin.

"Wait a second." Connor finally spoke up after watching Abby and I bounce words back and forth like two kids playing catch. "How do you know I'll like these new beans from Venezuela?"

"Everyone likes them."

"That's not true." Connor nodded his head in my direction. "She's having tea."

"Well, if she drank coffee she'd like them."

"Maybe I just want plain coffee," he argued.

After watching him order last night, I highly doubted that.

"Do you?" I asked. "Do you want plain coffee?"

Connor looked at me as if I were betraying him.

"No." Answering didn't stop the scowling. "But that doesn't mean I can't pick out my own coffee. I'm not an idiot."

I patted his hand where it rested on my shoulder really enjoying being the calm one for once.

"Okay. Tell Abby what you want." I gave him a sweet smile. He seemed like he needed it with the coffee emergency and all.

Connor frowned in my general direction before swinging his gaze toward the chalkboard over the counter. "What's the Pandora's Blend?"

"Oh." Abby brightened. I could see I was going to lose my ally before the conversation was over. "Good choice."

She went on to explain some complicated roasting and combining methods for the beans I couldn't have cared much less about. What I did care about was that Connor was doing that smile-welcome-attention-bonding thing and slowing down my chocolate muffin arrival.

Not to mention, winning Abby over.

I walked down the counter, eyeing the muffins as I went. I was two seconds away from pressing my nose against the glass and drooling when John popped out of the backroom again.

"Why don't I just get that for you before you swoon?"

"Thank you." I managed to tear my gaze off the pastries to smile at John. "You're a god among men."

He popped the muffin in the microwave and turned back, leaning on the display case.

"Speaking of god among men..." John nodded his head toward Connor. "Looks like he gained another fan. Didn't take him long."

"I know. It's disgusting." Even I noticed the distinct lack of heat in my words. I wanted to believe it was, but every time I saw him with someone, he came off as so genuine, I was beginning to believe what he'd said about the bad day and the challenge his brother had thrown at him.

"I meant more, what are you doing with him?" He waved a hand before I could go on the attack. I was sick of not being good enough. "You're smart, funny, successful, and pretty. Why are you with a guy who has a whole column every week dedicated to being shallow?"

I didn't know if Connor heard any of that. Part of me wished he had. He needed a reality check about how the real world viewed him. The other part didn't want to see his feelings hurt.

I started to politely tell him to mind his own business, but then I looked closer and saw the concern.

"He's settling down."

John just raised an eyebrow.

"What?" I asked.

"Go grab your chair. I'll bring your tea over while she explains every variety of coffee bean known to woman."

I wasn't going to argue. While I needed my Sunday morning muffin, I didn't *need* Connor. Even if it would have been fun to tell him all about The Brew while I ate. I could enjoy the deliciousness while he schmoozed.

I settled into one of the overstuffed sofas near the fireplace. We met there every weekend—me, Jenna, Kasey, and Kasey's boyfriend Max. Jayne came when she wasn't working one of her three jobs. When Jenna's guy Ben was around, he'd join us and we were also blessed with the effervescence of Dane when he wasn't: A. hungover, B. still in bed, or C. still in someone else's bed.

Any way you looked at it, Sundays were my chill-with-friends morning. One of my favorite parts of the week.

Connor finally got an order in and settled down in the chair next to me and propped his feet on the beat up coffee table before taking a sip of his steaming hot coffee.

John followed close behind him with my tea.

"This place is great. I'm surprised it's not packed."

I was glad we'd decided to discuss ground rules. The Brew Ha Ha was mine and he couldn't have it. I'd hand over Catherine before I handed over The Brew.

I also didn't want it to become *A Spot.*

"Connor, this place is where I work and meet my friends. I need you to not be bringing craziness here."

"I don't bring craziness."

"Please. Your life is the definition of craziness."

"Worst case scenario is John gets a little more business and keeps Abby out of trouble. I think it's pretty obvious he needs all the help he can get on that front."

"I'm serious, Connor." I leaned forward in my chair, desperate for him to understand what I was saying. "This place is more than a coffee shop. Do not ruin it for me."

I'd met Jenna for the first time here when she'd already had her first book out and I couldn't believe she'd take the time to have coffee with me. We'd met Kasey here when she'd lost her job and her boyfriend in one swoop. We'd cried together and eaten chocolate cookies fresh from the oven when Jenna's boyfriend, Ben, had gotten on a plane to London. We'd celebrated sales and bestsellers and mourned bad reviews and rejections. When Jayne showed up, this was the first place she asked Kasey to bring her.

This coffee shop was our equivalent of other girls' bars.

It was our Cheers. Our second home.

"If we can keep The Brew under the radar that would be great." I smiled, knowing how hard that might be. And, on a sudden whim, added, "I don't mind sharing."

Connor gazed back at me, no expression whatsoever on his face. That had to be something he'd perfected being chased by cameras all the time. One more reason I didn't need them staying in my life when he was gone.

"Hailey, the entire point of our being together is for people to see us together."

"I know." I did. Trust me. I'd been dealing with that fact for a few days now. "But, when this is over, what if you had to move out of your house? This is my second home. Please, Connor."

His gaze softened, an understanding smile shaping his lips. He leaned forward to speak when a voice interrupted me from behind.

"Hey." Jenna glanced between us, an unreadable expression on her face for once.

"Hey. You're here." Now that she was here, I had no idea what to say. I was glad she knew what was going on, but I was a bit embarrassed to be caught together.

Connor rose from his chair, probably glad not to have me challenging him any more, and stuck his hand out. I should have expected it. He'd shown perfect manners toward everyone else. He always went out of his way to put people at ease.

I guess I hadn't expected that to extend to my friends. The friends seemed to be the equivalent of "off hours" when you didn't have to do your job anymore.

"I'm Connor. You must be Jenna."

I'll admit it. I was surprised and impressed. Sure, he'd seen the pictures of my close friends and family in the apartment. He'd heard the brief overview of the girls at dinner. He knew they knew.

But that was it.

And yet, he'd picked out Jenna.

"Yes. I'm Jenna. The one who will be watching every step you take for the next several weeks and plotting my revenge well in advance if you hurt her." She leaned in, her usual pixie face taking on an almost threatening gleam. "I write fiction. I have a very active imagination. In my brain, nothing can stop me. It doesn't matter if you're bigger, faster, or richer. If you hurt her, they'll be looking for your body for years."

Connor's eyes had gone wider than those big night game lights and I have to admit, I was awed—I mean, shocked. Yeah. Shocked.

The writer in me couldn't wait to see what she was going to come up with next.

The faux girlfriend knew I had to step in.

"Connor, Jenna drinks chamomile in the morning. You can see why."

Proving once again that he was smarter than the public gave him credit for, Connor pulled his hand from the tiny one it was trapped in and headed toward the counter. Abby was whispering at him before he even made it all the way there.

Jenna collapsed in the seat next to me, watching them with an amused look on her face.

"Thank goodness you sent him off. I think that took up all my energy for the next three days. I'm going to have to power nap for seventy-two hours."

She was the sweetest person I'd ever met. She'd been hit hard, walked over, and left behind. But on the other side of that she'd come out with a heart still so sweet it sometimes made me feel guilty just to be around her.

"He's not that bad."

"If you say so." She watched Abby making her drink to make sure she put lemon in it. "He seems nice."

"Yes. He wins everyone over. He's got Abby roasting special beans for him."

"How Jack and the Beanstalk of him. Are you the golden goose?"

"I'm the something alright. I just don't know what yet."

I watched him lean against the counter as he pulled out his wallet and paid for Jenna's drink. Then I watched him stick another five in the tip jar. He definitely was generous...not in an insane attention catching way. Not in one of those MC Hammer-you'll-have-nothing-left-in-five-years way. Just in a little-bit-here little-bit-there way that no one really noticed if they weren't watching. It was sweet really.

"Oh my gosh!" Jenna grabbed my wrist, forcing my attention back to her. "You like him."

"No."

"Yes. You like him. You can't lie to me. I know you too well." Her voice dropped and she leaned in, careful to make sure our private conversation was staying as private as possible. "Remember when I knew you slept with Nate? Well, I know this too. You like him."

"Shhhh...Yes. Alright. I like him. He's likeable. But not how you mean."

Jenna was just grinning at me. Since she was living the fairy tale, she believed everyone should be...that everyone *could* be a happy pair. But I knew it wasn't true. She'd lucked out with Ben beyond belief. Not every good-looking, smart, successful guy turned out to be Prince Charming. Most of them just ended up being exactly what you thought they were.

Egotistical heart-bruisers.

Jenna gave me the hard stare that only a close friend can give and get away with. "Are you sure?"

"Can you see me wanting to be followed by cameras every day? To have my relationship monitored and judged? To know that my books were being second-guessed because of who I was dating? To be the center of attention every time I walked out of my house with my boyfriend?"

I could feel my anxiety level rising just listing things off.

"No. But that doesn't mean you don't like him." She gave me a sad smile. "You can fall for someone and not want to be part of the world their job is in."

I wasn't sure what to say to that. I knew she wasn't just talking about me and Connor, but her and Ben. Ben had made a hard choice and followed the job he'd already taken across the Atlantic in London for a year.

Jenna had decided not to follow him for Reasons.

"Ben's coming back."

Jenna's gaze shifted, falling across the empty space between us and half focusing on the fire burning in the grate behind me.

"I know." Her words came out on a quiver, low and hushed. The confidence I knew she was trying for all but missing. "But, that's not what I'm talking about. This isn't about me. I'm talking about you. Do not fall into something you can't crawl out of here."

Jenna's eyes focused and her gaze cut toward the counter where Connor stood.

"I'll be careful. And, the liking him thing?" I leaned in and lowered my voice. "We decided we might as well try to be friends after we argued everything out."

She froze, her tea forgotten as she gave me her full attention. "You argued with him?"

"Um, yeah. It's not like we didn't have to handle some things before we could move on." Obviously.

"You don't argue with anyone. It took you three years to tell me to mind my own business when I butt in."

"So?" I didn't like where this was going. Jenna was, if nothing else, astute.

"So, in less than a week he has you feeling like you can argue with him."

Jenna gave a little *huh* as I tried to see what she was reading into this.

"Well, yeah." Because it was a desperate attempt to hold onto some control in my own life. "And we decided there was no sense not enjoying ourselves while we're stuck together."

"That friendship wouldn't involve any type of overly-friendly activities, would it?" She waggled her eyebrows at me from behind her black-framed glasses.

"Nope. Just normal friendly activities."

"Fine." She still glared at the back of Connor's head.

"Thank you for your permission."

She wrapped a hand around my wrist and gave it a squeeze. Leave it to Jenna to nurture where she wanted to shout.

"So, ladies." Connor set Jenna's drink down on the coffee table. "Did that give you enough time to talk about me?"

Coming from anyone else it would have made me want to smack him. But Connor delivered the line with just the right amount of self-deprecation and a grin that would make you forgive him just about anything.

It was sad, really, how good he was at making people like him.

"For now." Jenna picked up her cup and took a sip, watching Connor over the rim. "But, I'm watching you. Don't mess with her. I can be scary."

"I believe you." Connor nodded as if Jenna being scary wasn't the most ridiculous thing anyone had ever heard.

Connor spent the next thirty minutes trying to charm Jenna. It was nice to know there was someone out there—besides me, of course—who was immune.

I was wondering when he was going to give up when Kasey and Max wandered in. Kasey eyed Connor and then gave Jenna A Look.

I gave Kasey A Look because I wasn't stupid and had been friends with both of them for a while and could translate just about any Look traded between the three of us.

Kasey, of course, gave me my own Look that clearly said, *Have you lost your mind?*

I glared back a, *No. And you knew he'd be here.*

In return I got a clear, *Don't get too cozy.*

As if I would.

In the meantime, Max had stuck his hand out and introduced himself to Connor.

Connor stood and grasped Max's hand. It was probably a guy thing to put himself on equal footing. "Nice to meet you."

"You too," Max said, but his tone said *We'll see.*

"Max is a cop." Jenna added. "In case I need help with the body." And gave Connor A Look.

Apparently all my friends were very skilled in subtext. Too bad I couldn't have used that to fulfill my foreign language credits.

Max went to grab their standard order as Kasey settled into the loveseat across from us.

"So, where did you guys go to dinner last night?" See? That's a true friend. Steering us toward the normal conversation. Not to mention, letting me off the hook.

I tried not to sigh. All this meant was that Jenna and Kasey were going to double team me later when there were no witnesses. They'd break me and force every secret I'd ever had out into the open.

I considered how much I wanted to hide the fact that my first crush had been on Weird Al in sixth grade.

I was just starting to relax when Connor shifted, crossing one of his ankles over the other knee and slipping a hand around my shoulder.

There was glaring. Much glaring. From all three of them. And Max was all the way over at the counter.

I couldn't say if Connor didn't notice or was ignoring them. He went on to discuss the way I'd tricked him with *The Notebook* and how relieved he was when I'd popped in the *Terminator* instead.

I was just starting to re-relax—*everyone* was just starting to re-relax—when a ticked off voice came from behind me.

"What the hell is going on here?"

Uh-oh.

Connor stood, a new tension I hadn't seen before rushing through him.

"I asked a question. What is he doing here?"

"Dane." I stood next to Connor and slipped a hand around his arm, wondering where this was going. "This is Connor."

"I know who he is." Dane's jaw was tight with a rage I wasn't used to seeing. "What I don't know is what he's doing here with you."

"Are you saying he's out of my league? You don't think I can date a hot guy."

"Sweetheart, I'm saying you're too good for a womanizing ass who shows up with a different warm body every week and blew a double play in the World Series."

I couldn't tell which Dane was more ticked at Connor for.

Slowly, like air seeping out of a tire, Connor relaxed next to me, his defenses dropping faster than a book's ranking after a bad Paige & Prejudice review.

"Is this your brother?" Connor started to reach out, to drop his hand down to my lower back like he seemed to do whenever we were standing next to one another. Instead, his hand dropped right to his side, his fingers flexed once. Twice.

"My brother?"

I turned toward Dane and studied what was probably the best-looking guy I'd ever see in my life. He made Jenna's Ben look frumpy, Kasey's Max look weak, and Connor look average.

In what world would that guy be my brother?

"He's just awfully protective." Connor's hand slipped across my waist to my back then, either as a warning or a taunt. Who could know?

"Connor, have you looked at him?" I waved a hand toward Dane. "What gene pool do you think would create him and a girl you weren't sure you wanted to be seen with at first glance?"

"That's it." Dane reached across the back of the sofa and grabbed at Connor's shirt. "Outside. I'm kicking your ass."

Before I could do more than collapse onto a chair as Connor pushed me out of the way, Max stepped between them. "As much as I'd love to allow that, I promised Kasey a movie this afternoon. Watching you two ladies rough each other up would be fun, but I'm going to have to say 'no' to that."

There was something magical about Max. He had this authority in his voice that convinced you to do exactly what he was telling you to do. Maybe it was a cop thing.

And so, while he stood between them, Dane let go of Connor and Connor took half a step back.

Dane stepped over the loveseat and dropped into Connor's seat next to me.

"Dane." Max jerked his head to the overstuffed chair at the end of the coffee table.

"Fine." Dane stood and glared at Connor. "But, I'm watching you."

"Join the club," Connor mumbled as he sat back down.

"I know you're going to say this is an apartment conversation." I patted his leg to get his attention as he stared down Dane and put his arm around me again. "But no one else is here. You're going to have to let me tell Dane if you want any peace in the land."

Connor glanced around before lowering his voice and saying, "Fine. But only because you're uncomfortable. Not because he's uncomfortable."

"Oh, you don't know uncomfortable. I'll—"

"Dane." Max gave a shake of his head and watched him subside.

As I filled Dane in—and everyone else more fully—no one relaxed as much as I expected. By the end, coffees were drunk, pastries were eaten, and the guys still looked like they didn't care for the arrangement one bit.

After an hour, Kasey and Max packed up to go to their movie, Jenna pulled out some work, and Dane headed home to finish recovering from his weekend. Dane's exit included a very long, pointed glare at Connor in which Connor sat there looking back as if he hadn't a care in the world.

"So, we have to go do a lap." Connor stood and began clearing our cups away surprising me with how he wasn't just letting *the help* take care of it.

If he thought I was going to train with Superman, he was dead wrong. "What?"

"You know, go run some errands while holding hands and getting fresh vegetables from the farmers market."

Oddly, that almost sounded like the perfect Sunday.

"Did we magically get a dog in the last hour and I don't know it?" I asked, rounding out the picture.

Connor broke out that grin that I was beginning to realize was his real one. Not the humoring-grin or the aren't-I-something-grin.

"Not yet, but I always wanted a dog. Between the traveling and the crazy hours I thought it wouldn't be fair to him, though. But, if you're volunteering to let him live with you and feed him and walk him and all that stuff, we could go to the pet store right now."

That's all I needed. To go from faux girlfriend to dog walker when this was over. The tabloids would have a field day with that. I could see the headlines already: *Con'd Into Doggy Day Care* or *Fever Pitch Custody Battle*.

"Um, no."

Connor handed me my jacket, then turned to Jenna. "It was nice to meet you. I know you'll be watching. Feel free to send your comments through Hailey."

Jenna shook her head at him, probably lost in that same feeling of what to make out of the bad boy who was just so darn likable. That's what made him dangerous. Jenna was lucky. She didn't have to deal with it non-stop. She only had to keep her shields up for small bursts of time. I, on the other hand, was going to have to buy special sunglasses to deflect the looks he tossed around.

You know, just to be safe.

"Connor, just because you're charming doesn't mean I trust you as far as I could carry a Suburban." She gave him the sweetest smile in her repertoire. "Have a fun afternoon, kids."

With that, she went back to her laptop and started flicking through the notes she'd been opening when we'd cleaned the table off.

I knew what that was. That was her trying not to be rude or argue but also not backing down. Jenna's heart was too soft for tough words. Knowing her, she was on the verge of apologizing to Connor and trying hard not to.

In Jennaland, what she had said was terribly mean.

I didn't know how she went through life without every person she passed taking advantage of her.

To be fair, the last few months had been a whirlwind of strength for her—ditching a horrible friend, taking a chance on a guy she considered out of her league, trusting him with her heart even as he took off to London.

Maybe I should take a lesson from her and all her newfound strength.

Connor was reaching past me to open the door when I turned back.

"Give me a second. I'll be right back."

I rushed over to Jenna and leaned down to wrap my arms around her.

"Thank you. Thank you for being such a good friend and for being you."

I could see her eyes get that pre-tearing-up glazy look.

"Let's do something later," I rushed on before she could say something. "Just the two of us. Let's go over to Betty's Pages and mock all the bad literature covers with their depressing endings telegraphed on the back cover copy and then go out and eat carbs."

She grinned, the tearing up complete. "That sounds good."

"I'll call you. You know, after I go be the oddest trophy girlfriend known to man."

She laughed like I knew she would and waved me off toward Connor standing at the door.

I dodged under his arm and out into the sunshine.

Free at last.

Eleven

EVERYTHING OKAY?" He dropped that arm around me and steered me toward the farmers market a few blocks away. When I just nodded, he stopped and looked me over.

"Oh. Yeah. Jenna's just having a hard couple months. I thought it might be good to get some girl time. Good for both of us."

We walked on, just enjoying the sunshine till he stopped in front of Starbucks.

"What are you doing?"

"I need more caffeine." He pulled the door open. "Do you want anything?"

"No. We just came from a place that has really good caffeine."

"Right, but today's goal is to have our picture taken out being couple'y. I know you didn't want The Brew to become a hangout, so I thought we should carry other cups."

I stopped halfway into the store. It was amazing how he could come up with things so...thoughtful.

"Thanks."

He shrugged as if it was no big deal. As if anyone would have thought of it. *I* hadn't thought of it and I was the one trying to protect my private life while dealing with living in his spotlight. Of course, I wasn't used to having to think things through like that. I was used to no one looking at me. The most I had to do was look reasonably cool when I went to a book signing or talk.

Which, yeah. Me, cool? But, people expected writers to look like writers, not actresses, so it was typically all good.

Connor went in and stood in line, me at his side. Almost right away people went from glancing our direction to out-and-out staring. It didn't take a genius to realize the old-fashioned shutter click was the sound of a cell camera snagging our image. How quickly it was texted or emailed or tweeted to the world was anyone's guess.

Part of me was annoyed. I mean, that was the entire point of the morning and yet in the irrational back part of my head I was thinking, *what's wrong with these people? Would they like their Sunday morning to be documented by the masses? Can't we just grab coffee and be left alone?*

Connor brushed my hair over my shoulder and ran his hand down my back and up again. Down and up. Every time I started to stress, Connor reached out. I'd never been around such a toucher before. It was like he needed ways to ground himself to the person he was with.

I leaned into him a bit, wishing instead of being lit up by his fame I could hide in his shadow.

He ordered himself another coffee and a tea for me. I listened as he made small talk with the girl behind the counter who kept giggling. She couldn't get through a sentence without the nervous sound squeaking out. Of course, he couldn't get through a sentence without her doing it either.

But, she was young and nice and star-struck. I tried not to blame her, but all I saw was the entire afternoon stretched out in front of me with a constant stream of giggling.

Somehow, he kindly separated us from her small talk and moved us toward the door. We were stopped twice by fans. Both times he was gracious.

Outwardly I smiled and stood by silently attempting to look trophy-like.

But Connor was patient with everyone, even when I could see the edges starting to fray. He stood with a little girl wearing a pink Nighthawks' shirt for a couple pictures. He introduced everyone to me as they introduced their friends.

He treated every single person like we were at a dinner party and he was excited to get to hangout with them. It was impressive. It was gracious.

It was exhausting.

When we finally cleared the doorway and hit the street, Connor took my hand in his and gave it a squeeze.

"You'll get used to it."

"I don't think so." I really didn't. And, I didn't see why anyone would want to. I was feeling a little shell-shocked and wondering if I could head home…and crawl under my bed.

"It's not so bad." He whispered, his nose just brushing by my ear. "The fans are the reason I have a job."

I stopped. Just stopped walking. It took him two steps to realize I wasn't with him, giving me a jolt when his hand gave mine a little yank.

"What?" He took a sip of his coffee and glanced around.

"It's just that..." I was more than a little surprised I was about to say this.

"It's just that what?" he asked.

"That's my job too."

He looked like I was speaking a different language and I realized how disjointed my entire thought process had become.

"Fans. That's my job too. I have to have fans or I don't have a job."

"Oh." Out came that grin. He was using it a lot today. "Well then, see? We *do* have something in common."

It was true, but it was unexpected. Of all the things I'd thought to find in common with Connor Ryan it hadn't been this.

Okay, so I hadn't really expected to find anything in common with him. But, if you'd told me there was something—*anything*— I'd have guessed something really stupid. Something obvious. Like, we both have agents. Or we both breathe air.

Not something as important as valuing people who made our jobs—our lives—possible.

He gave my hand a little tug as he grinned at me again.

I just fell in step with him and tried not to ponder the fact that he had a value system in at least one area that I didn't think was shallow and worthless.

It was a start.

Of course, in the power balance of value-systems, womanizing still outweighed his kindness to fans way more than a few photos could ever make up for.

TWELVE

THE FARMERS MARKET was more of the same. At first we walked around fairly inconspicuously. Then, one person noticed him and the whispering started.

The guys were easy. Unless they had a kid with them. Most of the guys just nodded and said, *Hey, man*, as if they knew him.

The girls were a different situation all together. It began to feel like every girl within a twenty-block radius had honed in on the fact that *OMGConnorRyan* was there and wanted to get a picture or autograph…or a date.

Six girls in fifteen minutes offered their number. One girl offered up more than that.

Each time Connor just smiled and said, "Sorry, darlin'. I'm off the market."

Half of them glowered at me. The other half just looked confused.

One poor girl asked if he'd started dating someone.

Connor looked at her like she must be a little slow.

"Yes. Hailey." He'd taken his hand from mine to sign her hat. Now he took my hand back and gave it a little squeeze, pulling me forward into their tiny circle that had felt so exclusive a moment ago.

The girl just looked at me, a long, confused stare.

"This is your...*girlfriend*?"

Her voice carried so much sarcastic doubt that it was as if she knew for a fact I couldn't be. That somehow she'd gotten word from someone in the know that this was all fake.

"Yes."

I stared, shocked by the vehemence in Connor's voice. He seemed really annoyed to be questioned. I guess I'd get that way too if my life was laid out for people to ask about and judge all the time.

She just kept looking at me, studying me like I was supposed to tell her something. Then it dawned on me she was running through some type of fan guide to celebrity. She was trying to figure out who I was. How I could possibly have snagged the elusive bachelor.

"Oh. Are you...?" She stared at me, looking for the answer in my face. "You're one of the Day-Martins? The tire family, right?"

I almost said yes. She sounded so desperate for me to fit somewhere. But the last thing I needed was to be outed for masquerading as one of the heiress daughters of the Tire King.

"Nope." I tried to think of something to add to that, but nothing else seemed to help.

"So, who are you? I mean, you're famous or *someone*, right?" She seemed so adamant that I had to be someone I

136

almost felt bad for her. "I mean, you couldn't be a model or actress, so you're someone's daughter or something, right?"

"Yes. She is." Connor's voice had dropped an octave to a place that showed, for the first time he was controlling his annoyance. "She's someone who is smart and kind and funny."

I squeezed his hand. I had no idea where this was going, but I knew it had to be something he really did not want to hear.

"But—"

I gave Connor's whole arm a tug, trying to get him those first few steps to get moving. "It was nice to meet you." I grinned at the girl, giving her my best, wasn't-this-great smile as I tried to ignore the fact that she was standing there all but outright insulting me to my face.

But Connor was deciding to show me yet another facet of his personality: Stubborn.

"But what?" He shifted toward the girl so he could look down at her and flashed her one of the most devastating smiles I'd ever seen. That would include on the big screen.

I wanted to shout, *Don't do it! Do not believe that smile!*

"Well, you only date famous women, so she's not...you know, your type."

I could feel the last bit of ease slip out of Connor's body only to be replaced with alert tension.

"She's not my type?" he asked very, very carefully.

"Not really."

"And yet, I asked her out. We've gone on dates. Last night I stayed at her place so we could spend today together. We were just talking about getting a dog."

I started laughing. It was amazing how he could get away with that absolute pile of absurdity when none of it was true because none of it was a lie.

"What?" Now *he* was giving me A Look. "Were we not just talking about a dog?"

"Oh, we were definitely talking about a dog." I shook my head at him because what else was I going to do at this point. "We were also talking about your crazy schedule and how I'm not going to go around picking up dog poo all the time because you're on the road."

Bit by bit, he started to relax. It was as if the moment had let him step away and realize how stupid it all was.

"I'd hire a dog walker," he stated as if that were going to solve all the problems of the world.

"And where's this dog sleeping when you're away?"

"At your place."

"Where in my place do you think a dog is going to fit?"

"There's a perfectly good corner in the bedroom behind that cushy chair thing."

"There's a lamp behind that chair."

"So, we move the lamp."

"To where, the fire escape?"

Connor was laughing, the tension gone, the girl all but forgotten. "Fine. I'll get a dog sitter for when I'm out of town."

"You're going to have a dog nanny. He's going to be so confused about who his daddy is. He's going to be one of those kids who calls the nanny *Mom* by accident. He'll chew up all your shoes because he's feeling angry and neglected and there's no way around that."

"Of course there is." He grinned, the last bit of tension seeping out. "Shoe trees."

"Shoe trees? That's your solution to doggy abandonment?"

"It's better than shipping him off to boarding school."

"Is it? Is it better?" I demanded, poking a finger into his very solid chest. "At boarding school, he could play with other dogs."

"He'll play with other dogs when the dog nanny takes him to the park."

"But all he'll want is for *you* to take him to the park, but you'll be too—"

"Wow." The girl, the one who'd started this absurd argument, was still standing there watching us argue over an imaginary dog we'd never get because we weren't really dating. "You guys really *are* dating."

She turned on her heel, shaking her head at what she must believe was the ruination of one of the hottest men in sports.

"Nice meeting you," I called after her as she headed toward the coffee shop. Then I pulled Connor toward the street, his hand still tight in mine as we got to the sidewalk.

"Sorry." He sounded embarrassed.

"For what?"

He shook his head and just kept walking, eyes straight ahead.

"What are you sorry for?" I asked again.

"I didn't expect anyone to talk to you like that. Even once she started, I thought I had to be misunderstanding her. And then, when I should have let it go I was just too ticked off."

"I don't mind." I did, but I didn't. I'd been expecting it.

"How can you not mind her insulting both of us like that?"

Maybe because she was just insulting me?

"Um, because?"

"She's standing there telling you you're not good enough to go out with me and that I'm so shallow I'd never date someone who wasn't..."

Hello corner. How's all that wet paint surrounding you?

I cocked an eyebrow and waited to see how he was going to extricate himself from this.

"Wasn't?" I let it sit out there, waiting to see how he'd finish it.

"Wasn't my typical date," he finished, pink rushing up his neck.

Nice save. Well, as nice as it was going to get.

"Alright then." I said, trying to let him off the hook. Trying to let both of us off the hook and just get back to our nice, laid-back weekend. "Let's just go do your walking-around-people-seeing-us thing."

I expected him to be all gung ho about it. It had been his idea to head somewhere really public. But now he seemed like he didn't want to go anywhere.

"Oh. I get it." I slipped out from under his arm and stepped away. "Let's just head back."

The look of relief was more insulting than anything that girl could have said.

"Sure," he agreed quickly, glancing around. "We can do that."

Obviously, he was done being seen in public with me for the day.

I couldn't believe how much that hurt. What had happened to, *let's be friends* and *let's just chill?*

"Yeah. Don't do me any favors." I passed by the Starbucks and wondered if tactless girl was looking out the window to see Connor following a few steps behind me.

"Hailey, wait up."

Storming off hadn't been my best idea. For one, it didn't fit in the plan. We already looked like we were fighting. For another point, Connor was an athlete, even if I'd started running down the street—which in these new shoes was so not an option—he'd have caught me before I'd gone four feet.

His hand wrapped around my upper arm, slowing me down but not spinning to face him.

"What are you so ticked off about?" He asked. It was a fair question.

Okay, no it wasn't. Anyone in his right mind would see that having people insult you would begin to wear.

"I know I'm not your type. Every person on the planet knows it. I know other people are going to point it out over and over again. I know I'm going to be humiliated in the magazines and online as girls just like her—ones who don't have the nerve in person—all go on the warpath. But I do not need it from you. I haven't exactly thrown myself at you so I think you can relax and realize that this 'not-my-type' thing goes both ways."

He looked kind of thunderstruck. Like he was really hearing me this time. I'm not sure anyone had ever told him that...besides me. Maybe it would sink in this time.

"I'm a writer. I work with words. I create guys who girls fall in love with. And, here's the thing. It takes smarts. I'm not an idiot. So, if we were in my world—if I took you to a writers' conference for instance—and everyone would *ooooh* and *awwww* over you and your chiseled looks and your flat abs, but at the end of the day, everyone would also know it wasn't going to last. The phrase *dumb jock* would be bandied around more than a boilerplate contract someone got her hands on that no one was supposed to see."

Connor looked like I'd just smacked him across the face. And, yes, what I was saying wasn't nice. But I'd had enough of being on the receiving end.

"Don't *look* at me like that." I was *not* going to feel bad about this. "*I'm* not saying you're a dumb jock. I know you're smart. I'm just saying that's how people would perceive you from your actions and media coverage. Your world judges based on looks. Mine judges based on books...or intelligence. *Perceived* intelligence."

I pulled my arm away as his grip loosened and started back toward my house. Connor soldiered on next to me, sipping at his coffee and keeping his mouth shut.

Which proved he wasn't a dumb jock, because his life was in serious jeopardy if one more wrong thing came out of his mouth.

At my building's front door, I expected him to just go on his way, but he trudged in behind me and followed me up the stairs. I was really hoping he wasn't planning on coming in. I wasn't in the mood for one of his Apartment Conversations. I'd already started calling them ACs in my head just because thinking about all the things I couldn't say in public now needed to be abbreviated.

I took out my key and tried to gauge what he was thinking.

When nothing came, I slid the key home and opened the door. Stepping in, I was relieved and annoyed to see him waiting in the hall. After all the liberties he'd taken with my home in the last twenty-four hours, this seemed a little silly.

"So. I'll give you a call," he said, not even looking at me this time. Just as done with me as I was with him. "We'll figure out what our next move is later."

"Okay." I walked back to the door when I realized he wouldn't even come in for an AC.

"I have to meet with Dex and my trainer. So, I'm not sure what my schedule is. I'll make sure to have my calendar in front of me so we can line up some dates…I mean, *outings.*"

"Okay."

"Great."

"Yup."

"See ya."

"Bye."

Brilliant.

THIRTEEN

W HAT WERE YOU thinking? This is an emergency." I looked at the bag wondering what could possibly have caused such a lack of planning. "What kind of friend shows up without chocolate to an emergency meeting?"

Jenna rolled her eyes. "Dude, this is just the alcohol. Kasey's bringing the chocolate."

"Oh."

"Yeah. *Oh*," Jenna echoed. "What has gotten into you?"

What hadn't? I'd been feeling guilty all day. I don't know why. I'd just fought fire with fire. It wasn't my fault he couldn't take what he dished out.

I'd left the door cracked so Kasey and Jayne could let themselves in and join us in the kitchen as I put together the drink mix Jenna brought.

I got out my blender and considered just pouring the whole bottle of booze in. Adding *drunk* on top of *confused* was probably not going to get me to a better place any quicker.

"We're here!" Kasey carried a Matteo's chocolate cake in, letting Jayne close the door behind them. She set it on the counter and tossed her jacket on the couch behind her. "I figured if we're going to pack on the calories, they might as well be the best darn calories I could find."

"Bless you." I handed her a knife and grabbed plates and silverware while Jenna took over the Margarita creation.

That was probably for the best.

We chit chatted while I cut very healthy slices of cake for each of us. Jayne wandered into the living room, turning on quiet background music and lighting candles. She slid the comfy chair so it faced the couch instead of the TV and cleared the coffee table for our drinks and dessert, shifting pillows and throw blankets around.

She was very visual. She could turn an empty room into a welcoming home in less than an hour. I was surprised HGTV hadn't somehow found her and given her a show.

She was also very careful about girl time. Always making sure she wasn't overstepping into our circle. Always seeming to remind herself that she was Kasey's tagalong friend, not ours.

We were going to have to fix that.

After we fixed the mess I'd landed in.

"So, spill..." Jenna directed from her perch on the counter. "The details, not the drink."

Now that they were here, I was oddly reluctant to share my messed up morning.

"Connor and I had a fight."

"A fight?" Jenna kept her voice carefully neutral as she took a sip of her drink.

"Kind of." I think. That was a fight, right? He didn't fight back, so maybe not. Maybe it was just a…something where I did all the talking in a negative fashion.

"Did you have a fight or not?" Kasey wasn't as careful. She was a facts girl. Unlike me and Jenna, Kasey wasn't a writer. She owned her own marketing company and sometimes she could be very cut and dry.

"I'm not sure." That was the worst part. "We went to the farmers market and this girl started making a big deal that we were together. She all but called me ugly right to my face. Totally couldn't believe Connor and I were together."

"Hailey," Jenna smiled at me softly to lighten the blow. "You and Connor *aren't* together."

"I know that. But she didn't!" I could still feel the frustration from the whole situation. The embarrassment from standing there being discussed as if I didn't exist. "She just kept going and going. Connor even gave her a chance to back out of what she was saying, but she wouldn't. He got ticked and we left."

"So, Connor came to your defense and you had a fight," Kasey stated as if I wasn't being completely emotional.

"Yes. No. Not exactly like that."

"Exactly like what?" Kasey pushed.

Why did I invite Facts Girl?

"Kasey," Jayne gave her a chill-the-heck-out warning look. I knew I liked her.

"Well, I was really mad," I explained.

"And?" Jayne prompted before Kasey could jump on that.

"And I may have said some things that—while absolutely true—might not have been so nice."

"Such as?" Now Jenna was in on the questions.

"Well, I said in my world people would assume he was a dumb jock."

Jayne just stared at me while Kasey shook her head a little and Jenna gave me another of those soft smiles that says what-were-you-thinking and it's-going-to-be-okay all at once.

"Anything else?"

"I said, something that sounded vaguely clever, like in his world people judge you by your looks in mine they judge you by your books. And then followed that up with a statement about having to be intelligent to write a book."

Kasey actually groaned this time.

"Hey!" This was not the support I needed. "At least I didn't go for the cliché judge-a-book-by-its-cover thing."

"Really?" Kasey set her drink down, probably afraid she'd spill it with all the arm waving she was doing. "Hailey you just insulted someone who was sticking up for you and you're worried about self-editing clichés?"

"I think what Kasey is trying to say is we should focus on what happened and how to fix it, right?" Jenna took a sip of her Margarita and glared at Kasey over the rim of her glass.

"To be fair," I added in my defense, "he agreed with her."

Kasey slammed her hand down on the table. "He *agreed* with her? I'm going to kick him so hard he'll still be limping when he starts Social Security."

Jayne patted Kasey's knee in her offhanded way. You could see that these two balanced each other out. It was surprising to find out they'd been estranged for a few years. "What exactly did he say?"

"Well, he said there was no way he could be seen with me and no one would buy that he'd be dating me."

"He said that in front of the girl?" Jenna asked, a bit surprised.

"Well, no."

"After she left?"

"Um, no."

"Hailey, when *exactly* did he say that?"

"When we met that first day."

They all just stared at me.

"*What?*" This was my emergency meeting. They had better be considering how to make me feel better. "He did. It's only been six days. I seriously doubt he suddenly thinks I'm good enough for him."

I sat there, drinking my drink and waiting for one of them to comment.

And waited.

And waited.

"Well?" I prompted. What kind of support meeting was this?

"Well," Jenna started. "He was a complete jerk the day you met."

"Yes. Exactly."

"But, and correct me if I'm wrong." Kasey set her drink down and leaned in, forcing me to meet her gaze. "He's apologized and been nothing but nice since then."

I really didn't want to have to agree with her.

"He's a bit pushy. The whole sleeping here thing is a little much."

"But, he's been nice. Polite. Suggested you guys be friends. Told off the girl who said you weren't famous or pretty enough for him."

"Even though he agreed with her." That was the point. Why was she not seeing the point?

"Okay, let's say he agrees with her," Kasey allowed, and I got suspicious this was going somewhere I wasn't going to like.

"Because he does." I gave her the squinty eyes.

"Fine. Say he does—"

"He *does*."

"Hailey, for the love of stars, let her finish." Jenna got up and headed toward the kitchen. "I would have brought the pitcher with us if I'd known how irrational this conversation was going to be."

I couldn't believe it. I watched her go and then turned toward Kasey who was using those too-knowing eyes on me now.

He'd won them over. One morning coffee and they were convinced he was a great guy. That all the tabloids and the wild behavior and the womanizing and the cheating was all...just...POOF! Nothing.

"You know what, if a guy said you weren't good enough to date him—that he wouldn't be seen with you—I'd stand by you no matter what. I don't care how nice he was after that."

I sat back, slouched in the comfy chair arms crossed.

"Hailey..."

"Don't *Hailey* me. You know I'm right."

"It's just, he sounds like he's trying to make up for it. Maybe he didn't mean it."

"Oh, trust me. He meant it. He meant it so much, he walked out of the meeting and left me standing there looking ugly *and* stupid."

"Hailey..." Jenna slid down the couch to get closer to me. "I know you're embarrassed and you're annoyed you like him, but, being mean back to him isn't going to make things better."

"Also," Kasey added, "that stopped working when we were twelve."

I gave her another squinty-eyed look, then turned back to Jenna.

"But, it's going to be on the news." I could feel the slight buzz making my head feel light, like it wanted to slip back and let the soft cushions hold me up. I downed the rest of my drink, just plain tired of having to explain myself to the three people who had always just *understood* before.

"Your fight is going to be on the news?"

"No. Everything." Weren't they listening? "Everything is going to be on the news. And they're all going to be making fun of me because I'm short and tubby and plain."

"Okay, first of all, you're like two inches taller than me. Just because you're not an Amazon does not make you short. And when a size six is fat, we have a problem."

"It's fat next to a zero."

Jayne snorted, and choked on her drink. "A stick figure is fat next to a zero."

"But, it's just going to happen over and over again. And every time he's going to have to defend me because he's pretending to be my boyfriend and I'm going to know he feels stupid and embarrassed because he agrees with them."

I sniffed and reached for the box of tissues Kasey produced.

"And every time he's going to get *more* annoyed and embarrassed." I sniffed into the tissue, blowing my nose and wondering if I could drink another Margarita and just forget this entire weekend ever happened.

"Hailey, if he's that shallow, he's a jerky-jerk. Look. It's not like this is new to us or something." Jenna took my drink away and forced me to face her.

"It isn't?"

"Nope. We all love Dane, right?"

"I guess. Well, most of the time." There was the occasional idiotic guy move, but other than that, yeah.

"I thought you guys were a couple when I met you," Kasey jumped in.

"You did?" That seemed—weird.

"Yup. You're super tight and he's really protective. I thought he was going to break Connor's nose today."

"And," Jenna added, "he's even better looking than Connor."

I nodded, although Dane was more of a model good-looking whereas Connor was just classic guy good-looking. Connor was real life good-looking ironically enough.

"And even more of a bed-hopper," Kasey threw out there as if we all needed reminding.

That was true also. Although, who knows how many girls Connor was picking up on the road and sneaking into over-priced hotel rooms.

Jenna kept going, "And, he says stupid stuff about women all the time."

I couldn't argue with that. Just last week Dane said if the world was coming to an end, he'd decided that only the redheads should be allowed into bomb shelters since they were already an endangered species.

I tried to explain the difference between *endangered* and *fewer*. I still have no idea if he didn't understand or he was just being Dane.

"What's your point?" I had a feeling I wasn't going to like where this was going.

"My point is, you can like the guy as a friend and still think he's a complete moron."

"I know. I know that." My head was spinning a bit. I'd downed those two drinks way too fast. Especially since I was typically a one-drink girl. Buzzed and dizzy was fine, but I was going to have to avoid drunk at all costs if I was going to win this argument. "It's just..."

"It's not like you don't get hit on." Jayne jumped in. "We can't go out without you getting hit on. You've dumped your last four boyfriends because you got bored with them. The last one left because he saw it coming. Just because this one guy has an obsessively wrong version in his head of what an attractive woman looks like, that's not your fault."

"Yeah," Jenna put in and went back to her own drink.

"Do you or do you not write books for girls trying to break the stereotype of those airbrushed magazine covers telling girls they're beautiful? That healthy is beautiful. That smart is beautiful. Am I correct?"

"Right. I know this isn't all about how I look." Kind of.

"Because, you look good."

I grinned at Kasey. Since we'd met her, she'd been Jenna's and my biggest cheerleader.

"I don't look bad."

"Whatever. You know you look good. You're at the gym making me feel guilty every day. Your hair is gorgeous with all those spangly highlights in chestnut. You're cute because you dress cute. You're actually really pretty, but that's not your thing—working to look pretty. You look good."

I let my head fall to the side so I could grin at her.

"So, what's the problem?" Kasey stared me down, leaving me no room to back away from her question. "Are you upset about what the girl said, what the newspapers may say, or what Connor said that first day?"

"Can't the answer be all those things?" I felt like crying. Like if I just had one good cry, everything would be better. I'd be out of this horrible situation and everything could go back to normal.

"Hailey, no one gets this upset—emergency chocolate and Margaritas upset—over *maybes*." It was never a good sign when even Jenna was pushing back. "We'll work on that. That's what friends do."

"But," Kasey jumped in. "If you're stressing about the guy, then let's just talk about it."

"Right." Jenna shrugged when I looked at her. "All we're saying is you should think about why you're upset. If it's the attention and the people and the pictures, forget about them. Your girls love you. You're one of those authors who fans flock to. They all dress up in costumes and want to have their picture taken with you. They don't care that you're not a size negative two. If it's Connor, then you're going to have to deal with it."

Jenna snagged another slice of cake and shrugged again.

I forced myself not to think about Connor. To think only about the next slice of cake, because, yeah. I was going to have to deal with something.

I just wasn't sure what.

FOURTEEN

O NE OF THE BEST things in the world about being a writer is the ability to ignore your alarm clock ninety-percent of the time.

Not that I do. I'm up most mornings at seven and off to the gym. But, after emergency margarita night, seven a.m. might as well have been yesterday. There was nothing in the world that made me feel better than a nice, hard workout. Except maybe hitting a deadline and turning a book in. But, physically, I was a gym addict. I'm not a fitness nut, but I like to move. It gets my creative juices flowing, lets me justify having a job that sometimes means fourteen-hour days on my butt, and allows for the emergency chocolate and margaritas that every girl caves to.

So, it wasn't odd to see those raised eyebrows from the girls behind the counter as I flashed my badge in front of the infrared scanner just before lunch. By this time on a Monday I'd typically be home, showered, and sitting in front of my computer typing away on the next great adventure of the undead and those who love them.

"Is Shawn in?"

"Rough weekend?" Kim pulled out the trainers' calendar and flipped through.

"You have no idea." Because, even I couldn't make this up.

"Oh," she gave me a look that could only be called *conspiratorial.* "I think I can imagine."

I started to laugh it off, but then thought about the look she gave me. "What?"

"Well, if *I* was dating Mr. Baseball, I don't think I'd be getting out of bed...well, *ever.*" She dropped the book open to Shawn's page and highlighted the rest of the hour. "Of course, that's assuming I could keep him in the bed. If not, then, yeah. Maybe I'd be here."

I wasn't ready for this. I knew it was coming and I knew I'd be dealing with it sooner rather than later, but I didn't expect it to start at one place I considered a refuge. Even Jenna and Kasey weren't part of my gym. This was the place you came to put on your headphones and block the world out. The last thing I needed was the world joining me here.

"Oh. Yeah." Lame response Hailey.

"How'd you meet him?"

I was relieved Connor and I had discussed these things. I'd thought we could put it off, but obviously I was wrong. People were far nosier than I anticipated.

"Our agents set us up."

I was getting good at the *truths that are a lie* thing.

"Wow." For the first time in my four years going there, she looked impressed. "I need an agent."

155

It was on the tip of my tongue to say, *You can have mine*, but I figured that was pushing my luck.

"I'm sure there's at least one who comes in here. Or, maybe one of those matchmakers." Wait. What was I saying? "Kim, every time I come in here a guy is hitting on you. You're gorgeous. I doubt you need any help meeting men."

"Yeah. Guys. But no one of the Connor Ryan caliber."

"Maybe you should get a job over at the Athletes Center." Because then I wouldn't have to be having this conversation. "I think a lot of them work out there."

She actually wrote that down on a sticky. As if it were a secret. Or that easy.

I avoided opening my mouth again for fear that this time I'd tell her she could have Connor too.

"Shawn had a cancellation. It's not a whole hour, but if you want to slip in now, I won't charge you. I mean, it's only half an hour." Kim smiled at me like there was something special going on.

With how small advances were, I wasn't going to stop and question my good fortune. But, I was curious if this was that celebrity thing. Would she be telling people, *Oh, Connor Ryan's girlfriend works out here. You can make an appointment with her trainer if he's free?*

My shoulders tightened up just as I should have been stretching them out. I loved my gym and didn't mind if there was a way that helped them. But after working out here for years, I also didn't want to become *Connor Ryan's Girlfriend*.

One of the best things about the gym was the small trainer spaces. Weights. Bands. Pads. A mirror. That was it. I rolled out my mat and started stretching.

"Hey kid." Shawn called everybody kid.

I asked him once if he knew my name and he just slapped me on the back and told me I was funny.

"I hear you need to work off some stress. That new boyfriend driving you crazy already?"

"You saw whatever there was to see wherever it was too?" Did Dex and Catherine take out a billboard I didn't know about?

"No. Kim told me on my way in."

"Great. Fine."

Shawn laughed. He had one of those full-gut laughs you expected to come out of overweight guys with lots of gold chains and slicked back hair. Or Santa Claus.

"Let's get some of that aggression out. Are you warmed up?"

I'd jogged to the gym and stretched, so, with only thirty-minutes to go, I wasn't giving up any of my time.

"Yup."

"Great. Pull on your gloves."

Oh, Shawn. You know just what a girl wants to hear.

I rolled my mat up and stowed it in the corner with my bag. I'd hoped he was going to be up for a little sparring as I really—*really*—needed to beat the snot out of something. I pulled off my yoga pants, comfortable in the little room in a pair of Lycra shorts and a loose tank over my sports bra.

I leaned over, doubling in half for one last stretch as I untied my shoes and pulled them off before tugging on my gloves.

He pulled on a set of sparring pads and started working me through a fast, hard round of pound-the-snot-out-of-A-Certain-Someone.

Every hit took out some of my frustration at the stupid situation I should have just walked away from. At myself for not walking. At the apology I owed Connor and would have to give. And at every single person who wanted a photo or an autograph for the next however many days we managed to pull this off.

And, especially at Kasey and her less than subtle implications that I was upset because I had feelings for Connor.

I ran the back of my arm across my forehead swiping at the sweat before it hit my eyes.

"There you go, killer. You're moving up in the world." Shawn pulled off his gloves and grabbed a stopwatch. "Let's check your pulse."

I counted while he timed and wasn't surprised how jacked my heart rate was.

"I wonder who you were thinking about as you beat the crap out of him."

I spun around. That voice wasn't supposed to be here. This was my happy place. My decompression zone. Connor was the last person I wanted walking in. And yet, there he was, leaning against the doorframe, just out of view of the mirrors. I'd been so focused I'm not sure I would have noticed him anyway.

"Connor." It was sad, and he probably liked it, but I practically panted his name. Of course, I was panting it because of thirty-minutes of hardcore cardio—unlike the majority of women who couldn't breathe when they made an attempt at those two syllables.

He grinned, watching me as I shifted, uncomfortable with his presence. "I had no idea you were such a bad ass." Slowly, his gaze shifted toward Shawn. "Hey, man. I'm Connor."

"I know." Shawn gave him one of those guy head-nod things. "One of the suits I train has season tickets but travels three weeks out of a month. It's a good way to get a tip."

Connor laughed and the two of them started talking baseball and training and injuries and I realized there was no reason for me to continue standing there feeling pretty much naked in the tiny amount of clothing I was wearing.

I rolled out my mat in the corner and swigged a couple swallows of water before grabbing my yoga pants. As I pulled them on, I caught a glimpse in the mirror of Connor staring at my rear end. I could only assume that was for Shawn's benefit. With a deep sigh and an even deeper yearning to be alone, I headed for my mat, collapsing into a few stretches.

"I'll let you cool her down." Shawn offered Connor his hand, and then waved as he deserted me.

The door fell shut behind him and I had no idea what to say.

I avoided Connor's gaze and stretched for my toes. I shouldn't have been surprised when he settled on the floor next to me.

"You're pretty hardcore with those little fists of yours." His tone was light but I wasn't fooled. "I had no idea you were so..."

Angry? Crazy? Prone to imagining the demise of those who tempted me?

"Athletic."

My head came up as he finished. Athletic?

"I'm not athletic." I tried to shake off the compliment, but he was still smiling at me. "I just like to keep in shape."

Anywhere outside the gym and I was off balance, but for some reason, the gym felt like a place I could relax my body awareness.

"Right. That's why you're pure muscle under those curves." His gaze went right down my body, heating it. He probably had a patent on that move too.

I pulled my legs up and sat cross-legged looking at him. I wasn't going to be swayed from dealing with yesterday based on a smarmy look and a sweet smile.

"Why are you here, Connor?"

That sounded rude. I meant it more as a question, but the inability to breathe yet made it sound shorter than I meant.

I didn't mean it that way, but all morning I'd been trying to work up the nerve to call him and apologize and now here he was.

And I was panicked.

"I wanted to talk about yesterday."

He scooted back until his back was against the wall, legs crossed in front of him.

I waited hoping he'd say something that would give me an open for my apology. But, I couldn't figure out where he'd head.

"Catherine's assistant said you'd be here if you weren't at home or The Brew." He glanced around the small training area, a look of appreciation for the space none of my other friends would have had. But, it also felt purposeful. Like he was stalling. "Hailey, I owe you an apology and after I realized that I didn't want to wait."

This was...unexpected.

"That first day we met," he continued, studying the edge of my mat as his finger flicked at the corner. "I was rude. You didn't catch me at my best. I'd gotten more bad news from Dex and his entire message that morning was basically, *Get your ass to this address where I will fix everything for you again.* I shouldn't have told you I wouldn't be caught dead with you or that you were..."

"Beneath you?"

"I don't think that's quite what I said, but I know that's how it came across." He finally looked at me. He looked tired. Almost as tired as I felt. "The truth is none of that was true. I don't think you're ugly or beneath me. I don't even know how I started dating all these women. If you saw a picture of my college girlfriend, she's...well, she's not that tall and she's definitely not ridiculously skinny. She was just really cute in a completely sexy kind of way."

I was having a rough time believing that. But the look on his face, the one a person got when they were remembering something long ago, far away, and very happy convinced me I was wrong.

"She was...well, you guys would have gotten along, that's for sure."

He looked my way, as though trying to gauge me. But, I wasn't sure what my part of this conversation was. He'd kept talking through so many points that I was afraid to interrupt and now I didn't know what I was supposed to say first.

"The thing is," he kept going. "Yesterday, when you called me a dumb jock, that really—" His gaze shifted away as he struggled with the next words.

If I didn't know better, I would have thought he was going to say I'd hurt his feelings.

"Connor, stop. I'm sorry. I feel horrible about the things I said to you. I don't even want to worry about the whole *type* thing." At all. Not from my side or his. I wanted to keep things even and fun and friendly. The best thing we could do was get back on track. "I doubt I'll be what your fans expect, but I can't worry about that either. No matter what, I shouldn't have implied that you're dumb. It wasn't right and it wasn't fair."

"Thanks." He still wouldn't meet my eye.

"No. Really. You've done nothing but show me how smart you are every time you have to handle people. To even insinuate anything else was mean and unfair."

He glanced away again, giving me one of those guy-nods that I hoped meant he accepted my apology.

I pushed myself back to sit next to him against the wall.

"And, I don't sleep with all those girls. Most of the time, we meet somewhere, go to an event and then I drop her off at home. I'm not saying I'm a saint. I sure wasn't during my rookie years. Being young and stupid, plus making a lot of money and being a starter on a pro-team, equals women throwing themselves at you. Then somehow it became part of the package."

"And, since your job is to catch things, you had that down, right?"

He grinned even as he looked embarrassed. "Let's just never talk numbers beyond my batting average."

I don't know why, but I believed him. Oh, he'd probably been a bad boy. Now, he was just a bad boy who'd become more discriminating. Women were still throwing themselves at him. I'd bet he was just pickier which ones he caught and how often.

I sat there, not sure what to say, but glad that was over. On both sides.

"So, what'd you do last night?" I asked trying to move past it.

"I went to my brother's, got drunk, and whined about you. It's like we're really dating." He grinned at me, that slick grin that always made me laugh.

"Great. Since we're so involved you can take me to lunch."

I stood up, stretching my arms above my head, a little bummed I was passing on my forty minutes on the elliptical. His gaze dropped to my stomach as it peeped out from below my tank—and then yanked back up again.

The boy really had too many hormones if he was looking at half-an-inch of skin on me.

"Give me ten minutes to shower and throw my clothes on."

"Ten means forty, right?"

"No. Ten means ten, maybe eleven."

"Alright. But if I'm standing out there for more than twelve minutes, we're going to Sports on Tap for lunch." He leaned against the wall looking smug.

"Deal."

That was the safest bet I'd been involved in all week.

FIFTEEN

I HADN'T SEEN Connor since the day at the gym when we both went on our small apologizing binges.

Part of me was afraid he was still upset with me...and maybe himself.

But the other part was trying to remember that I had a life outside of Connor Ryan.

I managed to get some work done, and go to a movie with Jenna, went over to Jenna's friend Jane's—yes, the other Jane—house so Jenna could play with her baby and I could play with their dog, and went to the gym.

All the stuff that had been normal and fun and made my life feel full before that darn Connor Ryan.

But, today, we were off on another one of our dating adventures. He'd called first thing that morning and asked if I wanted to get lunch. Since I had to be seen with him and needed to eat, I said yes.

Of course it had absolutely not a thing to do with not seeing him for a couple days.

I put on yet *another* set of casual clothes from Becca's binder. Amazingly, I still was tearing tags off things. She'd be horrified if she came over because two-thirds of the clothes were still in their bags.

It wasn't like I was hosting the Oscars and needed to do costume changes here.

I had no idea what we were doing, but Connor had said to put on "wander around shoes"—whatever that meant. I assumed that excluded all the cute heels I almost kept killing myself in on our messed up sidewalks.

He showed up almost on time—which was right on time for us—and gave me the prerequisite once-over before handing me my jacket. At this point they didn't even seem insulting. It just seemed like the thing he did. He was a people watcher and this was part of that.

We got to the sidewalk before I asked him where we were going.

"Oh, just to grab some lunch. I know this little place, it's a couple blocks away. I think you'll like it."

"What's in the bag?" I asked, nodding to a plastic bag he had tucked under his far arm.

He gave me a wink and answered, "Supplies."

Well, I guess that's all I was going to get.

He left it at that, tossed his arm over my shoulder, and soldiered on down the windy, fall-leaf covered sidewalk. We walked on, Connor telling me about Gavin's latest dating misadventure and how he was trying to find Ms. Right. Hilarity ensued. The girl ended up being the sister of someone he'd dated last year and had accidentally dumped in an email when he was trying to dump someone else so he could then be exclusive with the girl he accidentally dumped.

There was much groveling and flower sending, but in the end she wouldn't take him back.

He made the mistake of calling the sister the 2.0 version and got dumped by yet another member of that family halfway through a date.

Sounds like one Ryan boy was a picket fencer.

Failing miserably at it, but definitely a picket fencer.

He had me laughing the few blocks we went before we cut down a small, one-way side street I'd never been down before. Halfway down was a small glass fronted bistro with two wrought iron table and chair sets framing the doorway.

"What's this?" I asked, peeking in the window.

"This is my Brew." Connor gave me a grin and glanced both ways before pulling me in after him.

Inside was a cramped, but sweet little set up with only a few small booths lining each side of the room. We ordered at the counter, a mix of everything Connor felt like eating for his six meals that lunch and headed over to a corner where the sun still lit up the room and heated the air.

A young girl brought over our drinks and smiled at Connor, asking him how he was, but otherwise treating him like he was just some guy.

"Do they know who you are?" I asked, because I felt like I was in Bizarro World, where Bizarro World was normal world. Which was...bizarre.

Connor smiled at me, a huge smile and glanced around looking more relaxed than I'd seen him out in public. "I don't know. Maybe. Maybe not."

That seemed like an odd answer, but since he was perfectly happy with it, I was perfectly happy to let him be happy with it.

"Isn't it great?" He smiled at me and I realized he was sharing something very special for him. "Oh. The supplies." Connor grabbed the bag out from next to where it sat on the bench beside him, pulling out a *Sports Illustrated* then a *National Geographic*. He slipped me the *National Geographic* before flipping the *SI* open.

"This is great, right?" He asked before diving into his magazine.

I looked at the *National Geographic*, surprised he'd realized from the few sitting around my apartment that it was my favorite magazine. It was the newest copy and I hadn't even seen the topics, so...bonus.

We read in silence, sipping our drinks, reading our mags, enjoying the late fall sun, until our food came.

The waitress made small talk with Connor as if he were any regular before slipping away to where her husband shouted at her in French from the kitchen.

It was, by any stretch of my imagination, one of those perfect days.

"Why'd you pick this place? Didn't you want to go walk around and do the picture thing? Check off another day?" I thought about how quickly we were running through our time and hoping that everything had been enough to make a difference.

He shrugged. "I just wanted to chill out with you."

"Really?" I tried not to sound surprised, but...*really?*

"Yeah. Sometimes it's just nice to be quiet and eat some great food and be left alone."

Connor Ryan wanted to be left alone. With me.

And that's when I started to worry if I was going to make it out of this alive.

SIXTEEN

I NEED YOUR help."

No Hello, Hailey. How's your day going? Just cut right to the chase.

"Connor, so lovely to hear from you. How is your day going?"

"Horrible. You need to fix this." Connor breezed right past the sarcasm and circled back around to him needing something.

"Really, because, since it's a Tuesday, my day is going pretty well." I glanced at the flashing cursor on my screen where my day definitely wasn't going well. "Since it's a work day for those of us with real jobs."

"Oh, please. My job is as real as yours and I work with people who aren't imaginary." He paused, probably to let his point sink in as if it would bother me. "Now, you need to help me fix this or I'm never going to recover."

I was beginning to think something might actually be wrong.

"What's wrong?"

"I'm home, one of the first times in weeks I just get to be home and chill out." He was talking fast and if I wasn't mistaken, pacing. "I just want to relax, watch some boxing, have a beer. Right?"

"Okay, and?"

"And…you've ruined it. You and that old, broken in leather chair and comfy little apartment." He actually sounded mad. "I'm sitting on my seven-thousand-dollar couch that the designer woman said fit my décor and can't get comfortable."

"Again, okay, and?"

"And you need to fix it. I'm going to be there in thirty minutes."

"How exactly am I going to fix this?"

"You're my girlfriend. You shop, pick out a chair. I hand over money. Everyone's happy." I could hear a zipper and knew he was pulling on his jacket. Then a door. Then an elevator ding.

"I'm sorry. I'm in London." Or my pajamas. One or the other.

"You're in London?" He sounded suspicious.

"Yes. London. Jetted off last night. Harry just couldn't stand us being apart any longer. I'm sorry you had to find out this way. Please tell Catherine I'm sorry and make sure Dex doesn't go too hard on her."

"Right. How is the prince?"

"Excellent. I find him very attractive. That must be how I'm wired."

"Uh huh." Conner answered before I heard him hailing a cab.

"So, I need to go. It's dinner time here."

"Sure, Hails. No problem. See you when you get back." He hung up without another word and I went to take a shower knowing it would take all of fifteen minutes to get here by cab at this time of day.

I couldn't understand why he didn't believe me. Harry and I would be perfect for one another.

~*~

We passed down the tiny furniture salon I hadn't even known existed before Connor called someone to call someone to make us an appointment to view the furniture.

View furniture. This world of his was absurd.

After sitting in yet another ridiculously-priced chair, he turned to me, frustrated, and demanded I sit in it.

"It's just not...I don't know. What's wrong with it?" He asked looking at the chair as if it had purposefully offended him.

"Nothing. It's very comfortable." And expensive.

"I think it's too small. It's like it's built for short people." He eyed my feet comfortably resting on the floor. "See? Short people chair."

"Um, no. I'm not tiny." I rested my head back enjoying the supreme comfort while he paced around the chair. "My feet managed to reach the ground in every chair."

"I know!" He stopped and checked the chair out once more. "What if I buy you this chair and I take the one at your house?"

"You want my chair? Again, um, no." That was my chair and I earned it by putting up with an overbearing, pain in the rear ex.

"Yes, but you'd get this chair." He smiled, and I realized that not too long from now he'd also be an overbearing, pain in the rear ex.

But, still, no.

"You can't have my chair. It's already broken in and I like it. But," I said, watching him go from disappointed to hopeful. "I'll bring you to somewhere that you can get a chair you like."

And won't cost several thousand dollars.

"Really?" He sounded intrigued.

Without even asking where we were going, he called for another cab, thanked the sales woman, and dragged me out to the sidewalk to wait.

Apparently, this was a chair emergency.

We drove out to Jordan's, a beautiful, huge showroom of a furniture palace where normal people bought comfortable chairs every day.

Two hours, forty-three autographs, and six different chairs later, Connor had a flawlessly comfortable leather chair. There was no viewing, just a whole lot of sitting. Like normal people.

SEVENTEEN

I LOVED GAME night. Not so much because I was a huge game person, although Jenna was winning me over, but because the guys were insane.

In. Sane.

I'd been afraid when Ben had headed off to London that Jenna would stop having us over. I wouldn't have blamed her. Kasey and I were working on ways to make more Girl Time happen. But, instead, she'd doubled down, inviting John and Sarah to join us—leaving The Brew to the indelicate closing rituals of Abby.

But, John was trying to give Abby more responsibilities and being only three blocks away meant he could get there if she lit the building on fire or assaulted anyone. So far, she'd done a great job. Or at least hadn't done anything that got her and the café on the news. Of course, Jenna had asked John what night they had the fewest customers and shifted game night accordingly. So, Wednesday night it was. Weirdest night to play games, but whatever.

Our guy-to-girl ratio was off so I'd been afraid she'd suggest bringing Connor.

I should have known better.

"So, since we're down a player tonight, we're going to do something new," Jenna announced to everyone assembled in her living room. "Dane, you're disappointing me. I thought you'd bring one of the Danettes and I'd have Hailey to myself. But, since you didn't, we're going to do something a little different tonight. I've arranged—"

"Wait," Dane interrupted. "You're upset with me for *not* bringing a girl who you would mock for her low IQ and lack of pop culture knowledge?"

John glanced at Sarah, obviously worried that his inability to name anything culturally current might get him mocked.

"Don't worry." Sarah patted John's arm. "I have boy bands covered."

"Really?" He glanced at her as if he'd never seen her before. As if *boy bands* were such a unique knowledge base for a museum curator that she was way outside her intellectual comfort zone.

But, enough of that.

"Don't worry about the mocking," I said to John and Sarah, trying to put them at ease. "She means we mock them for sleeping with Dane, not for anything else."

"Hey!" Dane crossed his arms as if he had made a brilliant comeback.

"What? You pick them up, hang out with them for a week, and then move on."

Dane had *rules*.

"Right." He nodded. "But they know this going in."

"Where's Jayne?" I asked. "I'll take Jayne and you can have him." I nodded my head at Dane knowing that would annoy him.

"*Him* is sitting right here. Why would you want Jayne when you could have me?" He seemed genuinely confused.

"Maybe because all of your answers will be sexist when you think they're funny?"

"Hailey, sweetheart, I wasn't—"

"And, *that*," Jenna cut in, "is where I'll be stopping this argument. Jayne can't come. She had a gig working at a gallery tonight. So, yes. You get Dane."

"Fine, but—" My phone rang in the other room, cutting me off since everyone who might call me on a random Wednesday night was sitting in the room. I glanced toward the kitchen where *MMMBop* blared from, wondering who it could be.

"*As I was saying*," Jenna continued. "I have created a game that includes parts of all our favorites. I will moderate the play and referee any disagreements. The winner gets to pick the game next time. With three teams of two, we'll roll to see who goes first."

"I call Kasey!" I stuck my hand in the air, like someone might acknowledge me faster and hoping that my second attempt would make me Dane-free.

"What?" Max and Dane said at the same time.

"I get Kasey."

I was not being brought down by Dane again. We always lost. Not because he was stupid, but because he was easily distracted and his favorite part of game night was ticking off Ben and Max by picking the most absurd answers and fighting his stance to death.

"Um. No." Max shook his head before wrapping an arm around Kasey. "I've been stuck with Dane for a decade. I've upgraded."

"Also, you're prettier, and I always go with prettier." Dane gave me the look that had girls crossing clubs to climb into his lap before they even introduced themselves.

"But—"

"As the referee," Jenna interrupted, "I call the teams. Kasey and Max. Hailey and Dane."

"Challenge!" I shouted, jumping to my feet.

Sarah gave John a look that seemed to ask what they'd gotten themselves into. I don't think I'd ever seen either so quiet.

"Challenge? You can't challenge this. It's not a right or wrong answer." Jenna gave me The Look. "It's an official call."

She was tiny, but stern. I was stuck with Dane. Again.

"Fine, but I get a handicap for idiocy." I glanced at Dane, waiting for him to be insulted.

He shrugged. "I'm okay with that."

Geez.

My phone rang again as Jenna started laying out some complicated rules. I couldn't figure out who would be calling me two times in a row and started to worry something was wrong at home. I headed to the kitchen to grab my phone, surprised to see Connor's name on the screen.

My stomach dropped. Someone had outed us and my career was crashing into the mountains of authors past. I started making a mental list of everyone I'd have to call.

Crud, I was going to have to fire my agent. There's no way I could play this off without that. And, if I was no longer a viable brand, she deserved to be fired because this was all her fault.

I prepared myself for the worst and hit *answer*.

"Hey, Connor." Listen to how even my voice sounded. "What's up?"

"I was just calling to see what your schedule was for the rest of the week. I thought maybe you'd like to get dinner tomorrow night."

I gushed out a breath of relief, then sucked in one of panic. The call sounded way too much like a date.

Of course it was a date. We were *dating*. Just not for real. Or like sane people. But, the way he asked made it sound like a date-date.

I really needed to stop over-thinking everything. I took the phone away from my ear and started paging through my calendar. The color-coding Kasey had set up for events and launches helping me figure out my day at a glance.

"Um, yeah. I could do tomorrow night," I answered, blocking off seven to nine. "But I have an AMA at six."

"What's an AMA?" Connor sounded like he was in no rush to get off the phone.

"Ask Me Anything. We do one before every launch. The readers get to ask anything they want and, as long as it doesn't spoil the book, I'll tell them."

"That sounds like my worst nightmare." I could almost hear the tremble in his voice.

"Yeah, well I'm not out sleeping with supermodels, getting caught in elevators with co-worker's girls, or doing anything else to get me on the cover of any magazine I'd never buy. So, you know, I should be safe."

"Ha, ha." Obviously he thought that joke was too soon. "I'm going to create a fake account and ask you things like who you lost your virginity to." Connor laughed at his own joke as if teenage girls didn't want to know this stuff anyway.

It was often a careful balancing act to not give advice or become too personal.

"Who said I'd lost it?" I asked and smothered my own laughter when Connor went silent on the other end of the line.

"Hailey, that's not even funny."

"It's not like it matters to you any way you look at it."

"It would just be such a…" Connor struggled to find the right word and I shook my head confused about what my sexual activities had to do with him. "A waste. It would be a waste if a girl like you was—"

"Hailey!" Dane stomped into the kitchen looking annoyed. "We're already down three points. John must be the smartest person on the planet. What are you doing in here? And, don't give me that look, sweetheart. I'm not a complete moron. I can see you're on the phone."

"Who's that?" Connor asked—no. Demanded.

"It's just Dane." I shoved at Dane, pointing back to the living room.

Instead of moving, Dane crossed his arms and leaned against the counter settling in for the rest of my phone conversation.

"Dane? That…guy who had his hands all over you at The Brew?" Connor, man of the faulty memory.

"Um, no. No one had their hands all over me. Dane was *sitting* next to me. For a moment."

"Right. In my seat." It was like he was verbally pouting.

177

I didn't even know what to say to that.

"Anyway…" I glared at Dane more, thinking of all the ways I was going to torture him for being such a pain in the butt. "I have to go. It's our turn."

"Your turn for what?"

"It's game night." Maybe Connor and I needed to do a calendar sync and plan out everything for the next few weeks.

"And Adonis is your teammate?" Connor asked it like Dane was leading me down the path of seduction and debauchery.

"Yup. He's always my teammate." I pointed Dane toward the living room again, hoping he'd take off instead of staying there staring me down. "Lucky me."

"That's right," Dane shouted in my ear. "Partners. That's us."

I rolled my eyes. With Ben absent, Dane would settle for annoying some random guy on the phone.

"I have to go. Everyone's waiting for us." I pushed at Dane again, watching him smirk before heading back to the living room. "I'm up for dinner tomorrow. I'll call you in the morning."

"Right. Okay."

I waited, wondering if there was more, but apparently that was it.

"Okay. Night!" I hung up before the weirdness could multiply.

Back in the living room, Dane was sitting on our loveseat looking smug. "How is Mr. Baseball?"

"He's fine." I settled in and elbowed Dane when he slung his arm over my shoulder. "Dude, you're such a pain in the butt."

"Right, but when the ass looks like yours, I'm fine with that."

Lord save me from egotistical womanizing men.

~*~

I rinsed another plate and handed it to Jenna, glad to be down to just the two of us. If John and Sarah ever came back, we'd know they were either saints or just as crazy as the rest of us. I was leaning toward crazy.

"What the heck was up with Dane tonight?" I asked, more annoyed at him for the phone antics than the stupidity of our big loss.

Seriously, who says *green* when asked about van Gogh's famous colored phase? I swear he loses on purpose. The boy's IQ is off the charts."

Jenna laughed and I expected her to launch into a replay of Dane Highlights. But instead she looked at me like I was nuts.

"Are you kidding me?" she asked, as she squeezed another glass into the back of the dishwasher's rack.

"Um, no. He was worse than normal." And that had to have been a challenge.

"Yeah. *Of course* he was." There was way too much meaning behind those words.

"What's that supposed to mean?"

Jenna shut the dishwasher and grabbed the last of her wine before boosting herself up on one of the kitchen stools.

"He's in a panic. You're throwing off his plan."

"Dane has a plan?" A plan I could throw off? That was news. I wondered if it involved sleeping his way through

Europe, because that seemed like something he'd put on the calendar.

"Of course he does." Jenna took a sip, eyeing me over the rim of her glass and I wondered if I should have kept my wine fresh too. "He's actually very organized. Deadlines and stuff. He was ahead of schedule when he sold that website at twenty-four and I think it threw him off a bit."

"Okay. But, what does that have to do with me?"

"You're serious? You haven't figured it out?" She set the glass down and leaned in, looking as amused as she was surprised. "You're the girl he's going to marry after he's done screwing around."

"*What?*"

Jenna laughed and I was glad one of us thought that was funny. Maybe I'd think it was funny later.

No. Probably not.

"You're kidding, right?" Because, leave it to Jenna to think that was serious *and* funny.

"Nope." She smirked. She actually *smirked*. "I'm not even kidding a little."

"Did Ben tell you this?" Actual validation would be good. Or bad. Bad, it would be bad.

"Nope."

"Dude," I tried to stay calm, but this wasn't the type of news a girlfriend should just throw at you. "You're kind of driving me nuts right now."

"Hailey, anyone can see how much he cares for you. You're the girl. Smart, funny, cute. You know him, all of him, and still care about him. He's more than fond of you. You're the total package."

I snorted because, hey. It was so insane it deserved a snort. "That's ridiculous."

"You've met Dane, right? He's not always in step with the norm."

"So, he just thinks that when he's done sleeping around and figuring out what he wants to be when he grows up, I'll meet him at the front of a church and tie myself to his brand of insanity for the rest of my life."

"Yeah, that's pretty much how he thinks." She refreshed her glass and pulled a new one out from where they hung under the counter, splashing the rest of the bottle into it and sliding it over to me. "Now he's got competition and he's worried."

"Where are you getting all this?"

"Watching. Then talking to Ben about it. Then convincing Ben and watching more."

"So, Ben thinks you're right?" Crud.

Jenna nodded.

"But, I'm not going to marry Dane. And it's not because of Connor." Wait. "Why is *Connor* competition? What about all my other boyfriends?"

As if I was going to marry Connor. Ha.

"None of those guys were going to last." She took a sip of wine, a little smile playing around her lips. "They didn't get what we do. The crazy writer thing. All of us knew none of them would make it past a book cycle. Maybe two if they were patient."

"So?"

"So, Connor also has a job that isn't nine-to-five. He gets year cycles and having to be unavailable for stretches because of work." She made a little motion with her hand as if none of that really mattered. "He's also incredibly good looking, successful, rich, and famous. All the things Dane excels at, Connor does too."

"Yes. Because I'm looking for an idiot of my very own."

"Plus, Connor is looking to settle down."

"No, he isn't. That's the last thing he wants to do." Ever. And hadn't that been made clear?

"Are you sure?"

"Yes. Trust me. Dane will be a grandfather before Connor settles down." And that was a thought to avoid pondering.

"So, you'd be interested in Dane then?"

"Jenna." I set down my glass. "I feel like we're having a conversation where you forgot that I wasn't insane."

Jenna smiled a super, sticky sweet smile. The one she gave us when she knew something…or was up to something.

It was time to sleep with one eye open.

EIGHTEEN

THE ONLY THING Connor said about our "date" tonight was to dress casual.

After consulting Becca's binder, that still left me with too many options. Which meant, girlfriend consultation.

"Hailey, this is nuts. You're not really dating." Kasey's frustration threshold was a lot lower than Jenna's. "Just put on a pair of jeans and a nice top."

"I'm not dressing for him. I'm dressing for the pictures. I know that I'm going to get ambushed again by crazy people with cameras. I need to look the right type of casual."

Oddly, the pictures were easier than I'd expected. I hadn't had to pose for one yet. And still, there were pictures of us everywhere. It a lot easier emotionally not knowing pictures had been taken. Social media was, for once, my friend. Kasey said we even had a hashtag.

"What exactly is the right type of casual?" The sarcasm was more than implied.

"When you were figuring things out with Max, did I or did I not support you through your stupidity?"

"Wait, what?" Kasey sounded much more alert now. "Are you *interested* in Connor?"

"No. That's not the point. It's that when you were being an idiot about Max and your new business and your lack of home and your idiot ex-boyfriend and the fact that you almost got yourself arrested like fourteen times—"

"Four. Four times. Let's not get crazy."

"Sure. Because almost getting arrested four times in a week is totally normal." If she needed to be humored, I'd humor her. "And, all I'm asking is that while trapped in this insane world, a little support would be nice."

I waited, wondering what was going to come out of this, but I needed to not have to worry about my girls having my back.

"You're right." Kasey sighed. "I know you're right. I just think this is ridiculous. And unfair. And I'm worried about you. But, yeah. So, you should wear the Lucky jeans with that black, fitted Guess t-shirt. Add the red necklace you liked with the red ballet flats and put your hair up in a low ponytail. Make sure to wear a warm scarf since you don't know where you're going and the warmer jacket Becca got you. Just casual enough."

I pulled things out as she named them, half-annoyed I had that many high end brand names in my closet now, and pulled them on while I had her on speaker phone.

"Oh, this looks good." I turned sideways to look at the fitted-tee in the mirror. "Why do my t-shirts never look this nice?"

"First, that is your t-shirt now. And, second, we buy things at stores where the fabric isn't scientifically engineered to not lose its shape." She laughed at her own joke as I rolled my eyes. "Hailey, sorry about all that. Try to have fun tonight."

"You know," I edged into my statement, as though tiptoeing into a room where people were talking about you. "This isn't Connor's fault either."

I waited, knowing she'd have to admit that if I didn't fill in the silence.

"That doesn't mean I have to like it. You know I'm not pushing one way or the other, even if he's not the ogre you made him out to be while drunk and pitiful."

"Hey." I cut in. "I was neither drunk nor pitiful. I was just annoyed. And trapped."

"I know." She sighed as if this were all inevitable. "He's putting you in a tough position with the press even if it's not directly his fault." I could picture her pacing around her living room, waving her arms about. Kasey was nothing if not animated. "His agent wouldn't have had to make this bargain if he could just behave."

I bit my tongue knowing no matter what I said the jury was still out.

"But," Kasey went on. "I'll try to like him next time I see him. He sounds like he's playing nice. As long as he doesn't do anything to hurt or embarrass you, he's fine with me."

"Wow, Kasey," I jumped in, knowing that was as good as it was going to get. "Don't set the bar so high."

She laughed as I hung up on her. Fifteen minutes to go before Mr. Punctual arrived and I still had hair and makeup.

When did my life start to feel like a Broadway show? There better not be singing later.

I tamped down my excitement. Any girl would be excited to go out with a millionaire with a surprise, right? It had nothing to do with looking forward to seeing Connor.

That would be crazy pants.

~*~

Connor arrived ten minutes early.

If he was going to deviate from the plan, we were going to have words. I still had to do my makeup and make sure my ponytail was fuzz proof and figure out what earrings went with the necklace.

"Hey." He pushed his way into the apartment and looked at me and frowned. "You're ready."

"Um, no. I'm not." Obviously.

"But you look ready."

"I don't have makeup on yet."

"Well, you don't need that junk, then." Connor wandered into the kitchen and pulled the scotch from above the fridge. Pouring himself a glass, he went and settled into the leather chair. "See? This is how a date starts."

"Really?" I asked, trying to catch up from the accidental compliment. "That's why you're early?"

Part of me was ridiculously happy I'd bought the stuff. The other part of me was annoyed that while I went on primping, he got to hang out having an insanely marked up glass of liquor in a really comfortable chair.

"Yup." He took another sip. "But, don't let me distract you."

Picking up the remote, he turned the TV on. I shouldn't have been surprised it was still on SportsCenter.

Connor must have this down to a science, because he was taking the last sip of his drink as I came out and grabbed my jacket.

After getting ready with him lounging in the other room, I began to wonder what it was like to deal with this every day. How glad was I that my life as a writer mostly involved being around my girls, writing for my readers, and wearing yoga pants?

"You look cute." He grinned at me and I tried not to roll my eyes at the word *cute*.

"So, where are we going?" I figured I should check before we left in case I needed to update my look. Not that I'd know how to update it.

"Nope. It's a surprise."

That was not going to help me. "Do I look okay?"

"I told you, you look cute."

"I mean, do I look right? For where we're going?" I swatted at the panic rising up.

"Sure." He held my jacket out for me to slip into as I contemplated not killing him.

~*~

The cab drove us downtown. Every time it slowed, I thought we might be at our destination. But, it took us all the way to the arena and pulled into the VIP parking. Connor gave me a goofy smile.

"I thought we'd go low-key tonight." He paid the cabbie and slid out, holding his hand to me even though a girl in flats and jeans could hop out on her own.

Or, at least I think most of us could. Maybe really tall model girls can't. Their giraffe legs got in the way or something.

"We're going to a game?" I'm not sure I liked the sound of that. I wasn't really a sports fan and Connor was…well, fan is a weird word to use for a guy who other people were fans of.

"Yup. Courtside seats. We can hangout and chill and not worry about interacting with people." He grinned. "It's one of the few events we can go to and security is there to keep people away from a place we just happen to be."

Okay. That didn't sound so bad. But…

"Are you going to feed me or not?" Because, honestly, as far as dates went, that's all that really mattered to me at this point. Food was always an important part of every evening. Maybe he didn't expect me to eat anything. Did the giraffes eat when he brought them out?

"I would pay half a million dollars to know what you're thinking right now." He ushered me toward the arena, giving me the side-eye as we went.

"*Really*?" Because that would solve a lot of problems.

"Um, no." Connor laughed, dropping his hand to my back and steering me to a side entrance where he flashed some credentials. "But, yes. I will be feeding you. They have people who take care of that. You can have whatever you want. There's a really nice restaurant. We could have something brought down." He paused, and I could see he was thinking something over. Food did not seem very controversial to me. "Or, if you wanted, we could go eat up there."

I glanced up at him looking straight ahead and realized he was playing nice. If I wanted to go up to a restaurant to eat for part of the game, he'd take me. Chivalry in the face of missing out on his favorite pastime.

"Well, as long as you're going to feed me, we can eat wherever you want."

The look of relief was almost comical. "Great!"

We got to another security guard and Connor went to flash our credentials again, but the guard beat him to it.

"Mr. Ryan. Mr. Johnson called ahead to make sure your tickets were waiting for you. Mike will show you to your seats."

A young man in a team shirt stepped away from the wall and motioned for us to follow him. "Mr. Ryan, it's great to have you here."

Connor stuck his hand out toward the teen. "It's Connor. How's it going, Mike?"

I thought the boy was going to pass out. "Connor. Wow. Nice." He shook his hand, not letting go as Connor smiled at him.

"This is Hailey." Connor motioned to me with his head since his hand wasn't free.

"Oh. Hailey Tate. I think you're so cute!" The teenager turned bright red after he said it. "I mean—"

"Thanks, Mike." Finally. It took a fifteen-year-old to appreciate my not-quite-hotness.

Connor freed his hand to slap Mike on the back. "A man after my own heart."

By this point, we were coming out of a tunnel right at court level and ushered to our seats in the front row, just off to the right of the bench.

"I asked for seats off to the side since you're so little. I know center court is great, but you'd never see over those guys."

That was oddly sweet. Connor wrapped my hand in his huge mitt and glanced around like a kid excited to be at his first game. Our seats were lower than I expected, forcing Connor's knees up.

"You're a fan, right?" He looked anxious, like this was a make or break question. If we were really dating, I'd be worried. "I mean, you like basketball?"

"Yeah. It's *way* better than baseball." I grinned, waiting for the retort.

"You're a pain in the butt, Hails. It's a good thing you're adorable."

"You're just saying that because Mike said it. Now you're competing with a fifteen-year-old."

"It's only competition if I might not win."

I had no idea what to do with that. But… "You sound like Dane."

"Dane?" He made it sound like a curse word. "There's no way I sound like that—him."

"I don't know. Apparently he thinks you guys are competing too." I laughed, because, seriously. When did this become my life? As if I was going to date either of them, let alone marry them.

"What does he think we're competing over?"

I was glancing around the arena, not paying attention, otherwise I might have noticed the absurd tone of voice he asked this in.

"Me." I snorted.

"*Really?*"

"Yup. I guess in a few years Dane is going to get bored dating and marry me." I still couldn't say it with a straight face.

"He's *what?*"

Connor's tone finally broke through and I shifted my gaze to meet his, surprised to see how annoyed he was.

"Marry me?" I suddenly wasn't sure why this conversation wasn't the *ha ha ha* I expected it to me.

"He thinks he can just sleep around until he runs out of women, and then you're just going to trip over your feet to jump into bed with him?" His eyes had narrowed to little slits as he glared at me as if I were the one running around sleeping with people and discarding them.

"Um, I guess he assumed we'd sleep together, but the bigger issue is he thinks we're getting *married*." I rushed on because Connor's ears were tipping pink at this point. "Or, that's what Jenna thinks."

Connor gave me a hard look, completely different than the at-ease one he'd carried when we'd sat down. "You're not going to marry him, right?"

"Seriously, Connor? Of course not." Why were we even having this conversation?

"Good." He sat back, dropping his arm across the back of my little seat and snorted. "As if there were any real competition there."

I patted his leg, figuring everyone was way too out of control. "I know, right? I don't know why he was worried."

It took him a second before he realized what I'd said and let out an affronted huff.

Served him right.

NINETEEN

BASKETBALL WAS SURPRISINGLY exciting when seven-foot guys kept running by you with a piece of hard rubber that could break your nose. Connor had a rough time staying in his seat as things got tight. He was all but trying to rush the court to help as we fell behind.

Most of the fun was from just hanging out with him. He'd been right about us going low key and not having to worry about people. Being in the VIP section meant there was an invisible fence around us.

He spent a large portion of the night trying to win me over to the world of the sports obsessed. I was less than sad to disappoint him. At halftime, Connor pulled it together enough to ask me what I wanted to eat.

"Can I have a beer and a pretzel with cheese sauce?"

"A beer and a pretzel?" He looked like I'd asked for filet mignon and champagne.

"Well, I saw those other people with beer and pretzels and nachos and that looked good." It felt very what-you-eat-at-a-game to me.

He gave me a smile like I'd bought him a gift. "Do you want nachos too?"

"I don't think I could eat that much."

"We could share them." He waved over the server who seemed to appear out of the nowhere.

"You'd share your nachos with me?" Most of my boyfriends weren't much on sharing food.

"Sure. If we eat it all, we can just order more." Connor gave our order to the girl. He turned back to me, wrapping an arm around my shoulder while he grinned and kissed my temple. "You are the best girlfriend ever."

I laughed, surprised that was all it took to make him happy. A basketball game and beer and nachos.

When the game ended, I was afraid of Connor getting mobbed, but we were pointed toward an underground exit just off to the side of the court.

We wove through the small crowd of people in the secure tunnel, pushing through the heat toward the cool night air.

"That was so fun. I can't believe I've never been to a game before."

"Well, sorry to have ruined you for all other games, but sitting courtside is pretty much the only way to do it." Connor smirked, proud of himself for doing what no other guy had done...get me to a basketball game.

"That was a great way to spend one of our nights out." Which, yes. I was keeping track in my head. A countdown back to normalcy, if you will. I needed it to stay grounded. "Thanks."

"I was thinking we could grab some coffee and pie at The Brew on the way home. See what kind of chaos Abby is creating tonight." Connor flagged down a cab, which of course stopped right in front of us.

Golden boy.

"Actually," I put a hand on his arm to stop him as he reached for the cab door. "I have to go home and work. I need to get this outline and proposal to my editor by the end of the day tomorrow and with everything going on I'm behind."

"Oh." Connor looked at me as if this was a new idea. That I might actually work. "Right. You have to do stuff."

"*Work* stuff," I added because he looked as if he thought I was trying to blow him off. Especially since part of me *was* blowing him off. After talking to Kasey I realized I needed some space. I got that we were on a mission, but I'd never spent this much time with a new boyfriend and I just wanted some time away from him.

It wasn't that I was falling for him. It was that I wanted to make sure I didn't. Space was a good thing. For any type of relationship. Ever.

And moving to the Arctic was shockingly not an option.

"No. I know. Work stuff." He grabbed the handle, and motioned for me to slide in before him. "I'll just drop you off and you can see how much you can get done tonight."

He gave the cabbie my address then picked up my hand, running a thumb over the back of it. As the lights went by, I rested my head against the back of the seat, trying to get myself in writing mode before I got home. I was behind. The downside of my faux boyfriend was that, unlike a real one, I

THE CATCHING KIND

couldn't put him off for a few days. The deal with Connor
meant meeting my obligations to the T.

Plus, he was just so much fun. I enjoyed hanging out with
him.

"How far behind are you?" he asked, sounding a little
worried. Which was sweet.

Again with the sweet.

"Not horribly. If I just work late tonight and then deal
with all of it tomorrow, I'll probably have enough to hand
in." I was never late. I might push the very boundaries of
what that looked like, but I was never late.

This wasn't going to be the first time.

The cab pulled up in front of my house and Connor let
me out on the sidewalk side, leaning in to tell the driver to
wait.

"I'll walk you up." He motioned toward the door and
waited for me to lead the way.

"You don't have to do that." Because, why should he?

"Yes. I really do." Connor gave me a small push against
my lower back to get me moving and, at the front door, took
my keys to let us in.

We climbed the stairs, me already in my story world,
Connor climbing behind me. At my door, he used my keys to
let us in and paced the floor for a moment. I watched the
nervous energy get caged while I hung my coat up and tossed
my purse into my room, hoping it hit the bed so I could find
it again later.

"What exactly are you doing?" I asked when he did
another lap around my little living room.

Connor stopped, glanced my way, and shook his head. "I'm thinking about how long it would take me to say goodnight to you if we were really dating."

Yeah. Eye roll.

"Okay, got it." I shoved him toward the door. "Out you go."

"No. No way." He stood his ground, becoming an immovable object. "There's no way that if I was kissing you goodnight, you'd kick me out that quickly."

"You're paying a man to sit in a car and wait for you. Do you know how much that costs?"

"Less than my reputation." He shot me a grin, as if his reputation were really worth all this and not the reason he was stuck pacing my apartment in the first place.

I stared at the clock, wondering just how long it typically took him to say goodnight. "There's something wrong with you."

"Right. We already established that."

I rolled my eyes because, well, if he already knew there was something wrong with him, my work here was done.

"So, I'm pacing around your living room, wondering...just how serious are you about my body."

"Excuse me?" I didn't glance at said body as I set my kettle on the stove to make tea and crossed to turn my computer on.

"I'm here, saying good night—"

"Paying a cab to wait."

"Right, because, you're worth it." He winked at me and went back to pacing, which, with his long legs was three steps one way, three steps back. "And, I have to wonder, just how long I'd be willing to humor you and those crazy wandering hands of yours while I was paying this cab."

I just stared at him, wondering how exactly that incredibly intelligent brain came up with this stuff. Giving him a push toward the door, I figured, there was only one answer.

"Again," I said, as I pushed him out the door. "There really is something wrong with you."

Or me, because unfortunately, I was beginning to think the idiot was adorable.

TWENTY

ARE YOU INSANE?" Catherine definitely didn't sound like she expected a real answer to that question. "What were you thinking? You know this is fake, don't you? This is my fault. This is all my fault. Hailey, I'm sorry. I should have known you couldn't handle him. I'm fifty-two, have had three husbands and an affair with a diplomat who shall not be named, and I'm not sure *I* could handle Connor Ryan."

So much for thinking I'd get the easy call out of the way first.

"Catherine, what are you flipping out about?" Not that I was sure I wanted to know.

"Have you *looked* at Twitter? Facebook? Anything?"

"Um, no." Which was more on purpose than normal. As soon as I'd seen how half the girls with cameras had reacted to Connor being *off the market* when we'd been out and about, I knew the last thing I wanted to do was see the worst collection of candid photos of me possible and read the comments section.

She huffed out a breath on the other end. "There's pictures of the two of you being all cute everywhere. Cafes, parks, sidewalks, coming out of the gym." Her voice raised to a bit of a hysterical level on the last one as if going to the gym together led to a secret betrothal forced upon us by our fathers at birth. "Hailey you have to remember. This is a game to him. That's it. You're just a teammate. Not even. You're like the ball he needs to kick in the net or the bases he has to run."

"Beyond your slightly mixed metaphors, you're just wrong." I should have known this was going to be how my morning went. "We're playing a part. Stop worrying. I can handle this. Trust me."

Which may have been asking for too much if I was already worried about trusting myself.

"Sure. I trust you." Catherine was typing in the background, which wasn't uncommon. But you'd think when she was on a mission to protect my virtue she'd at least manage to do it without multi-tasking. "I just emailed you something. Why don't you open that up and jump to about the minute and a half mark."

"Okay." I downloaded the zipped file and watched as it started playing shorts of me and Connor throughout the night. Him with his arm across the back of my chair, him leaning in to tell me something, me wiping mustard off his face from the pretzel. Him leaning over and kissing my temple when he'd told me I was the best girlfriend ever.

I looked dazed.

I'd been dazed.

Well, crud.

"Are you watching this?" Catherine demanded, as if I was sitting there silently on the other end of the phone doing nothing.

"Yes. I am. I'm not seeing a problem." Because what I saw was a reminder.

I was sucked in by him. Who wouldn't be? He was fun and thoughtful and attractive…let's be honest, everyone was wired to be attracted to him. Brad Pitt who?

"Hailey—"

"Catherine," I interrupted, because I couldn't deal with this on top of everything else right now. "I appreciate you looking out for me. I realize you feel guilty about this. And, to be honest, you should. Connor is a friend and when this is over, maybe he'll even be someone I stay in touch with. But he's not a guy I'm going to fall for. That's not a life I want. And, I have a deadline my insane agent is pushing so I really don't have time for this."

I waited of her response, afraid this was going to turn into an argument, but relieved when she just told me again to be careful and hung up.

Oh, I'd be careful. I'd be so careful I'd be mistaken for a human traffic cone.

I took a screenshot of my dazed face and saved it, forwarding it to my phone for when I needed a reminder.

Because when you didn't realize how deep in you were, you could only fall further.

TWENTY-ONE

"WOW. YOU LOOK GREAT."

That was the exact reaction I was going for. I'd tried not to let him see how happy his comment made me. I might have even succeeded because he was behind me when he said it. I glanced over my shoulder wondering what he was looking at back there.

"Surprised?" I figured he must be.

"Nope." He gave me that cocky smile, the one that said he knew exactly where his place in the world was and it was at the top. "Just flattered you'd bring your A-game for me."

I shook my head. Of course. Leave it to Connor Ryan to make my appearance about him.

"Yup. I went through three hours of being plucked and blown out and made-up for you. It had nothing to do with wanting to look nice or the chance to dress up—which writers don't get very often. Or," I added, because I wasn't looking forward to this part, "all those darn photos."

"That's okay." He grinned, giving me another once-over. "You keep telling yourself it's for the photos."

He looked so darn sure of himself. He looked the same way he looked when girls were flirting with him or slipping him their number.

Grabbing my bag off the arm of the couch, I made sure my keys, ID, lipstick, cell, and a mini Moleskin were in it— which pretty much packed the tiny thing full—and grabbed my wrap. Before I could wing it out and around to cover my shoulders, Connor had taken it from me and gently— probably even elegantly—laid it over my shoulders.

I stood, studying that face which had begun to look almost normal to me. The crinkles at the edge of his eyes from squinting into the sun, the light dusting of freckles that rode over the bridge of his nose, all the little things you couldn't see in the photos and didn't notice right away when you met him. Somehow in the last two weeks he'd become more…human. Less the ideal every woman seemed to hold him up to and more just a guy with a really different job.

"Ready?" He was looking back at me as if I'd lost my mind.

How long had I been staring at him? The last thing I needed him thinking was that I was *interested*. Because, I definitely was not *interested*.

I was just—intrigued.

It wasn't very often you found out someone was nothing like you thought they were. I had several close friends, but generally we didn't surprise each other anymore. And even those surprises weren't the types that made you stop and stare.

THE CATCHING KIND

But, as we stood there in my doorway, Connor dressed in a Hugo Boss suit and looking like he could take over a corporation instead of just field a grounder, my whole world shifted.

Okay. Melodramatic much?

But, my whole idea of Connor shifted. What if he was what he claimed instead of how he was portrayed? It wasn't like it was his fault he was a good-looking, rich, successful celebrity athlete.

He was just doing his job.

And, I couldn't forget all the nasty reviews I got when I hit the *USA Today* bestseller list. I knew in my heart that was the best book I'd written. If I was ever going to make the *Times*, it would have been with that book. No. More than that. It *should* have been with that book. But, as soon as it was listed, my reviews took a nosedive.

Every YA hater in the reading world decided to tell everyone why it was the biggest piece of trash ever written. I could never help but think if I'd just stayed under the radar, if I'd just written for those people who liked my style and genre, I'd never have read about how I must be stupid and fat and all the other words people throw around. It always confused me why people would hate a book for the sole reason that it was written for teens. As if teens didn't deserve books and were too dumb to understand complex sentences.

Jenna had to talk me down for two weeks straight and then threatened to child-lock all my Internet access points.

Was Connor's world as toxic? How much was truth and how much was just the celebrity laid over the man—so they could sell magazines?

"Hailey?" His curiosity was beginning to look like worry.

"Sorry. I was thinking about my story."

"Oh." His shoulders dropped back to relaxed mode and a small, little smile stretched, softening his lips. "Do you want to make some notes real fast before we leave?"

It took everything I had not to drop the bag in my hand. Only Jenna—and now Kasey that we'd trained her—knew that when an idea hit, I had to write it down. Write it or lose it. That was the way my stories worked.

"Um. Yeah." Because, what was I going to say.

I crossed to my desk, took out my notebook, and wrote in block letters Do Not Fall Prey to Charm.

I should have it tattooed to the inside of my eyelids.

Shoving the notebook back in the drawer, I took a deep breath. This was going to be a fun night. I was going to a home that cost more than my entire block. I'd never have another chance to go there or drink what was most likely three-hundred-dollar champagne again.

"Thanks." I turned back to him, re-adjusting my inner sanity meter. "All set."

Connor pulled the door open and held it for me. I listened to him give me a run down again of the people who would be there.

"It's one of the few reasons I've considered buying a house in Europe. I couldn't be expected to fly back from Europe just for this party every year."

The idea that *that* idea would even cross his mind was absurd. Most people just got headaches. Connor considered foreign property.

"But, then I realized," he continued, "what a jackass I sound like just saying things like that out loud. What do I need with a house in Europe?"

And there went my clever quip opportunity.

"Skiing?" I started down the stairs, listening to his footfalls behind me.

"I can ski here. My brother and I used to ski all the time." There was something in his voice. Something...wistful?

"Why don't you ski anymore?"

"Can't. It's in my contract. No skiing, parachuting, rock climbing, car racing. Nothing that puts my knees or shoulder at risk."

That seemed excessive. I mean, no one had ever told me I can't cook because I might cut my fingers.

Of course, I wasn't making millions a year and costing other people millions a year if I didn't come out with a book. Who would have considered celebrity to be that limiting?

"Hey. Don't feel bad for me." He slipped his arm around my shoulder. "I have the best life. I just have to let my brother know he needs to keep in shape because as soon as I'm retired we're hitting every extreme sport venue in the western hemisphere."

I stepped into the cold night air and glanced around for the cab. Instead, as we stood there, a man dressed in a black suit stepped away from a Town Car and opened the back door. Connor steered me toward it, his hand finding its spot on my lower back.

"Thanks, Mac."

"No problem, Con. Miss." The driver winked at me as I slid in, trying not to let my high-slit skirt ride up too much in front of the two men.

Once we were all settled, Mac pulled the car away from the curb.

"So, Mac," Connor called as he let his hand fall over mine and wrap around it. "Did you end up driving that rock star guy while he was here?"

"Yep." He adjusted his rearview mirror so he could see us. "Be glad you hadn't rented the car the next night. It reeked of booze and cheap perfume."

"Really?" Connor leaned forward, obviously fascinated by the idea of car gossip.

This was a human chink in his armor I didn't see coming.

"Yep. Nothing like driving you. Two women, three bottles. He kept lighting up no matter how much I reminded him there's no smoking in my car. Said he'd buy me a new fu—um, new car." He glanced in the rear-view mirror, meeting my gaze. "Excuse me, Miss Tate."

"Don't worry, Mac." Connor waved the apology meant for me off. "Hailey puts up with me so she can put up with just about anything."

"I believe that must be true." Mac winked at me again, letting me know this was an ongoing joke between the two men.

"So," Connor got the conversation back where he wanted it, "you pick him up after the concert, and…?"

"Yep. He's an hour late, which isn't a surprise. We build that into the bill with musicians."

This was fascinating. I was glad Connor was just as interested because otherwise I'd feel like a nosy fan…and I didn't even know who we were talking about. Still, I asked, "Why?"

"There are…backstage activities that often slow them down from getting right to the car."

"I assume you're not talking about encores?" When Mac just snorted, I gave him a little grin. "How late do ballplayers usually run?"

Mac had one of those big laughs. Not the kind that forces your attention on him. But the kind that makes you want to smile. As if just knowing he was laughing was part of an inside joke.

"Con, you better keep an eye on this one. She's a hot ticket."

"She could also kick my ass." He gave my hand a squeeze. "I learned to never go near her when she's hung over and has her sparring gloves on."

A little bit of warmth rose up my neck at the compliment. From any other guy to any other girl it may not have been one. But I knew in his athlete's mind, allowing that I could beat him at anything physical—whether it was true or not— was the biggest compliment he could give me.

It was better than the *Wow* he'd handed me earlier.

I pictured the notebook shoved in my desk and repeated the words again.

TWENTY–TWO

WE CLIMBED THE stairs to the foyer of a home I may have seen featured on a show about a billionaire and I questioned every single thing I was wearing right down to my underwear.

This was one of those times the binder of outfits hadn't been enough. Becca had been in heaven. She even offered to come over and help me dress. I almost took her up on it.

But, between the phone call and a slew of emails with step-by-step for a simple hairdo and makeup that was just a touch more than I'd been wearing lately, I felt like I could almost pull this off.

And wouldn't that be a miracle.

But, Connor had a great point. Tonight would bring us a long way in finishing this whole thing. Half the reason Dex had him doing this was to get his bosses to chill out. Unfortunately, I was learning that if you're a pro-athlete, your bosses consisted of owners, managers, coaches, agents, fans, and who knows how many other groups of people.

Since I was the perfect girl-next-door and I was on the job, this party was the right opportunity for us to hit most of the key players and make them believe this social mirage we were creating.

Just inside the door, I'd done a quick scan of the room to make sure that not only did my clothes look good on me, but they weren't too formal or flashy or too under- or over-done.

Now, I needed to remember to send Becca flowers. Not only did I look good, but I looked right.

Connor slid his hand from my back to my waist, giving me a little pull into his side.

"Don't worry," he whispered. "Most of the girls have been where you are. The majority of them seem pretty nice from what I can tell." He pulled us out of the doorway and scanned the room with me.

Was I that obvious?

"See that one in the red with the slit that goes way too high up her leg?"

"How could I miss her?"

"Trust me. You want to. If you see her heading toward you, divert. Fast."

"Got it."

"That older man, the one actually wearing a tux with a cummerbund." He nodded to the man picking up two champagne glasses off a tray as it passed. "Jason's wife says he's handsie, so keep a safe distance."

"Handsie old man. Distance. Check."

"See that—?" Connor's hand stiffened, his fingers biting a bit into my hip.

"What?"

"Nothing."

"Yeah. No. Not nothing. What?"

"The blonde in the black dress with the huge bracelet?"

I glanced toward the way he'd nodded his head. Oh.

"Yeah?"

"That's Ackerman's girlfriend."

"The one you hooked up with?"

His step faltered. Not enough that anyone would have noticed, but with his arm around me, I couldn't help but feel it.

"The one who told him we hooked up. Unlike the reports, no one caught us. No one caught us because nothing happened. She came onto me in an elevator. I said no and the next thing you know I'm getting my nose checked to see if it's broken or not."

I tried to ignore the way his arm had tightened around me. How angry he sounded.

"And?" Because, I couldn't imagine that you got from a pass in an elevator to a nationally-televised brawl in one step.

"And, she went to Ackerman right before the game. She played it up, cried. Made it sound like I was hitting on her and was making her uncomfortable with my inability to take no for an answer."

A part of my heart raged at that. At the fact that anyone would do that, let alone to Connor.

"He held it together for most of the game," Connor continued, his voice even lower now. "But toward the end, as it was clear we were going to be out for the post-season, he started throwing little barbs my way. I didn't even know what they were about until right before he came at me. And, who would you believe?"

I felt horrible. Guilty. I'd assumed it was true. No matter how much I learned about Connor, I still thought it was true. Part of me, even as I was berating myself, still questioned it...wondered if he'd caved for one night. One hook-up. One kiss. Maybe just one flirtation. Just something that put him in that situation. That he wasn't just the victim. He was one of the players.

"Why would she do that?" I knew as soon as the words came out of my mouth that I'd messed up. It wasn't the question. It was the tone of my voice. Even I could hear the doubt tinged with sarcasm. "I mean—"

"No. Don't worry about it." He moved to step away, but I grabbed his hand at my waist. "Why would you not wonder what everyone else has? It's her word against mine. We don't want to ever believe the woman in the relationship. It must be the jock. He gets around, right?"

So much bitterness. And I caused it. Well, not all of it. But tonight's version. I did that. Before we were even officially in the party I'd ruined our night.

"Connor, I'm sorry. I didn't mean it like that." And, just like that I realized I hadn't. It wasn't that I was judging him or calling him a liar. It was that I was afraid that he was *that guy*. Because of how desperately I needed him not to be. "I swear. I didn't."

He shifted, his arm still around me so I stood in a half-embrace as he bent to come closer to my height.

He studied my face, his free hand lightly cupping my chin to force my gaze up to his. "I believe you."

It's what I should have said. But, I was glad one of us had gotten a chance to.

"Good."

We stood there, grinning at each other like idiots.

"That's our first fight." He winked, that cocky grin coming back. "We should find a broom closet and make up."

My heart skipped a beat at the ridiculously over-the-top pick-up line my fake boyfriend just threw at me.

"I think our first fight was the moment we laid eyes on each other and you wouldn't get out of the elevator so I could get to my meeting."

"Doesn't count. We hadn't met yet."

"Or maybe the second moment we laid eyes on each other when you said you'd never be caught dead with me on your arm."

"Doesn't count. We weren't dating yet."

"Or the time at the farmers market."

"Doesn't count. That was a misunderstanding. Not a fight."

"You have an answer for everything."

"It's a gift."

"You're a nerd."

"Only secretly."

I grinned, absurdly happy at the way he had a comeback for everything I said. The flow of give and take. Amazed at the sweet silliness he was willing to show when it was just us.

His eyes crinkled as he bit off a laugh. "So, about that broom closet..."

"We don't have broom closets. In a house this size we have pantries." The deep voice broke between us and had Connor stiffening before he straightened.

"Mr. Johnson." He unwrapped his arm from around me and offered it to Mr. Johnson. "Thanks for having us, sir."

"And, if I'm not a complete idiot, you'd like to be just about anywhere besides here." His gaze drifted toward me. "Can't say as I blame you. Looks like this one has brains and beauty. About time."

He didn't even ask for an introduction. Just wandered away.

Connor went lax, letting out the most relieved sigh I'd ever heard from an adult male. "We could probably leave now that we've been seen and spoken to."

"I haven't gotten my overly expensive glass of champagne."

"I'll buy you a bottle."

"Or to mingle."

"We'll go to a club."

"Or let the other girlfriends tell me horrible stories about you."

"I'll buy you last week's *People*."

You'd think he was four years old and stuck at his grandparents' house for the weekend.

I took his hand, forcing him to look at me and take me seriously. "It took three hours to look like this. We're not leaving yet."

"I don't see how *that* could possibly have taken three hours."

I considered smacking him. Who says stuff like that?

"I mean," he continued. "You look dressed up and everything, but you don't look much different than normal. You know. You don't look...airbrushed. You just look like you, but with fancy clothes on."

"Oh."

"I'm not saying this right." He pushed a hand through his hair. "You don't need all this to look pretty."

He sounded like he meant it. Like I was just me and just me wasn't too bad now.

"But, I thought you thought..."

"I thought, what?"

"Ugly." I tried not to blush, not to worry as I said it. "I thought you thought I was ugly."

Connor's arm tightened around me and he pulled me into him. "I never thought you were ugly. I thought you were...I don't know. Different."

"Great." Just what every girl wants to be. Forget glamorous or dazzling or even cute. *Different.*

I braced my hand against him, trying to push back but not getting anywhere.

"Hold still." His voice was low and tight. "Here's the thing. I'm not going to apologize again. But, I want you to understand, because...well, you deserve to see the whole picture."

"I'm not angry. I swear. I—"

"Hails, you obviously think that how I behaved that day is how I feel. I don't blame you, so here's the deal." He ran down my back and up again. Down and up. I began to wonder if the motion, the touching was for me or for him. "When I walked in there, Dex blindsided me. I knew something was coming, but I didn't know what. I was planning on finding a way out no matter what and there you were. I said the first thing I could think of that might get him off my case. Even though you were standing there looking like Miss Girl Next Door. Granted, an annoying and messy girl next door, but still. If I'd said the first thing I thought..."

I waited, looking up into his face as he stared out over my head. *What?* I wanted to shout. *What had you thought?*

Connor cleared his throat. "Anyway. I was used to these women who couldn't leave their rooms without hair, makeup, and three wardrobe changes. One girl I know changes her nail polish twice a day. Once for her daytime look and once for her evening look. We might have had a bet going on as to when her nails were finally going to fall off."

I laughed, turning my head down into his shoulder to avoid doing something tacky—like spit in his face.

"Now." He eased me away, straightening his cuffs before dropping his hands to his sides and stepping back. "We have a party to impress. Half of them have already noticed we're here, but now we get to really go wow them."

His hand dropped to the middle of my back and he led me toward the main room where everyone mingled in an elegant dance of casual conversation.

"Con, it's about time you showed up." A man slightly shorter and a whole lot broader than Connor slapped him on the back.

If he'd slapped me like that, I'd be face down and unconscious. But, Connor barely noticed it.

"Crowded rooms aren't exactly a favorite for me, you know." Connor ran his hand down my arm until he could slip his fingers through mine and pull me forward. "Hailey, I'd like you to meet Marcus Holder. Marcus, this is Hailey Tate. Hails is a writer."

He sounded so darn proud of the fact.

I just couldn't figure him out. Part of me liked the idea that *he* liked the idea that I was a writer. Another part worried that this was just part of the plan. That my writerliness was one more way to show people he wasn't stupid. *See? I'm smart enough to date someone who's smart enough to be a writer.*

Marcus stuck out his hand. It was huge. I wondered if they had to have special gloves made for him. My hand was basically hidden in his.

"I know," he said, surprising both of us. "My daughter was really excited when she saw the news online. You're one of her favorite writers, Miss Tate."

"Oh. That's so sweet." It never got old hearing that I wrote something someone enjoyed. That's the entire point, to give people a few hours of pleasure. "How old is your daughter?"

"Thirteen." Marcus pulled out his phone and started showing pictures. He let me know how much his daughter read and her favorite topics in school. After a few minutes, he glanced at Connor, a bit embarrassed. "I don't mean to be rude, but...Stacia sent me with a copy of her favorite book. If you have a minute before you leave, I was hoping you could sign it for her."

"Of course! Let's do it now so we don't miss each other at the end of the night."

Marcus looked so relieved I almost laughed. "Oh, thank you. If I'd come home without it, there would have been a special kind of daddy torture planned I'm sure. I considered forging your signature. The book's with my wife."

Connor just shook his head when I motioned for him to join us. "I'll grab you that champagne you wanted. You can drink it in the car."

With a quick kiss on my cheek before I could figure out if he was joking or not, he gave me a little push after Marcus. I followed him toward the far side of the room, glancing over my shoulder to see Connor watching us go. He raised his hand, a little smile playing about the edges of his lips.

In an alcove, several comfortable—not to mention expensive—looking couches crowded around a coffee table, a fireplace lit off to one side contrasting to the open French doors that led to a terrace.

"Chantelle, this is Hailey Tate."

"Oh," Her perfect features relaxed so quickly it was almost comical. "Thank goodness."

"Wow. I guess from hearing that reaction twice we know who runs the Holder house."

"You aren't kidding." The woman rose, coming toward me with an outstretched hand. Talk about former models. She was gorgeous, tall, and elegant. I felt frumpy at best standing next to her. She looked like a young Lena Horn. But, when she smiled I couldn't help but feel like I was exactly where I was supposed to be. "I'm Chantelle. Yes, that's my real name. I lucked out and became a model or I would have had to go by Sandy."

How could you not like someone who introduced herself like that?

After I signed the book, Marcus started eyeing the guys in the corner.

"Chantelle..."

"Go ahead. I'll keep Hailey company." She smiled my way. "Don't worry. I won't throw you to the wolves."

I felt myself relax, not realizing how stressed I'd been after I lost sight of Connor. "How did you know?"

"Honey, I've been doing this for sixteen years. Marcus and I have been together since high school. When those recruiters came around, I was already doing magazine shoots and making sure I was home so they weren't hooking my man up with some college coed to get him thinking the wrong way. Even after all that, *I* have no interest in navigating one of these parties on my own."

"Really?" I found it difficult to believe that someone as polished as Chantelle wasn't at home at these things by now.

"And anyway, this is better than the season premiere of *Grey's Anatomy*. Half the group is cheating, half the group is fighting to keep his job, half the group is clueless."

I may not be great at math, but even I saw the problem there. "That's an extra half."

"Oh, trust me. There's a lot of overlap. Especially in the clueless one."

Chantelle kept me company, pointing out the who's who of the team, staff, girlfriends, and wives.

"I love watching the new crop come in. They're hopeful, eager or, manipulative. The best are the ones who are manipulative trying to play hopeful but come off eager in the worst possible way. At this point, most of the girls are here to stay. At least till the next season."

I glanced away. I was officially New Crop. But even worse than that, I was Fake New Crop.

"Oh, honey. I didn't mean you. You're a totally different caliber. You're in the has-a-brain-and-isn't-using-it-for-evil category."

I was about to say something witty—or, I'm pretty sure I was—when a glance across the room caught Connor with another tall blonde. Her arm was draped across his shoulder and it looked like she was running her hand through the back of his hair. Connor, for his part, was standing there smiling at her.

Smiling. At her.

My whole body went hot. There he was, flirting with some hot woman right in front of me. I didn't know if I wanted to melt into the floor and disappear or walk across the room and stab him in the eye with those little spears they put my drink's cherry on.

"Oh." Yeah. Clever, that's me.

Chantelle turned toward where I stared at my supposed boyfriend being fondled by a bombshell.

"You better get over there."

"What?" Why should I get over there? If he wasn't going to step away, then I wasn't going to cause a scene and drag him away. That was the one deal breaker. That he didn't embarrass me. This was going to be pretty embarrassing anyway you looked at it.

"That's Trish. Trish is on the prowl for her next Nighthawk."

"Well, if she can sway him that easily, she can have him." I wrapped my hands around one another so they'd stop shaking.

Chantelle slammed her drink down on the table, her smile turning less friendly. "I don't think you get how it works here. It's not like out in the normal world. Right now, she's setting Connor up to be the center of attention in the worst possible way. Guys are probably noticing that he's over there with her instead of here with you."

"Yeah. I'm kind of noticing that myself."

"Only, the problem is, she's got him and she knows it. If he just turns and walks away or if he's rude, he's disrespected one of the senior guy's girlfriends. If he doesn't, he's trying to steal her." She cocked an eyebrow at me. "You seem less than surprised to see him with someone else."

I wasn't sure if it was an accusation or a question. I just knew it was true. I wasn't surprised. What surprised me was that Connor had made it weeks without us having this problem before.

"I'm not exactly his typical type."

Chantelle was shaking her head before I was even done talking. "That's a good thing. First, because his typical type is airheads he goes out with once. And also because when a guy diverts from type, it's for a reason. Now, get your butt over there."

There was no way I could just sit in the corner and stew. I had to go fight for "my man" against the technologically tampered-with-plastic beauty wrapped around him.

I could feel the stares as I wound my way through the room, smiling, and nodding to people who Chantelle had introduced me to. Some of the women wore Cruella de Vil smirks and were waiting for a scene or for me to just plain embarrass myself. Others looked at me and did everything but high-five me as I went by.

"Hey, Connor." I ignored the woman's hand still on him and wrapped my arm around his waist. I darn near jumped when he lashed his arm around my shoulder and pulled me into him. "Want to introduce me to your friend?"

"Hails, this is Trish. Trish is McPhee's girlfriend. She works at *Vogue*."

Vogue. Bummer. Another writer. There go all my originality points.

"Oh, you're a writer?" I smiled my most welcoming smile as I fought to not push the hand still touching Connor away.

"A writer? What a waste of time they are. I do layout designs for our cover story pages."

"That sounds interesting." Now my smile wasn't so welcoming. "So, anyway, *I'm* a writer."

Try to steal Connor, fine. Have your hands all over him, fine. Insult writers? Oh, we're going to Throw. Down.

"Really? You couldn't get a real job?"

"Why bother getting a real job when I get paid to work at home in my pajamas while I respond to fan mail? But, you must know what that's like. I'm sure you get lots of fan mail telling you that picture of those shoes was put at just the right angle."

Connor snorted and covered it up with a coughing fit.

"The hardest part of my job is all the travelling." Trish smirked. "London. Rome. Paris. It's such a struggle."

"I believe you. There's nothing like jumping time zones to age a girl quickly." Bravado was coming out of my fingertips at this point. It must have been flowing right out of Connor and into me, because I had no other idea where these words were coming from. I rushed on, "You look great, though."

And she knew she did, so what could she say?

"So, it was nice to meet you," I said and gave her a smile that would have insulted even a blind woman.

Trish stood there staring at me for a long moment before giving back a smile that threatened bodily harm if we ran into each other in a dark alley. "Have a nice evening."

She wandered away, an extra snap in her sway that had me checking to see if Connor was watching her rear end. Instead, his gaze was locked on me, that little smile still playing around his lips.

"That was awesome."

"Thanks."

I snuggled under his arm trying not to enjoy being there too much. Trying not to let the happy glow of just the two of us mean anything.

"But, Hails, where have you been? That woman had been trying to sink her claws into me for half an hour. You were supposed to come rescue me."

"Connor, you're not exactly known for fighting off the attention of beautiful women."

"Exactly." He winked at me and turned to lead us back over to where the others milled around the bar.

Well, crud.

TWENTY–THREE

MAC PULLED TO the curb outside my door and threw the car in park. I knew there was no way I was getting upstairs without Connor right behind me. Him and that stupid bag sitting in my bedroom.

I tried not to think about the extra toothbrush in my bathroom or the oversized t-shirts that still managed to be tight on him that somehow made it into my laundry basket this week.

As if I wanted to have even more stuff to carry to the basement and back.

Mac went to open his door, but Connor reached over the seat and patted him on the shoulder.

"No need to be all official with us." Connor slid out and reached back in for me.

"Thanks for the ride, Mac. I've never been driven around in such high class before." I grinned, knowing he wouldn't be insulted by my lack of fancy-schmancy'ness.

"Ms. Tate, it was an absolute pleasure. I don't think I've enjoyed driving Connor around so much before. I hope we see a lot of each other."

I took Connor's hand and let him help me out of the low car onto the sidewalk. He gave a last wave and turned me toward the building.

"You know," I started, knowing this was a losing battle. "You don't have to stay."

"Oh, I'm staying."

"It's gotta be an even harder decision knowing how uncomfortable the couch is now."

"I'm a stronger man than you give me credit for."

"Connor—"

Before I could finish whatever I was going to say to try to get America's Sexiest Athlete to not sleep at my place, a bright flash broke off to my right blinding me for a quick second.

Connor's arm went around me, tucking me into him as he rushed us toward the front door. When we got there, he stalled, realizing he didn't have keys. Another light flashed behind us.

"Hailey, your keys."

I tried not to let him see my hands shaking as I struggled to dig them out of the bottom of my tiny clutch with all that stuff shoved in it. As soon as they'd cleared the edge of my purse, he pulled them from my hand and unlocked the door, all but pushing me through it.

"Go." He gave me a small shove. "Around the corner and up a few stairs."

Flash.

"Hailey. Go."

Flash.

I rushed to the stairs and climbed three while I listened to him pull the door shut and give it a tug making sure the lock fell into place.

I sunk down on the step, shocked that this is what my life had become. Paparazzi. Who in the normal world was staked out by paparazzi?

I pictured my life narrowing down to my tiny—*cozy*—apartment for fear of dealing with the flash and click of cameras again. The loss of privacy reaching all the way to my home and invading it, pulling my private life onto tabloid pages and viral websites.

No freedom to go out alone. To walk to the gym. To throw on a cap and avoid makeup and hair and matchy-matchy clothes. To have to go the long route to see the girls or hang out at The Brew.

It narrowed and narrowed and narrowed until I was getting anxious just sitting there on the stairs.

He barreled around the corner, stopping short of stepping on me as he began to rush up the stairs.

"Hey." His voice softened, floating down to where I sat at his feet. "Hey, Hailey. It's okay. I know it takes some getting used to. And, we're so low profile, it might hit a website, but that's about it. It's not like it was *TMZ* or something."

Getting used to? I hated having my picture taken at book events when I'd had time to prepare. Having some strange guy hiding behind a post office box to take your picture in the middle of the night was just insane. I couldn't imagine any more invasions of privacy that were legal…and had the threat of becoming constant.

"I know it's a big adjustment," he continued. "I know we talked about this and you probably didn't think it was going to be an issue. This isn't what you expected even as everyone told you this was how it would be. I guess…I guess I've just learned to block it out."

"You can block that out?" My own voice sounded smaller than I expected.

"Well, block it out might be a little bit of an exaggeration." He turned and sat beside me. "But, don't forget, what I do means having my picture taken all the time. For a large part of the year, I'm on TV several times a week and that's a week where all I do is play ball."

"There aren't a lot of live book events." The joke fell flat even to my own ears.

"Well, that's true." I could hear him trying not to humor me but still stay positive. "Also, the girls I'm usually out with are with me so someone will take their picture. I typically have to stop for them. There's also the whole acting like I'm excited for whatever the purpose of the date is that night thing."

"What about when you're really dating someone?"

I thought about the way he rushed me into the building, keeping me as much out of any shot as possible while getting me out of sight, and then staying to secure the door. If he was that protective of my privacy and safety, he must go all out for his girlfriends.

Connor loosened his tie and leaned back on the stairs behind us, propping himself up on his elbows.

"Some of the women I've gone out with have become good friends, but as for really dating—the way you mean it?" He glanced away as if he didn't want to have this talk…or maybe felt guilty. "That's not what I want. I'm not that guy. I told you, I'm not looking for the white picket fence."

I thought of my brick walk-up and laughed. "Is anyone?"

"You know what I mean, Hailey." He wasn't meeting my gaze as he rambled on. "I'm not that guy. I'm not looking to settle down or for the love of a good woman. I'm not feeling lonely or less than I am because I'm not one half of a marriage or partnership. I like my life the way it is."

I stared at his overly photographed profile and realized what he was doing. He was warning me off.

"Yeah, well. I like my life the way it is too." I stood, brushing the dirt off the rear of my dress. "I like my privacy. I like coming and going as I please. I like having my space be *my* space. I like that if I allow someone in it, I know that he and I share certain priorities. So, Mr. I'm-Not-That-Guy, don't worry. I'm not looking to fence you in."

I turned and started climbing the stairs waiting to see if he'd follow me up, knowing that—in his head at least—he didn't have a lot of options.

And suddenly, I felt out of options too.

T WENTY–FOUR

I T'S THE ODDEST thing to wake up in the morning and know that the night after a real fight your fake boyfriend is asleep on the couch.

I stretched in my bed wondering how he was going to play it this morning. Wondering how *I* was going to play it.

There was too real a chance that he was going to take from last night's argument that I was looking for something from him. And that was definitely not true. I wasn't looking for a fence or a ring or even a real date. The flash of the photographer was just a reminder of how different we were and that what we wanted wouldn't ever line up.

Not that it mattered.

It would only matter if we really *were* dating. Or if we were interested in really dating.

But I wasn't stupid and he wasn't changing, so it was all good.

I got out of bed knowing I couldn't put this off all morning. Know that after an event we'd have to go out together and there'd be more pictures and we'd have to look all happy and comfortable together.

So, it was time to be reasonable.

I headed out to the living room to find Connor playing some type of game on my TV...a game I didn't own. With controllers.

"Hey. I had this delivered last night." He gave me a quick look. "I couldn't sleep."

I don't even want to know where a millionaire called to have video games delivered in the middle of the night.

"Listen—" I started and then waited for him to pause the game.

And waited.

"Connor, for real." I might have to demand my place stay a video-game-free zone.

He paused the game and tossed the controller on my table to give me what, he made clear with an exaggerated sigh, was his full attention.

"About last night—"

"Yeah, I shouldn't have—"

"No. Stop." I cut him off, knowing if I didn't go first this wasn't going to go the way I wanted it to. "I want to talk first this time. I was upset. I don't like surprises and I hate having my picture taken or being the center of attention. Together was horrible. But, here's the thing. I get it. I do. I don't want you to think that this," I waved a hand between us, "is something that's confusing me. We're friends. Great. But that's it. And, I get that. I more than get it. I *agree with it.* We're on the same page, but that doesn't mean that even as your friend I like your world. It's going to make me uncomfortable and that sucks for me."

I took in a breath, figuring that was all I had to say. Everything else, about how unbalanced our deal was and how he didn't have to do uncomfortable book stuff, wasn't going to change even if I complained about it. So, I left it where it was and hoped that Catherine was right. That at the end of the day, I was going to walk away from this with some advantages because I was beginning to wonder how I was going to walk away from this at all.

Before the flash, before everything, we'd just been feeling so...*right*. And there was nothing *more wrong* than that.

Last night's disastrous end couldn't have happened at a better time.

Connor rose from his slouch in the leather chair and stuck his hands in the pockets of his track pants.

"Right. So." He cleared his throat. "I was out of line last night. You didn't need a lecture about what kind of guy I am. You've been clear about the fact that I'm not your type. Which is great, because we're not each other's type and we can just hang and it's cool. Right? I mean, it's not often I get to just chill out with a friend. I don't want you to think I assume just because I'm me, you're going to go mad with lust and throw yourself at me."

He was saying all the right words, but part of me thought the last bit was exactly what he thought would happen. I fought back the desire to roll my eyes at him.

"Good." There was no sense arguing if he was saying the right things. "So, is there a reason we're always here? I'm betting you have a nice apartment with a guest room I could live in if I wanted to."

Because, getting him out of my space might help to keep him out of my heart.

"That's true, but I also have a housekeeper who comes in every other day, a nosy doorman who I'm pretty sure has a contact at the tabloids, and I've never had a girl stay over."

He...what?

"I'm sorry, what?"

"For real. My family stays there when they visit, but that's it. If you stayed over, they'd think we were getting married. And since we just hit their radar that might be weird even for what we're trying to pull off."

"You *never* have a girl stay over?"

"No."

"So, you always go to their house?"

"Yes."

"That's a bit..." I wasn't sure what that was.

"Guys think it's genius." Connor wasn't one to smirk, but he did now.

"Yeah, that's not the word I was looking for, but thanks for trying to help me out."

"Well, either way, that's what it would look like. And, by the time we'd be willing to have them think that, it would be time for us to break up." His gaze shifted away. Just like last night when he thought he was telling me something I didn't want to hear.

Ha! I should let him sweat it out.

I gave him the sweetest smile I could and headed toward the bathroom.

"I'm going to shower and we can go get coffee. I'm shocked you were able to have an entire conversation without caffeine." I gave him my best *in awe* look. "Impressed even."

"Right. Thanks. Glad to see *something* impresses you."

I shut the door since I didn't have a witty come back and started getting ready with Casual Outfit #7A and a new found attitude to just go with the flow.

Because, this was a ride with an end date and I wanted to enjoy every moment.

~*~

"A Parisian blend, a green tea, the banana, and a heated up chocolate muffin." Connor slipped Abby a twenty and shooed me away from the counter as if I were going to ruin his coffee experience.

Which was probably true. This was the third time we'd been in and the third special blend Connor had tried. I think he was about to hire John to make special caffeine deliveries to my place in the morning so he wouldn't have to suffer while I did things like, wake up and brush my teeth.

You know. High maintenance stuff.

I settled into my chair, picking up a copy of the paper someone had left behind and flipped through the pages, trying to find the arts and entertainment section. I loved to follow the book reviews. It wasn't the same getting the updates online. There was just something about having a newspaper in print that said chilling out on a Sunday morning.

I skipped right to the second to last page where the reviews were, hoping they'd picked up a YA. It happened so infrequently that I tried not to get frustrated. I'd considered offering to do a monthly guest post, but the idea of publicly reviewing my peers was just…bad. So very, very bad.

And potentially career damaging.

Some authors could get away with stuff like that, but not me. Jenna could. She could probably, very sweetly, tell someone that their writing was dry and unimaginative and they'd thank her. With my luck I'd be like, this is worth reading and the author would get ticked off at my heavy criticism.

"Um, Hails?"

I glanced over the top of the paper, expecting him to hand me my yummy chocolate goodness, but instead he set everything down. Reaching for the paper, he turned down the front page of the section I was holding.

"So…" He dragged the word out as he pulled the paper from my hands. "I just need to look at this for a second."

He stood, opening to the page that had caught his attention, and scanned it.

"Right." Connor cleared his throat and came around to sit in the comfy chair next to mine. "Remember how I said the picture from last night was probably an amateur and it might just hit a small website?"

I did not like where this was going. "Yes."

"Well, it might have hit the local paper." He folded the paper up and set it on his lap, his hands creased over it where I couldn't see anything.

Since our local paper was one of the biggest print papers on the east coast, this was not such a bargain. It wasn't like it was the *Tab* or something.

"How bad is it?" I pictured me with my dress all crinkled and askew, my hair falling down, makeup running, and a deer in headlight blind stare and…well, whatever else could go wrong in a photo, it was in this one.

"It depends on how you define *bad*." Connor gave me what I could only assume was a reassuring smile. Since I'd never seen one from him before, this was strictly a best guess. "Honestly, we knew this was going to happen. I'm surprised they didn't try to go through our reps first is all."

"Our reps?" I had a rep?

"Well, your agent. My business manager."

Right.

"Okay, let me see it." I reached for the paper and he held it away, just out of reach. "Connor. Seriously."

"Just, be open-minded. Now that the first piece of national gossip is out there, our people will spin it the way they want."

"Stop saying that." I could feel the panic rising up and choking me from the inside out. "I don't have *people*. I have an agent who deals with editors who try to give us horrible, cheap contracts."

"Really? They don't have a PR person or anything?" He looked confused, and for the first time, concerned.

"I don't think so. None of us is celebrity status. They don't even have in-house, film-rights agents."

"Well, that's not going to work." He stuck the paper under his thigh, a place we were both pretty sure I wasn't going to reach for it, and picked up his phone. "Amy, hey. Sorry to call on a Sunday morning. How's it going? Uh-huh. Right. And Mike?...Really?...He did? Well, that's great...Yeah. We saw it. That's why I'm calling...No, of course I'm up. Bright and early, that's how we do it at Hailey's house...Ha. Right. So, anyway, Hailey just told me she doesn't have, and I quote, *people*...I know, right? Just her agent and the woman's sole job is to be a contract pit bull...I'm not sure. But, I'm going out of town and I hate to leave her with no backup. Could you have one of the guys make a call…Yeah, play it so it looks like we're both in your house, roll it together for Dex. He'll take care of it…Great. Thanks…Oh." Connor glanced my way for the first time since picking up the phone. "Yeah, I think so too. Thanks."

Connor shoved his phone back in his pocket and turned back. "Amy is creating people for you. We'll put out a joint statement and they'll just state it as if our teams wrote it together."

This was all very nice and thoughtful and kind, but in the land of Hailandia, completely unnecessary. I needed to slow this roll before it got out of hand. "I don't think I really need people."

"Well, you might." Connor sipped at his coffee, his focus going wide for a moment. "I'm going to talk to Dex about this. I don't want you to be tsunamied when we break up and have no one to handle the media for you."

Oh, I hadn't thought about that. I just figured I'd be old news and they'd leave me alone to chase him and his next model.

He glanced at the paper again. "Plus, I'm going out of town for that first interview, and the timing is pretty bad. I don't want you to be stuck here with no resources. Especially since this guy knows where you live."

A strange man knew where I lived and Connor was going away.

I could feel my heart picking up speed and wondered just how fast it had to go before heart attack land.

"Hey." Connor took my hand and gave it a squeeze. "Don't look like that. It's going to be fine. This is what Amy does. She'll make sure you're protected and everything goes smoothly."

"Thanks. I'm glad you called her." I wasn't in a place to be prideful about making my own way.

"No problem. I can't believe Dex and Catherine didn't think of this already. Or they just figured they'd handle it as it came." He pulled the newspaper out and started to unfold it. "Ready?"

"Sure. How bad could it be?"

He held the paper up so I could see the photo. They'd been incredibly kind, picking what was one of the first shots. I looked a bit dazed, probably from the flash. Connor had all but picked me up and looked like if you got in his way he'd cut you down. The caption read, Nighthawk Gets Protective.

Connor cleared his throat and read the headline with announcer guy voice, before running through the few short paragraphs. "The Nighthawk and the Raven. I don't get it...Wait, that's your heroine, right? Raven?" He glanced my way for confirmation before diving back in. "Connor Ryan has been seen out and about with a petite writer for the last few weeks doing the most ordinary things. No cat fights or gossip mags for this girl. Hailey Tate is what we in the industry call a class act. A good girl persona of writing for children and donating her time, Ms. Tate is taking a walk on the wild side with Ryan. But will she tame the bad boy or will he sully this angel's halo?"

Connor folded the paper back up and frowned at me as if it were my fault we'd been written up.

"What?"

He was glaring at the far wall and I wasn't sure he was going to answer me at first.

"They make you sound too good for me."

I tried not to laugh, but it was kind of sweet to have him notice.

"No. They just said I wasn't a cat-fighting floozy."

And that I'm too good for him.

"Yeah." He reached for his coffee, obviously still put out. "Whatever."

Nothing like a grown man pouting.

TWENTY-FIVE

"HELLO?" I GLANCED at the clock. Who in their right mind would be calling at 2:53 in the morning?

"Hey. Did I wake you up?"

"Connor?"

"Yeah."

Well, that answered that question. Someone not in his right mind.

"Is something wrong?" I shifted, trying to wake up, worried something had happened, that he was stuck somewhere.

He was traveling and anything could have happened. Would his new, mysterious *people* be able to take care of things in other towns?

"No. You know I'm just..."

"You're just what?"

"I'm just..."

Seriously, he did not wake me up to say the same half-sentence over and over?

"Connor, it's the middle of the night."

"Oh. Yeah. Well." I heard a gush of breath as if he was pushing all the air out of his lungs at once. His words were soft and had the slight slur of sleep like he was exhausted but couldn't rest. "Sorry. I couldn't sleep."

I squished my pillow up behind me and sat up, pulling the blankets with me.

"How was the interview?"

Connor laughed, a light, breathy sound like he was trying to swallow it instead of letting it out. "Different."

"That's all? Different?"

"Well, I'm used to guys asking me about the models I go out with, but it's usually more of a guy thing. Like, once I got asked if Genevieve Alexander's boobs were real."

"*Oh.*" Well, that would make for an interesting conversation. And… "Are they?"

"Seriously, Hails?" He was laughing now, his voice less worn. "How would I know?"

"Well, you went out with her."

"We went to a charity event as a set up. I told you. I don't sleep with all those girls." He made a sharp *pfft* sound on the other end of the line. "What am I, some eighteen year old rookie?"

He sounded insulted that people assumed he was sleeping with a different model every week. That was just a different level of guydom.

"So what did they ask you this time? Oh, and, by the way. Just to clear it up in case it's ever an interview question. My boobs? Totally real. Not worth a multimillion-dollar insurance policy impressive, but still, real."

"I kind of figured no one invested thousands in A-cups."

"Hey, mister. These are Bs. Definitely Bs." I rolled to my side, staring at the dim light coming through my curtains. "Someone just measured me during that great Hailey-needs-a-new-look shopping spree."

I let him laugh at my expense, wondering what was wrong that had him calling me in the middle of the night. Wondering who this girl was in my skin flirting with him in the dark.

"They asked me a lot of questions about us. Like how we met and how long had we secretly been dating and how serious we were and what it was like to date someone like you."

"Someone like me?" I wasn't sure I was going to like this one.

"Yeah, you know."

"Um, no?"

"*You know.*" He drew it out like I was being dense. "Someone who's famous for her brain."

I was famous for my brain. Huh.

Of course, I wasn't really famous. Most writers weren't. It took a ridiculous number of books and movies or television shows sold to become famous. But still, it added to the warm fuzzy night-talk feeling I had.

"What did you say?"

"I told them we'd been dating a while, that we kept it quiet because you weren't comfortable being called one of my flavors of the week on every tabloid out there. And, that I didn't mind because I knew you weren't a flavor of the week and I could just wait you out. And that you were the funniest, smartest, nicest girl I knew. And that brainy girls were a different level of sexy."

Oh.

Wow.

Even if he was just saying those things, it was still really sweet. Exactly what I'd want him to say if he'd meant it.

"Then the rest was just sports talk." He cleared his throat, a move I was realizing he did when he was uncomfortable. "Nothing you want to hear about."

"Maybe I do." I was thinking I could listen to his voice lull me back to sleep, let it wrap around me in the dark until even RBIs sounded sweet and sexy.

He chuckled again. Maybe he did think I was funny.

"Do you want to do something tomorrow when I get back?"

"The tomorrow in a few hours or the real tomorrow after I sleep-recover from this?"

"The real tomorrow. It looks like they booked me an extra day here for some reason. I'm not flying back till tomorrow morning. Why, you have a hot date tonight?"

"Yup."

"What?" The sleepiness left his voice, quick, like he'd just come to. "You do?"

"Yup. Fifteen teenage girls. My pre-launch party is tonight. They get the book before it comes out on Tuesday. There'll be a few local bookstore owners and some bloggers there too. It's the final book in my series that hit the *USA Today Bestseller List* so we're doing it up big."

"Wow." He actually sounded impressed. "Look at you Ms. Big Time Author."

"I know, right?" It never got old getting to hang out with teen readers.

"So, you should be getting your beauty sleep right now." He stopped and with the long pause it felt like he was going to say something else. But, instead he just said, "Sorry I woke you up."

"It's okay."

"Sleep well. I'm sure you'll knock it out of the park tomorrow."

There was nothing like a good baseball analogy for a book signing.

TWENTY–SIX

I STOOD ON the threshold, afraid of what I'd find. A death-dark flower dripping a dim glowing nectar called to me from across the room. No matter how I fought, I couldn't break free of its spell. The Professor had warned me not to come here. But after two years of fighting all those things that crept past good people's houses each night, the things that killed and stole and haunted, how could I know the evil behind this door was more than anything I'd ever faced—anything I'd ever even heard of.

'Raven!'

As soon as I heard his voice, I knew. I knew who it was and I knew the right man had come for me.

I closed the book with a snap to a chorus of *no* coming from the girls sitting on the floor around me. I rested the book on my lap and smiled.

"I know. You've been waiting for a lot of books to find out who she picks. Michael or Priam. The bad news is, I'm not going to tell you. The good news is that Mary from the bookstore has a book for each of you before you leave."

As soon as I'd said the words *good news* they guessed what was coming.

"You all just have to promise not to give the ending away since people are still waiting for it."

After everyone had raised her right hand and taken a solemn oath to never tell the ending of the book, the bookstore brought out cupcakes for everyone while I did a question and answer period.

"But, if Priam has lived twelve lives, he's at the end of the zodiac, what happens to his next life?"

"That's a great question...and maybe you'll find out when you read *One Last Tomorrow*."

"Excuse me." A deep voice came from the back of the reading area. Connor. Leaning against the doorframe, his carry-on sitting at his feet. "But, what kind of girl is this Raven chick? Michael and Priam both sound like good guys. Is she just leading them on?"

The gasps from the group around me would have put an end to that line of questioning from anyone else. But not Connor.

"I mean, how long has this been going on?" Connor asked.

"Mister," a little voice piped up from the front row. "You don't understand. She loves them both."

"Yeah." One of the chattier girls threw in. "She has so much in common with Michael, but she and Priam have lived other lives together. You can't just discount that."

"But Michael is always there for her." Another girl added, making the battle lines very clear. "He never lets her down. He isn't all, *Oh. I'm Mr. Mysterious. I can't be here for you all the time. You can't trust me.*"

"But he wants her to trust him. He just has other responsibilities."

"If he loved her, he'd be there for her like Michael. He'd always be there for her."

"See?" Connor jumped in before the Michael/Priam contingents came to blows. "If he really cared for her, he'd always be there for her."

He glanced up and smiled at me.

It took a moment to break free from that gaze, but I held my hand up, knowing how teenagers could get when they were passionate about something. I wished I could bottle their passion, but right now I was too flabbergasted.

"Well, girls. Mr. Ryan seems to be on Team Michael. I'm sure one or two of you might want to put that on your blog. Maybe he'll answer a few questions after the cupcakes. In the meantime, feel free to get your book from Mary and if anyone wants me to sign it, they're setting up a table in the corner."

They moved in a flash, rushing Mary as if she was going to run out of books. She had the bookstore staff handing out cupcakes with ravens on them and trading cards with Michael, Priam, and some of the villains over the last couple years.

"So..." I grinned as Connor picked his way through discarded jackets and backpacks to where I sat. "Team Michael, huh?"

"Team Hails." He reached down and pulled me up from my cross-legged seat on the floor. "Wow. You're amazing at this. You had them eating out of your hands."

Before I knew it, he'd kissed me. Just a quick sweep of his lips across mine, but my knees almost gave out and dropped me back down.

"What are you doing here?" I asked, recovering as quickly as possible. "You weren't supposed to be back until tomorrow afternoon."

"I wasn't going to miss your big night. Why didn't you tell me about this? You just said we had a dinner for the launch with your friends."

"It's—"

"Hailey, is this your boyfriend?" A small, suspicious voice interrupted from just behind Connor's elbow. "The baseball player guy?"

Wow. If the news had even trickled down to my readers, we were definitely in Couple City.

"How'd you hear about that?" I asked.

"My brother is a huge fan. He says you should date more actresses. Or another one of the girls on Big Brother. But I told him Hailey was wicked pretty and her books are my favorite." She grinned up at Connor and darn it all if she didn't bat her little thirteen-year-old eyelashes. "Then, when he said no you weren't, I hit him with one of your hard covers."

And I hadn't believed the publisher when she said hard covers had more diversity.

"That's very sweet of you, but maybe not so much with the hitting."

"Will you sign my book?"

"Of course."

Connor kissed my cheek and stepped away. "I'll let you go make dreams come true."

He worked his way back to his luggage, stopping for each girl interested and brave enough to challenge him and explain Raven and her love interests. I couldn't help but watch him as he headed toward the closed café at the front of the store and disappeared behind a bookshelf, most likely sinking into one of the overstuffed chairs.

I hadn't realized I'd missed him until he was here and gone again, the surprise of it all catching me off my stride and throwing me off my game.

Wow. Even I was thinking in baseball analogies now.

TWENTY–SEVEN

CONNOR TOOK THE cab back to my place and
got out...probably force of habit because he was so
exhausted.

Now, I was curled up in the corner of my couch, my feet
stuck under Connor's leg, one of his arms wrapped around
my calves the other holding the glass of the scotch.

"Why have you never had me come over to your place?"
It suddenly seemed important now that he'd invaded every
corner of my life, I'd never gone anywhere into his that
wasn't related to the deal. Maybe he was afraid it would be
harder to get rid of me when this was over. "I mean,
regardless of the paparazzi-partnering doorman, now that
we're tabloid fodder. Not to stay over, just to see it."

"Why would you want to go there?" I know he was tired
from the insane trip back to go to my launch party, but it
seemed like a pretty straightforward question.

"I don't know. I mean, why wouldn't I? Is there a reason
you haven't had me over?"

"Yes."

Oh, dear.

"It's big and spacious and cold. It's much nicer here. I have a nosy doorman. There's an elevator that you have to be nice to people for like fifteen floors. I've barely decorated. And you would mock my TV." He took another sip and rolled his head to look my way. "Your apartment has made me think about downsizing. As long as I have a guest room for my folks, that's all I need. It's not like I throw big parties or anything. I don't like to bring all that schmoozing home with me. So, you'd probably hate my place."

Yeah. I'm sure I'd totally hate the three-million-dollar penthouse overlooking the river that was featured on *Million Dollar Views* last year.

Not that I Googled it or anything.

"So, you like it better here?"

That seemed too simple.

"Yup. Remember? Cozy." He tilted his head back again, his eyes half-shut.

No matter how happy I was to see him, it was going to have to be bedtime before he passed out and dropped that glass.

I slid my feet out from under him and stretched before getting up to go get his blanket.

When I turned back, he was standing in my bedroom doorway.

"Hails, I'm sleeping in that bed with you. I'm exhausted and jet lagged and I'm keeping my clothes on, but I am sleeping there."

He stood there, half challenging me, half waiting for me to say yes or no. He looked dead on his feet, partially because he raced back to celebrate with me. My friends and Catherine didn't even go to my closed events anymore. They were having the launch dinner for me next week. And so, Connor had been the only adult there just to support me for no reason to do with money.

"Fine."

I grabbed my pajamas and changed in the bathroom, washing my face and brushing my teeth and wondering if I'd lost my mind.

When I came out, Connor was folding down the covers on the far side of the bed wearing those mesh shorts again.

Only the mesh shorts.

"You said you'd keep your clothes on.

"These are clothes."

"Where are the rest of them?"

"Hails, the important stuff is covered." He crawled into the far side and fluffed the pillow I usually threw at his head in the living room. "Get in bed."

I knew it was a bad idea as I slid under the covers and reached for the bedside lamp. Nothing good came of sharing a bed with someone you were attracted to. And darn him. It was bad enough he was so good looking. But showing up at my event, calling me just because, kissing me—no matter how casually—it just wasn't going to end up with me in a good place.

I turned away, hoping to just fall asleep.

"Hails. You need to calm down. I'm not going to molest you in your sleep. If I haven't slapped you on your rear end yet, I think you're safe for one night."

He was absolutely right. The more I thought about it, the more stupid I felt. Of course he wasn't going to jump me.

One, he'd promised. And, two, it wasn't how he was wired. So, everything was good in the world.

I was just getting comfortable as an arm was thrown across me. Before I could say anything, Connor was already pulling me up against him.

"Stop freaking out." He sounded half asleep, already fading out. "I'm going to end up wrapped half around you once I'm asleep anyway. Might as well get it out of the way."

Before I could figure out how to respond, he was snoring.

I laid awake, trying to not cuddle back and questioning if it were cuddling if only one person was doing it.

Eventually, I closed my eyes and just enjoyed the feel of his heat at my back and the warm strength of him holding me.

I'd let tomorrow worry about tomorrow.

TWENTY-EIGHT

I BARELY SLEPT as I focused on staying on my side of the bed. This had "accidental cuddle" written all over it, and I really didn't need to go there. Friends don't cuddle friends in their sleep. Unless they were Connor. With his amazing way of seeing things, him cuddling was okay. Me cuddling meant I wanted an engagement ring.

But, when I woke up, my bed was empty and I was wrapped around my pillow just like always.

Voices were coming from my living room. Because I wasn't nuts about someone being in my house who I didn't know, I considered texting Connor from my room. The upside was, I could throw something over my Becca-approved pajamas—Yes, Becca bought me PJs. She also bought me non-sleepwear PJs, if you get what I'm saying. Those were stuffed in the back of my closet, in the bag, with the tags still on, because friends also didn't let friends wear inappropriate *sleepwear*.

"I did that. It still doesn't taste the same." Connor's voice slipped through the door sounding frustrated.

I ran a brush through my hair as I listened for the muffled response. It sounded high and fast. Was Jenna here? I found it hard to believe she'd just be hanging out with Connor while I slept.

"Right. Okay, so I've put those in the oven and I split the two K-cups." Something banged shut. "Wait, the oven isn't warm. I put the little preheat button…"

Mumble, mumble, mumble.

I snuck down the hall and peeked around the corner to see Connor glaring at his phone.

"I did. Why isn't the oven warm?"

"Did you pick a temperature and set the timer and everything?" Abby's voice asked over speakerphone. "I should have known you'd need the cooking virgin directions."

"Don't mock me, Abigail."

I smothered a laugh as Connor pulled a muffin tray back out of the oven and dropped it on the counter.

"You're extremely mockable, Connor," Abby taunted.

"Can I just stick these in the microwave?" I watched him slide a glance at the appliance like it might solve whatever issues he was having.

"No. You can't. Also, your pan is probably metal." Abby sighed as if this were the biggest struggle ever. "I told you to just come down here and get her a muffin, but nooooo. You want to be all Cute Morning-After Guy."

"Hey! That's not what this is," Connor sounded almost as annoyed by that as by the betrayal of his beloved microwave. His head jerked up, as he realized what he'd said. "I mean—"

"Dude, trust me," Abby interrupted. "I'm not an idiot. You guys aren't dating. It's a secret. Dane wants to kick your butt and Jenna's watching you, and you're—"

"Um…" Connor picked up the phone and took it off speaker. "What do you mean?"

He nodded and scowled and checked the oven to see how warm it was.

"Abby, you get the weirdest ideas." He forced a smile as if Abby could see him. "You need to get out more."

I could hear her high-pitched voice memer-memer-memering from where I'd snuck to the edge of the counter to watch as Connor continued to scowl.

"It is not cute," he declared. "We're just friends. And, she likes muffins…Right…So, once the oven is warm, put them in for how long?…*That long*?…Fine, right. Okay. Thanks. And, Abby?" He waited for her reply. "Not a word of any of this, got it?"

He hung up the phone, shaking his head as he did and went back to the Keurig that had magically appeared in my apartment. He better figure out where that thing was getting stored, because it wasn't on my counter top. I stood there, wondering what was going on and if I should just go back to bed while my—hopefully edible—muffin baked. But, just as I was thinking of slipping back to my room, Connor caught me out of the corner of his eye.

"Hey, Hails." His smile was surprised, like he didn't expect me to be up yet. "I figured after your big night you'd sleep in a bit."

"It's almost nine." Which *was* sleeping in.

Connor glanced at the clock then back at the oven before mumbling, "Exactly how long is it supposed to take to make muffins?"

Since I'm pretty sure this question was rhetorical, I wandered over to the counter and pulled out a stool, waiting to see what exactly was going on. Connor turned to the sink and worked through rinsing everything and putting them in the tiny dishwasher squeezed next to my fridge.

"I was making you a muffin." He looked almost guilty as he explained.

"I heard." I waited for him to expound, but instead he just went back to cleaning the kitchen.

Don't get me wrong, after I'd gotten over the cuteness of pro-athlete sized Connor trying to bake in my tiny kitchen, I'd wondered who was going to clean this mess up. But, now that he was doing it, I was more curious about what was going on.

"Connor, you didn't have to make me a muffin." Because, four blocks away were the best muffins on Earth, but why set the bar impossibly high. I'd settle for "edible and didn't light the kitchen on fire" at this point.

"I know."

Well, that didn't give me a lot to work with.

"Okay, let's try this a different way." I waited until he glanced my way and went on. "Connor, why are you up early, making me a muffin?"

His nose squished up in a way that made him look much younger and he set the sponge down and came to stand across the counter from me.

"You know the other day, the fight we had?" He asked as if our post-paparazzi throw down was easily forgotten.

"Yes." I hoped this wasn't his way of fixing something we'd already gotten past. I didn't want to go backward.

"And, how we talked about being friends?"

"Yes." Now I was worried he was going to brush me off for good.

Maybe he realized he had opened the door for something he didn't want. Our time was almost over. He's probably trying to soften the blow that we're not *really* friends. As if I don't know this.

But, he should have waited until the last day. Which was tomorrow, but I wanted to enjoy my last day. Maybe he just wanted to get it out of the way, though, instead of waiting and then being all, *Hey, this was great and I'll see you around but probably not.* Maybe even roll it into the whole fake breakup thing. *You know, we can't really hang out because people think we broke up.*

I slid my hands down my pajama-covered thighs, realizing I was sweating a bit. How was I supposed to be friends with someone who announced ahead of time we weren't really friends?

"Well," he drew the word out like he didn't know where he was going to go from there. "I just wanted to say...thanks."

"Thanks?" The shock in my voice came through so clear, I smiled to try to lessen the blow.

"Yeah. I know this is lame, but I don't have a lot of friends. My brother, a few guys from home, and a couple from my old team. But..." He ran his hand through his hair, the pink staining his cheeks giving away his discomfort even more. "I told you I burned a lot of bridges on my old team. That means that no one here wanted to take a chance on me until they saw if I was going to be an as—a jerk. It's been nice to have a friend. I just, you know, wanted to say that."

"Oh." I guess I shouldn't have been surprised. It had to be hard being in the spotlight all the time and not knowing who was a real friend. And, he'd been honest about the bridges thing.

Part of me was amazingly flattered and thankful. It's not often someone so private—because he was about the important stuff like his family—and so untrusting would welcome me into his world as a friend.

The other part of me took the hit. It was one thing to know it, and another thing to hear it. But still, the place he'd offered me, it was valuable—coveted even—and not easily earned. So, I'd cherish it for what it was.

"Well, then, at least we got something out of this whole mess, right?" I asked. "I could use another friend myself. I mean, you've basically met all my friends. Writers are hard to be friends with. In three weeks I have to start writing my next book after I finish this outline and, trust me, that's a whole different Hailey. Then, when deadlines come around…Yeah, that's known as the breakup segment of the writing cycle because the hours and focus are nuts."

"Like the playoffs." He grinned, seeming pleased with himself to have found a correlation.

"Sure. That makes sense." I smiled back, taking in a breath of the chocolate scent starting to come from my oven. "So, this is good."

He gave me a smile so sincere it almost broke my heart. No wonder the guy didn't believe in picket fences. If he couldn't find people he trusted to be a friend, how could he trust anyone in further than that?

Right. Good.
Yeah.

TWENTY-NINE

I DID A once-over of the outfit Becca had suggested.
She'd been a bit melancholy when I told her what the
occasion was. I doubt she ever had to put together a
last-date outfit. But, in her line of business, anything was
possible. Plus, I think following us online had convinced her
we'd get a happily ever after. And, if we could convince
Becca, who was in on it from the beginning, we could
probably convince just about everyone.

Now, if I could just keep from convincing myself I'd be all
set.

The door buzzed and I let Connor in even though I'd
given him a key after the first paparazzi incident. I'd never
wanted to leave him standing out there vulnerable. But, if
there was no reason for him to worry, he always rang the
buzzer.

It was a simple thing that made me feel like he appreciated
the fact that this was my space.

I opened the door, my heart flipping over more than a little at the sight of him. Somewhere along the line he'd stopped being the media sensation and had just become Connor.

And that was more dangerous than anything else.

He smiled down at me, looking as at ease as ever.

"You look beautiful." His gaze traveled over me in an assessment far less critical than the one I'd just given myself.

I gave a little snort as I reached for my jacket and scarf knowing the night air wasn't what it had been even a few weeks ago. The leaves were rushing off the trees, fall was rushing toward winter, and we were rushing to a finish.

"Hailey." He grabbed my hand, tugging me back around to face him as I went to grab my bag. "You look beautiful."

I looked up at him, really looked and saw there was nothing but sincerity in his gaze. So honest that I couldn't even bring myself to throw out a comment about how we met or the women he dated. Instead, I stood there, enjoying the compliment and living for once in the moment of appreciation.

"Thank you."

"You're welcome." He laughed before adding, "Was that so hard?"

I rolled my eyes. Leave it to Connor to challenge me with a compliment.

We got to the stoop and he reached out and wrapped my glove-covered hand in his, turning me down the sidewalk.

"I thought we'd walk. It's only a couple blocks."

I nodded, feeling stilted and slow. Feeling like a woman walking to her own execution.

Everyone had warned me. Even Catherine, once I was too far in to care, had tried to pull me out of this emotional nose-dive. But, knowing it was too late, I decided to enjoy our last evening out together. The idea that after everything we'd been through together we'd be this uncomfortable was ridiculous.

I gave his hand a squeeze and asked, "Are you excited about the SportsCenter thing?"

He glanced down, blinking as if I'd pulled him out of another world. With a shake of the head, he gave me a Connor-smile that began to feel like it was just for me.

"Honestly? I'm really nervous." He rolled his eyes at himself as if to make his statement less important. "It's a great opportunity. It's basically a job interview. If you can't pull off a guest spot, there's no way you could carry a host position."

"And you're thinking that's what you want to do?" I guess I hadn't considered what he'd do when his career on the field was done.

"Maybe. I had thought…" He glanced away looking, for the first time ever, embarrassed.

"What?" There was no way I was letting him off the hook with that blush creeping up his neck. Maybe he'd hoped to be an actor or a Playgirl bunny. Were the male versions bunnies too? That seemed a little emasculating.

"I had thought I'd coach." He shrugged, and glanced away, not meeting my gaze. "But, I'm afraid maybe I burned too many bridges. A coach needs a good reputation and starting out, coming off the field, mine isn't that hot."

"You still have time to turn that around. I'm sure the next couple years you could work with some of the younger guys and see if it's even something you like."

I wanted to add, don't head out and sleep with the first leggy blonde you see after I leave on book tour, but that seemed a little proprietary. And, also, not the Connor I'd come to know.

That was just my fear talking.

I was going to have to stop watching TV. And stay off the Internet. And have my groceries delivered so I didn't get bombarded with tabloids.

This was going to be a long recovery.

I didn't want to talk about what this month had done for me. It wasn't something that was measurable. It made me want things, things I thought were further down the road for me. Things I had assumed would take a backseat to my writing career 'til I could hopefully build a stronger foundation and get another series or a movie deal, or something.

Things I was realizing I wanted with Connor.

My love for Connor had snuck in like a soft breeze on a summer's day—so light and refreshing that it was just what you needed and you didn't even notice it until you felt better.

He'd become My First.

Not like the *first* people talk about. But my first for all the important now stuff. The person I wanted to tell things to first and call first and talk to first in the morning and hear his news first and be there for him when he needed support before he reached out to others.

It was not something I'd expected. As much as Connor had warned me, he had warned me about something ridiculous and not real. Something that would never happen. An infatuation would have been a relief, but what I felt for him was so much more solid than that.

Walking to our last date felt like walking to my own ending, because Connor had become such a part of me that when he was gone, part of me would surely be dead.

And I doubted the loss would be as soft-footed as the falling.

"And what about you, Hails? Is it making a difference for you?"

I watched my feet move, one in front of the other, down the dust-grey sidewalk, ignoring how his voice had turned serious. Because, yes. It was making a difference for me and I was going to have to figure out what to do with that now.

I'm not even sure how I answered him, but the joke I made seemed to fall flat.

Neither of us seemed in the mood for funny.

We got to dinner and were seated right away—the magic of the celebrity reservation.

I'd sure miss that.

There was a script, we were supposed to play it out. A little bit melancholy, still happy to be with one another but both of us worried about where this was going.

It wasn't hard to act out since it was almost true. Except I did know where it was going.

Connor reached across the table and took my hand, pulling my attention back from the flashbacks of the last few weeks running through my head.

"Hey." He whispered it before getting up and moving his chair around to sit next to me. "This is…this sucks. Hails, this just sucks. I know the plan and I get it. I even know that it's right that we play it out like this, but that doesn't mean we can't be friends any more, right?"

"Of course." Because what was I supposed to say? *No, I'm sorry. Being friends with you might kill me?*

"I mean, I need you, Hailey. You're one of my best friends and I don't think that if you were going to kick me out of your life now I'd be okay with that." He ran a hand through his hair, giving it a tight tug at the end. "Of course I'd be okay with that. I'm not like a friend-stalker guy or anything but…when I told you how limited my friend pool was, that was true. Some of it's my job. Some of it's bad choices I made. But, Hailey, you're one of those few people I trust. I'm *glad* we've gotten to know each other."

"Me too." I nearly whispered it because it was true. My heart was breaking but it was true.

"So, we'll do the rest of this. You'll go on your book tour. I'll go do that guest host gig. We'll stick to the plan and maybe in a couple weeks we could do something. You know, hang out?"

"Sure."

That was a lie. That was a bald-faced lie. For a moment I feared he saw through it and realized that when he left, when he took his little bag home with him tonight, that was the last time I'd see him for a long time. Distance and time were going to have to do their job getting me over him before I could consider seeing him again.

We sat there, his hand wrapping mine tight in its shell as he waited for the bill to come. The walk home was just as quiet. Neither of us talking but the heat of his hand seeping through my thin, fall gloves to warm my palm. He followed me up to my apartment, where his bag was sitting on the table next to the door waiting for him.

He glanced around, as if taking it all in for the last time. No matter what he had said in the restaurant it seemed like he was saying goodbye too.

"So, we're taking off tonight." He stared ahead, his gaze going straight past my shoulder as if the most interesting thing in the world was in the kitchen. "I texted Gavin when we left. He should be downstairs in a few."

"Great. That's good." I stood as still as possible, trying not to break. "I'm glad he's going with you. New York's a lot of fun."

"Yeah." Connor dropped the bag and stepped to me, pulling me into a tight, solid hug that went on until my body finally relaxed against his. "Thanks, Hails. Thanks for everything."

I didn't know what everything was, but I knew if it was even a portion of my everything, he felt like he was losing something. Maybe not his heart or a friend. Maybe just a favorite pair of shoes. But still.

"Have a safe trip." I gave him the warmest smile I could, opening the door and hoping that he'd be safely down to the lobby before I started to cry.

He looked at me like I'd just hurt him. Like there was something else I was supposed to say. Maybe the script I thought we were going off of wasn't the same one he had. But, as far as I knew, this was when he left and didn't look back.

This was when I got ready to leave on book tour in a few days and hoped that the hectic schedule and the time away made coming home to my suddenly huge apartment seem bearable.

He pulled his bag over his shoulder and crossed to the door, pausing to look down at me.

"I'll talk to you later." He made a declaration. One I wanted to believe.

I gave him a nod and a smile, not trusting myself to speak.

"Hails." He laughed, filling the apartment with that Connor light again. Who knows what he was thinking, but I glanced away. Not wanting to have this conversation any more.

Before I knew it, he'd kissed me on the cheek and headed down the stairs.

I listened, standing with my body leaning out the doorway of my apartment as if it wanted to follow him but was anchored there in the real world. After a moment, his feet on the stairs silenced, then the echoey click of the front door falling shut. I ran to my window, wanting to make sure he wasn't left standing there just in time to see him climb into a dark SUV and it pull away.

I sat down, waiting to feel grief or whatever it was a person felt when their pretend romance ended and they realized they were actually in love with the idiot.

Instead I just felt sad. A tiny, overused word for a huge, gaping emotion.

~*~

The phone rang a few hours later and I figured it was Jenna checking in. Maybe making sure I hadn't joined a convent or any other ridiculous thing. But, when I glanced at the screen, Connor's name lit it up.

My hand almost immediately went to accept the call, but stopped when my brain kicked in. I wanted the time to figure out how to deal with him and be fair to both of us. To be fair to the man who had warned me in more ways than words that he wasn't a long-term relationship guy.

After a moment, the voicemail indicator dinged and I stared at the hunk of electronics in my hand silently mocking me.

Since I had already proven I was a glutton for punishment, I pulled up my voicemail.

"Hey, Hails." Connor sounded normal. As if we'd just had dinner and he was on a trip with his brother…and we'd see each other again soon. "Just wanted to let you know we got here. I'm taking Gavin to that restaurant you talked about. He's being what I think you'd call mopey guy because of his most recent dating disaster, but I'm glad he came." There was a long pause as if he was confused or looking for words. "Just wanted to call you before you left tomorrow."

There was some mumbled shouting in the background that sounded an awful lot like Gavin giving him a rough time. Then the phone got quiet and scratchy as I pictured Connor holding it against his jacket.

"Seriously, jackass." Connor shouted. "Shut up."

I laughed, listening to the two of them bicker before the phone cleared and Connor came back.

"Sorry about that. Anyway. Hope you're all set for your trip. I'll talk to you after mine."

The phone went dead and I hit nine to save it because—as we've established—I'm a glutton for punishment.

THIRTY

TURNED OUT, I was even more of a glutton for punishment than I thought, because there I was sitting in my illegally gained leather chair, wrapped in a blanket with a Whiskey Neat watching SportsCenter.

Alone.

Because Connor was going to be on. He was still on the road doing all the good PR Dex had wrung from our *relationship*. And tonight was his guest run as a host. The World Series was over and apparently getting the gig of post mortem on the season was a big deal. The first step into post-ball retirement as a commentator.

And here I was watching it.

Because I was an idiot.

I didn't understand a quarter of what they talked about, but it was clear that Connor was engaging, knowledgeable, and fair-minded. Even when he was critiquing one of the teams, he did it in a way that felt more like sharing a secret with them than blasting their errors. There was that legendary charm.

"So, Connor," a huge gentleman in a very nice suit grinned in a way I completely didn't trust. "It's been great having you here, but we didn't discuss the *highlights* from your season. And we have just enough time to do that."

Connor gave him a pained grin and I knew what was coming.

My phone dinged. I ignored it, wanting to see what was about to happen.

It dinged again, which was never good.

Turn it off.

I know you're watching it.

Jenna. Figured.

I texted back, wanting to be left alone. *I'm working. Too much to do.*

DING. *Fine. Call me tomorrow.*

"Well," Connor deflected. "I had some great highlights between my move to the Nighthawks or maybe that ninth inning homer against the Sox."

He winked at them as if they were in on a joke that was funny and not a near career-ending incident.

"We might just have a highlight reel." The man smiled again and I wondered if all reporters were just evil at the core and should be avoided at all costs.

A clip of Connor during his first game with the Nighthawks came up. To be fair, they showed a bunch of great highlights of him making some gravity defying moves. Then a few more game shots. Then, because grown men could be as mean as thirteen-year-old girls, the shot of Ackerman coming off the bench at Connor in what would become the season defining moment after the alleged elevator incident.

Then, as if that had never happened, a quick collage of photos that had to be from social media of the two of us out, then Connor—his face tightened in anger I hadn't noticed that night—rushing me into my building after the paparazzi had jumped out of the bushes. More of us, us, us everywhere. And all the shots of us looking happy and relaxed. A completely different Connor than the intent focused one from the game shots.

"Word on the street is you and Hailey Tate are taking a break. Any truth to that, Connor? And, if so, how is that going to impact your time with the team? I know they're focusing more on the whole *family values* thing. The thing is, without Ms. Tate, you're just another playboy ballplayer." The guy grinned at Connor as if he hadn't just said words that ripped my heart out. As if the end of a relationship was just another piece of news, something to cover while we waited for the next sports event on the calendar. As if lives weren't changed or hurt or healed by being separated from someone you had cared about.

I took another sip of Connor's scotch, curled up in the chair watching for him to tell the world he'd moved on.

"Well," Connor's open, easy persona dropped for the first time all night. "It wouldn't surprise anyone, would it?"

I was pretty sure that someone snuck in and stabbed me with an invisible knife at that point. I hadn't expected Connor to revert so quickly. To use me as his media shield.

The man across the shiny counter from him laughed. Of course he did.

"Hailey Tate is so far out of my league that I'm surprised she's put up with me for as long as she has." Connor shifted, making sure his gaze came right through the camera, that charm-boy smile fleshing out his face. "I'm not exactly the guy who knows how to make relationships work and with two schedules as crazy as ours, it's not going to be easy. But, I am a man who knows when something is worth the effort."

He gave another one of his smiles, the one that said this-conversation-is-over, and transitioned them back to post-season discussion.

And I died a little more.

DING.

Call me!

I stared at my phone afraid of the I-told-you-so's that were going to be coming my way. I tossed the phone across the room, not wanting to see whatever Jenna texted next.

DING.

See? And I totally wasn't getting up to go get it. No matter if I—

DING.

Oh, for the love of stars. Seriously. I wasn't getting up.

The phone, sticking out from under the entertainment center, started to ring, vibrating itself across the floor. I had a feeling it had come to either answer the phone or answer the door. And, since it was raining out I went and grabbed the phone figuring Jenna didn't need to be wandering the streets at night in the rain.

"Is this Jovi's? Is my pizza here?" I asked, trying to throw her off the fact that I'd collapsed in a hot mess of tears a few minutes ago.

"Really? You were so busy ordering pizza you couldn't text me back?" And the little dictator was in full swing.

"Jenna? Well, this is a disappointment. Unless you're outside holding a meat lover's with ricotta cheese."

"Please." Even her snorts were delicate. "Some of us would rather not have to spend hours a week on torture devices to keep a relatively reasonable figure."

Right. Because the tiny girl needed to think about her figure.

"I know why you're calling." I figured I might as well just head it all off. "Yes, I watched it. Yes, I heard what he said about me. No, I'm not stupid enough to assume he means it. Especially since it was in response to a question about his career falling apart if he went back to his non-picket-fence ways."

"His what?" Jenna asked, obviously thrown off like I'd hoped for.

"Picket fence. He says he's not a picket fence guy." I listened to the silence on the other end of the phone. "You know. Not a guy who is ever going to settle down. Etcetera, etcetera, etcetera."

"Right. Because you've always been aiming at the whole picket fence thing. You're a city girl. We've never even talked about if you want kids to go inside a picket fence that you don't want."

"Jenna, you know it's a metaphor. Stop being difficult."

"I'm not being difficult."

Yeah, right.

"So, anyway." I anti-segued. "Good talk. Gotta go."

"Oh, no. No you don't." In the background, something made a heavy dull thud of a sound, and Jenna made the appropriate painful reply before refocusing back on me. "Hailey, are you sure?"

"Sure about what?" Because this time she'd lost me.

"Are you sure about Connor?" She asked before rushing on. "Because, what if, and I know this is the last thing you want to hear, but what if he meant it? What if he wants to make this work?"

The problem was, it *wasn't* the last thing I wanted to hear. It was the thing I wanted most in my world right now. Maybe the thing I'd ever wanted most, making my first book deal fall to a very close second place.

"Don't do this." I meant to sound strong, to demand it. But instead it came out as a whispered plea. "Please, Jenna. Don't do this. If you do this, then I have no defenses at all if you tear them down. You know that's not him. You know it. And it was one thing for it to end when I knew it was nothing, but if you start making me think there's hope, then I'm done for. There's no real quick recovery from that, you know?"

"Oh, Hailey. I know. I really, *really* know." She sniffed on the other end of the phone. "I just—I want you to be happy. And, that overly charming jock made you happy. And I'd bet the farm you made him happy too. But, I know that fear. I'm living it and I'm a huge hypocrite to tell you to take the chance on hope. To not give up and fear what may be inevitable, but…"

I waited, wondering what the *but* was.

She sucked in a deep breath and I could almost feel her bracing herself across the line. "But, I believed him."

"Of course you believed him." I was almost shouting. Was she trying to kill me? "He's Connor Ryan. His entire life is selling himself to coaches and fans and the media. He's born for this."

"Hailey." Her voice was even, calm. A juxtaposition of my near manic panic. "You don't have to believe him. Just don't count him out yet either."

"We already decided. He'll start his press junket. Then I'll go on a short book tour. When I get back he'll be down doing the guest host thing. All this traveling for both of us. We'll just let things fizzle in the media through that and let it die a peaceful death. No one gets blamed. No one gets hurt."

In theory.

"Right. So, that's not working." Jenna laughed, as if this were funny. "All I'm saying is, when he comes back around, don't shut him out."

"Okay," I said because all I wanted was to end this conversation and go back to eating enough chocolate ice cream to drown a small nation.

Part of me wanted to snap at her, to strike out. I wasn't the one with the perfect guy begging me weekly to move across the ocean to be with him. I wasn't the one staying away for no reason.

I had reasons. I had *Good Reasons*.

To remind myself what they were, I Googled "Connor Ryan Girls" and waited for the barrage of models, actresses, senator's daughters, etc. Only, what seemed to have taken over every search of Connor Ryan were pictures of us. My faux romance laid out in color from events to just walking down the street, his arm resting across my shoulder. It took seven pages to find him with anything resembling a supermodel.

No matter what Jenna said, I knew I had to do what I had to do. And that meant that a relationship for career reasons couldn't go any further. I needed to get some distance, some perspective about my time with Connor. But I knew one thing.

No matter how good it had been for either of our careers, I was now only looking out for my heart.

And that meant putting up a big fence when he came back to propose we continue our charade.

I turned my phone off and started packing for my tour. I was looking at five days out on the road wearing Becca approved outfits and avoiding all the conversations about my personal life, which had never been an issue before, so hopefully it wouldn't be an issue now.

But, with a five A.M. cab call, I had to focus.

And, focusing on anything but the idea Jenna was trying to plant in my head was the only thing I could do. I grabbed my laptop and started typing away, forcing a painful, heartbreaking opening scene to my next series on to the page. I typed 'til I was too tired to worry about anything else. 'Til I was worried I'd miss my flight if I didn't fall into bed right then. 'Til the only thing running through my head was my new world and the characters I was ripping apart in it.

Better than wine, chocolate, and therapy.

THIRTY-ONE

A WEEK LATER, I wandered home from my book tour. My apartment was cold. Turned out, I hadn't left the heat up enough to come home to cozy. But, exhausted, I dragged my butt around trying to unpack and sort my laundry and send thank you notes to all the bookstores who had hosted me.

Anything to make me even more exhausted.

Because, the moment I'd stepped back into my apartment everything had just swept right over me again, washing the modicum of peace I'd gained being so busy on my trip right out. From the fact that Connor's games and coffee machine were sitting out and ready to go, to the fact that half of my hamper was filled with oversized t-shirts, everything caused my apartment to feel tainted with Connor. As if he'd just stepped out and would be back any moment.

I'd forced myself not to watch any more of the interviews or gigs. I stayed offline. I avoided the magazine racks at the bookstores. I did everything but delete his phone number from my phone—everything I could think of to get to the other side of this.

And then I walked back into my apartment and it was all here waiting for me.

I grabbed one of the boxes of ARCs on my desk and dumped them out to shove all his stuff in there, but then felt bad because it wasn't his fault I felt bad. Which made me feel worse.

The girls had been texting me all day, trying to make plans for the upcoming weekend. I had a feeling they were afraid I'd become a slobbering mass of emotions while Connor was gone.

Of course, I had, but I wasn't telling anyone that.

Part of me was glad he was traveling again. There was something about us not being in the same city that made it feel easier.

I was fine. It had been a deal. We had paid the bet. Move along, nothing to see here.

That's what I kept telling myself too.

So, I worked myself to fall down tired and headed to bed, planning on diving back into the book I was nearly finished with from constant fear-driven work, and knowing it would suck me in to a world that was not this one.

~*~

The knock at my door was as much of a surprise as anything could be. I crawled out of bed, exhausted in too many ways to count. Wrapping my robe around me, I ignored the second pounding on the door wondering who in their right mind would need me in the middle of the night.

I pulled it open, expecting one of my neighbors, but instead found a tired, rumpled Connor standing there looking better than most men look rested and ready to go. He had an overnight bag slung over his shoulder and the same suit he'd worn last week on TV.

I stared at him, trying to rationalize just closing the door again and going back to bed where it was safe. I didn't need to add *alone* to that statement, did I? But, knowing that anything he said was going to hurt more than my daily recovery pain, I braced myself. I wasn't ready for us to be just friends—even though that's all we'd ever been.

My heart stopped and then triple timed at the sight of him. I took a deep breath, then another trying to get myself under control. Trying not to show him the thing he wanted to see the least...how in love with him I was.

"Hey," he stepped in, dropping his bag and facing me on the threshold of my home. "Did I wake you up?"

Since it was almost two A.M. and I didn't know what I'd say. I just nodded, biting back the sarcasm. But, even with that, I was just too exhausted to deal with the emotions rushing over me at the sight of him.

"What do you want, Connor?" Even I could hear it in my voice. The whole *strong front* thing wasn't going to hold up for very long. Or at all.

My tone, my words—I watched them hit him as if I'd slapped him in the face. I know, it wasn't very friendly, but I wasn't feeling friendly.

"Seriously, Hails?" He gave me a look of such disbelief that I didn't know what I'd missed. I didn't know why he was even here. Why he'd shown up now, why he had to be standing on my doorstep.

Every defensive wall I had went up around me. Emotional moats were dug, trebuchets armed.

"Connor, I'm tired, exhausted. I've been traveling. And, aren't you supposed to be in Atlanta or something today?" I asked as if I hadn't memorized the schedule I'd avoided watching. As if I couldn't tell better than Dex at this point where you could see—or avoid seeing so your heart wasn't further bruised—Connor Ryan.

"Right. I was in Atlanta." He spoke each word carefully, seeming to measure out where he was going with this. "But now I'm here."

As if I could avoid noticing that. I wanted to hit him, raise my smaller fists to his thick, solid chest and beat on it. I wanted to beg him to leave and just let me be. I wanted to scream and cry and demand to know if he knew he was killing me little by little.

I wanted to wrap my arms around him and never let him go.

I sucked in a deep breath, blinking to make sure there were no tears in my eyes, before raising my gaze again to meet him head on and repeating my question, "So, what do you want?"

Red-flash heat crept up his neck and he looked angry and uncertain and annoyed and a million other things at once before he stepped in further and slammed the door, pacing away and coming back to hover over me.

"You want to know what I want? You don't know or you want to hear it?" He pushed, the tone of his words forcing me back a step. "I want to be us. I want to not worry about…" He stopped, ran his hand through his hair, and glanced away. "I want to know if I get traded, we'll make it work. I want a little place like this, something with an office for you and a guest room because no matter how much money I make, my mother won't let me pay for a hotel. And we're keeping that chair because it's comfortable and your ex is an idiot. I want a dog. I don't care if we have to get a dog nanny. That dog will know he's our family. I want to come home to you every night I'm not on the road. I want to be the person who orders your meals and makes sure you eat more than sugar when you're on deadlines. I want to celebrate launches and deals and bestsellers and buy you the booze when that Paige woman slams you. I want to hold you every night and I *don't* want to have to wear eight layers of clothes to be in your bed. I want your friends to at least put up with me. I want you to never ask if Gavin is single again. I want our lives to become so mixed up that I don't know where mine ends and yours begins. I want to be the guy who I was supposed to be while we were together."

He sucked in a breath, his gaze slipping away as he ran out of steam before flashing back up to slam into mine, almost knocking me off my feet.

"What do you want?" he asked, looking more unsure than I thought he was capable.

I leaned back, feeling the ridges of the doorframe support me as my legs threatened to give out. I closed my eyes, shaking, shaking to my core and praying I wasn't asleep or delusional or part of some weird plan. But when I opened them, he was there, still hovering looking anxious and worried and like he was going to spring forward if I continued to slip down the wall. And I realized that the only way to have what I wanted was to take that risk. To reach out and trust that those words, those perfect, perfect words were the truth of it all.

"You." My hands were shaking so badly I was afraid to reach for him. Afraid I'd miss or fall or that he was an oasis in my emotional desert that would disappear if I reached out. "I just want you."

And I knew, as the words slipped out, that it was true. I just wanted him and I was willing to risk it.

Connor laughed, an exhale of nerves as he swung out and caught me against him. "That's what I said."

His mouth came down on mine, sending a jolt through me and waking me from the hazy world I'd been walking around in since my slow fall into love with Connor Ryan.

There was nothing slow about my feelings now. I'd lost my breath either from the kiss knocking it out of me or the strong arms banded around me. But, I'd rather pass out than let go.

Connor kissed like he did everything, smooth and hot. My toes tingled as he pulled away, kissing my cheek, my eyes, my forehead before coming back to my lips and taking them again.

After long, drunk kisses convincing me I was right where I should be, Connor lifted his head from mine, kissing his way up my jaw to whisper in my ear. "I love you, but I'm never sleeping on that tiny couch again."

I gave him a little grin and reached up to kiss him again. "If you insist."

~~*~~

Thanks so much for reading *The Catching Kind*. I've been so happy at how Connor won the crowd over even before he won over Hailey. They were amazingly fun to write.

Want More Brew?
THE BREW HA HA SERIES

It's in His Kiss
The Last Single Girl
Worth The Fall
The Catching Kind

BREW AFTER DARK Shorts
Love in Tune
Sweet as Cake

~*~

YA Books by Bria Quinlan

Secret Girlfriend (RVHS #1)
Secret Life (RVHS #2)
Wreckless

~~*~~

Bria Quinlan writes sweet and sassy rom coms because if you can't laugh in love…when can you? Check out her non-story ramblings www.briaquinlan.com.

~~*~~

CPSIA information can be obtained
at www.ICGtesting.com
Printed in the USA
LVHW051024100219
607024LV00001B/140